# THE HANDYMAN
# METHOD

# THE HANDYMAN
# METHOD

### A STORY OF TERROR

## NICK CUTTER
## ANDREW F. SULLIVAN

SAGA PRESS

LONDON  SYDNEY  **NEW YORK**  TORONTO  NEW DELHI

SAGA S PRESS

AN IMPRINT OF SIMON & SCHUSTER, INC.

1230 AVENUE OF THE AMERICAS, NEW YORK, NEW YORK 10020

Excerpt from *A Feast of Snakes* by Harry Crews. Reprinted by permission of John Hawkins and Associates, Inc. Copyright © Harry Crews 1976.

"I'm a Lover, but I Still Fight" by Dale Hollow. Copyright © Hollow Headed Enterprises LLC. All rights reserved. Used with permission.

First Saga Press trade paperback edition August 2023

For information about special discounts for bulk purchases, please contact Simon & Schuster Special Sales at 1-866-506-1949 or business@simonandschuster.com.

The Simon & Schuster Speakers Bureau can bring authors to your live event. For more information or to book an event, contact the Simon & Schuster Speakers Bureau at 1-866-248-3049 or visit our website at www.simonspeakers.com.

Interior design by Hope Herr-Cardillo

Manufactured in the United States of America

3   5   7   9   10   8   6   4   2

Library of Congress Cataloging-in-Publication Data has been applied for.

ISBN 978-1-9821-9672-1
ISBN 978-1-9821-9671-4 (pbk)
ISBN 978-1-9821-9673-8 (ebook)

*For the boys at the card table*

"His life terrified him. He didn't see how he was going to get through the rest of it."

—Harry Crews, *A Feast of Snakes*


"Well I've seen *Road House* thirty times
Instead of the dialogue I memorized the fights."

—Dale Hollow, "I'm a Lover, but I'll Still Fight"

## PART I

# JUNE

# 1

**THERE'S A SECRET** *at the heart of every marriage.*

The thought hit Trent Saban without warning as he pulled up to the new house. He didn't consider it an omen, but he did wish his brain—that malignant turd in the punchbowl socked between his ears—hadn't conjured it at the moment he first set eyes on the place.

He reached across the armrest and squeezed Rita's thigh. "We're here."

"Yup," his wife said. "Thar she blows."

Trent reeled his hand back with an audible exhale. The Toyota Sienna idled under a broiling midday sun. The house filled the windshield. The tempered glass had a magnifying effect, dragging their new home closer to them.

"That's it, huh?" came Milo's voice from the backseat.

Their son threw the rear door open and strode parallel to the driver's-side door. He planted his hands on his hips with an exaggerated squint, a pint-sized foreman assessing a construction site.

"It sure is big."

Trent got out beside the boy and stretched. The shadow of the house's roof touched the tips of his loafers. The driveway gave way to hard-packed yellow dirt that fanned out to every point on the compass. There was no sidewalk. Trent knew he shouldn't have expected one, but still, its lack bugged him . . .

. . . and where in blue fuck was his grass?

"It's going to be awesome, big guy," he said, rallying. "Build you a playset right over there, or there . . . or, uh, there. Lots of room."

"*You're* gonna build it?"

The skin tightened up Trent's spine. "Yeah. Why wouldn't I?"

Rita hadn't got out. Trent rapped on the windshield. When this earned no response, he rubbed his jaw, scissoring the bones side to side.

"Wait here," he told Milo. He walked up the drive flanking the garage to the front door. A plastic placard dangled from the knob:

WELCOME TO DUNSANY ESTATES

WELCOME HOME!

Trent snapped it off and flipped it over his shoulder. He slid the key in and turned the knob but only let the door fall open a scant inch, not wanting to spoil the surprise.

"Let's *do* this!" he said, jogging back to the Sienna. "We'll go in together as a—"

The wind gusted, flinging grit in Trent's face. With a dread premonition, he turned just in time to see the front door blow open, banging lustily on its hinges.

The placard lifted off the flagstones with a whippy *thwip!*; it cartwheeled up the steps and zephyred merrily inside the house.

"*Shit.*"

Milo was standing back at the Sienna. He'd fetched his turtle, Morty, from his tank in the backseat. "Were you saying something, Dad?"

"Door's open," Trent told him flatly.

Cradling Morty protectively to his belly button, Milo dashed up the drive.

"Take your shoes off, kiddo!" Trent called. "And don't be dripping salmonella water all over the floor!"

Rita was still rooted in the passenger seat. The hell was her problem? At times like this, Trent imagined a trick zipper at the back of his dear wife's head. He saw himself gripping the pull-tab and peeling the teeth of that zipper open, *pok-pok-pok . . .*

*What's the weather like inside that beautiful skull of yours, baby?* It bothered Trent not to know, not to have a friggin' clue. *What storms are brewing in that swirling cumulus?*

Ah, but did anyone want to know what their partner was really thinking? Take today, for instance, on the drive in. They'd stopped for gas, Rita and Milo heading into the convenience store for snacks, leaving Trent alone at the pumps. A train had been rumbling down the tracks behind the station. Trent pictured himself dashing up the berm and leaping onto a passing railcar. Ditching his wallet on the minivan hood and hightailing it with nothing but the clothes on his back, embracing a new life of adventure with mischievous hobos, scamps, and cutpurses . . . This unbidden daydream had filled him with the joy that a ground-bound bird must feel, were it miraculously to take flight.

Trent knuckle-rapped the windshield, harder this time. "I see Hector's on his way, hon. Come on, now, be friendly."

Rita stepped out and drew a jumpy breath. The wind purred along the earth, as if gusting across a vast lake. Trent watched earwax-colored dirt sift over the toes of Rita's Dior loafers. . . .

They turned from the house to chart Hector's pickup as it jounced toward them, lifting a rooster-tail of dust. It came through nothingness: no houses, no trees, no street signs or signs of life. The outlines of the neighboring development were barely visible to the south: Trent could make out the roofs of the nearest houses, fuzzy sawteeth against the horizon.

The Sabans' new home sat in moody isolation, a single unit in an otherwise uninhabited vista. Oh, there was the odd foundation sunk forlornly in the dirt; the skeletal suggestion of a frame rose from a few of them. But Trent could fire a shotgun—hell, a bazooka—and the blast would go unheard by human ears.

"Look, we know it's not going to be this way for long," he said.

"Of course not," Rita replied mechanically.

Hector Hannah—chief homeowners' liaison for Dunsany Estates—had assured them that construction would be ramping into phase two shortly. Dunsany would be transformed into a community with green lawns, families who shared the Sabans' interests, and plenty of children for Milo to horse around with at the park that would lie at the very center.

Though Trent was loath to admit it, they'd been lucky to land this place. It had gotten so a decent living wasn't enough to earn a roof over your head: these snaky developers practically demanded your kidney, your lungs, your *balls*. Hector had made this point clear during negotiations.

*This is the buy-low chance of a lifetime, Mr. and Mrs. Saban. You know how lucky you are, with everyone clawing tooth and nail to get a place these days?*

Hector's pickup truck pulled up next to Trent's Sienna, dwarfing it. Hector stepped down from the running board and spread his arms to Trent, Rita, the house.

*"Guys."* Hector's smile cut his face apart under his aviator sunglasses. "Is this a bit of all right, or is this a bit of *all right*?"

Hector was a garrulous blade of a man with the neck-popping strut of a bantam chicken. He was their liaison, but Trent had another title for him: professional turd polisher.

"Hey, quick question . . . where the hell's our grass, Hector?"

You couldn't allow the Hector Hannahs of this world to pull a fast one. These spring-heeled bastards would nickel-and-dime you, sass you, rob you blind.

Hector threw a chummy arm around Trent's shoulders. "We lay down sod in this weather, my friend, what's going to happen?" Hector simpered. "I'll tell you—it dies. Then you have to buy your own sod, and guess what? *That* stuff'll die too."

Hector's arm slithered off Trent, as cold and boneless as a dead python. He sauntered over to Rita, tossing a final bon mot over his shoulder: "Until the neighborhood is complete, there's just a couple things you're gonna have to live without. Sacrifices must be made."

*Sacrifices?* What did this bum know about that? Look at that truck of his. The chrome alone could . . . ahh, fuck it.

Trent allowed himself to look, really *look*, at his new house. The façade was a mingling of iron-gray brick and stone cladding: big flat slabs that looked like they'd been chipped off a mountainside. A shake-shingle roof and three peaks facing what would soon be the road: two canopying the front windows and a third peak over the oak door. It had the feel of something Mennonites could have built in its solemnity and forthright angles.

Hector hunkered on one knee in the driveway, directing Rita's attention toward some feature of the interlocking brick. Trent stalked past, barely checking the impulse to knock Hector's hairpiece off. He was 95 percent sure it was a rug anyway, a glossy pelt stuck on with double-sided tape or sticky-tack or scalp-gum. He'd caught a whiff of it earlier during that phony shoulder-hug, astringent as airplane glue.

The front door was shut again; Milo must have closed it behind him. Trent hesitated. The house was like a gift he was resistant to opening—how could it match his expectations?

As soon as he stepped over the threshold, he let out an honest-to-goodness gasp.

Sunlight filtered through a dozen tall north-facing windows. To the right was the kitchen with a deep farmhouse sink, an eight-burner stove, a stainless steel fridge, and an island with a mahogany topper.

To the left sat the living area: a white leather couch spacious enough for all three of them to lie end-to-end facing a fifty-five-inch flat-screen TV. Everything brand-spanking-new.

Trent stepped into the center of the open concept design. He was glad Hector wasn't watching. He had a dopey grin on his face.

"Is that . . . ?" he said, his smile widening.

Tucked into the space under the stairs—which ran up the left-hand wall, switchbacking at a landing before ascending to the second floor—was a built-in wine cabinet. Trent eased the glass door open. Climate-controlled coolness bathed his face. He let it fall closed, speechless.

A pair of spotless bay windows dominated the rear of the house, looking out over a vista of that soul-rotting yellow dirt. A forest lay past that barrenness, maybe a few football fields away. Thousands of telephone-pole pines formed an impenetrable wall.

Trent let his feet carry him up the stairs in a daze. A horseshoe-shaped hall ran around the upper story, with rooms branching off. He could look down onto the main floor over the hallway railing. He poked his head into each of the rooms. All were pristine, as if they had been finished with a jeweler's attention to detail.

He left the master bedroom door closed. He'd wait for Rita. They'd open it together.

He found Milo in the last bedroom he checked, pacing from wall to wall.

"Seven, eight, *nine!*" The boy beamed. "Nine steps from that wall to this one, Dad. And I was taking big steps."

"Is this the room you and Morty want?"

"Well, I can't have the *big*-big room, right?"

As he looked at his son, an uncharitable image flew into Trent's mind: the pink skin under a picked scab.

"There are three other rooms besides the big one," said Trent. "You choose."

"Mom says one's for me, one's the spare room, and one's for my new sister."

Trent folded his arms. "What's this about a sister?"

Milo retrieved Morty, who'd ambled over to the wall. The turtle's crimson fléchette of a tongue was probing the floor trim.

"Mom said I'd have a sister."

"She did, huh? It's a regular old hen party when you and your mommy chat."

Trent stepped back into the hall, nettled about these secret meetings between his wife and son, the ones he wasn't invited to. What was this about a second kid? Did Rita think she could just decide for both of them?

He indulged in the peculiar fantasy of getting a vasectomy without telling her. *Guess what, Reets? I got my wires snipped. Surprise, your hubby's firing blanks from this day on!*

His mood brightened at the sight of the chandelier descending from the coffered ceiling: dozens of cloudlike glass globes suspended on filament wires, lit from within by a spectral light.

Trent buttonhooked at the bottom of the stairs, backtracking past the TV to the far-left edge of the main floor. The door back there opened into the basement. He stood at the top of the steps, peering down. A breeze curled around his ankles. He went down to a standard basement. The air was dank. But had Trent ever met a basement that *wasn't* dank?

Walking back up to the main floor, he found a mudroom down a narrow hallway. Its door opened into a double-car garage, appointed with sensible shelving units.

"This place is . . ." He was giddy in a way he couldn't remember feeling as an adult: the intense pleasure of a child who'd stumbled upon a fifty-dollar bill left in a library book. ". . . holy *shit*."

Flanking back into the main area, he saw Rita standing outside the front door.

"It's even nicer inside, hon."

Trent eased out behind her. When it seemed clear she wasn't moving, Trent cupped one arm behind her knees and lifted her up, his free hand cradling her neck as he swept her off her feet. Rita let out a strangled squawk as he carted her across the threshold like a sack of corn.

"Trent, stop!"

She clutched at the doorframe, her fingers tensed into claws. Grunting, Trent shoved them both inside. Rita spilled from his arms, splayed onto the tiles.

"For fuck's sake, Reets!"

She sat with her head tucked between her knees—the position flight attendants tell you to assume in the event of a plane crash—with her breath coming in raw heaves.

"What's your problem?" he said, his anger brimming. "You had to come in eventually. Unless you're gonna sleep in the friggin' yard."

His wife jammed her thumb into her mouth, a gesture that Trent found mildly revolting.

"Reets?" Worried now, he settled a finger on the topmost knob of her spine, jutting above the collar of her blouse. "Hey, Rita, are you—?"

"Fine!"

Pulling her feet under her, his wife sprang up like some eerie jack-in-the-box. She laughed, a gabbling goose-like honk.

"I'm being a silly Billy," she said, tossing her hair back. "I just had this vision of how I'd step into my new house but, *aaah*, it's goofy—it's like your wedding day, right? You have these grand hopes and then there's the reality, you know?"

She showed him her thumbnail, leaking blood. She must have torn it on the doorframe. A few hours later, Trent would find a streak of blood on the wood and wipe it away with vicious swipes.

"I'm sorry." He grabbed a tissue from the box on the coffee table and handed it to her. "Shit, Reets, I wanted it to be perfect."

She stanched her bloody thumb with the Kleenex. "It was me. I was being a pill."

*"Guuuuuuuys."*

Hector breezed in, stooping to pick up the DUNSANY placard on the floor. He held his arms out, Christ-on-his-cross style, and turned a showy circle.

"Damn, I wish this was *my* house. Wanna trade?"

Hector's phone chirped. The liaison consulted it, frowning. "Duty calls. I gotta bounce, but if there's anything you need—"

"The *lawn*, Hecto—"

"The sod, the sod, my kingdom for the sod!" Hector hooted. "You're a dog with a bone, Trent. A regular Rottweiler!"

He was already out the door, flouncing down the drive: "I'll talk to my horticulture guys and let you know!"

"If that fast-talking jackass thinks he's gonna rip me off," Trent fumed, "he's about to get a hard lesson in accountability."

Rita set her fingertips on Trent's wrist. "Show me our bedroom."

Energized by this new calling, Trent led her up the stairs. "See, Mrs. Saban, how everything has been built so exactingly? Not a stitch out of place."

Rita played along. "Mm-hmm, oh yes, this all seems quite in order."

"Imagine once it's full of all our stuff, baby."

The movers were scheduled to arrive the very next day. Trent led Rita to the center of the upstairs hall, stopping in front of the master bedroom door. He gripped her hand. "Ready?"

They both put one hand on the knob and turned it together.

Spectacular. No other word applied. Nothing gilt, nothing gold-plated. Just clean lines that created a serene harmony. Immediately Trent knew he'd sleep deeply and peacefully in this room.

Letting go of her hand, he made his way to the walk-in closet. "I believe this should be *juuust* big enough to fit your Imelda Marcos–ian assortment of shoes, milady."

Trent threw the door open with a flourish—

His jaw hung down like a drawbridge, a hoarse gag coming out of his mouth.

A gruesome crack slashed up the closet wall.

"Mother*fuck*!"

Trent dashed to the bedroom window. There went Hector's truck, burring away over the featureless dirt toward that scalloped ridge of roofs marking the closest human habitation.

"Those fucking shoddy-ass—"

"Honey, it's nothing really."

"Rita, I swear. Just *stop*."

Trent stalked back to the closet. He couldn't believe it. The place was just finished . . . and it was *perfect*. Almost perfect.

"Daddy?"

Milo stood at the door, eyeing him. Feeling like an automaton operating on wonky servos, Trent teased his lips into a smile.

"Hey, it's fine, buddy. Just something here I'll need to deal with. Every house has a few warts, even brand-new ones."

# 2

*"NOW, YOU'RE PROBABLY WONDERING, 'What if I screw this up?'"*

The man on Trent's laptop screen wore denim overalls and a green plaid shirt. His beard was graying down the center and when he smiled, he didn't show any teeth, just dimples.

*"My friend, that's why the Good Lord put erasers on pencils."*

Trent hit pause on the YouTube clip and shifted his focus to the crack zigzagging up the back wall of Rita's walk-in closet. It rose as a hairline from the base molding to become a two-inch gap near the ceiling. Trent swore it had grown overnight.

His disbelief remained epic. A . . . *crack*. In the wall. Of his brand. Fucking. New—

He bit his tongue, severing the anger rising up his gorge; the little rage-worm squirmed back down his throat. Just last night he'd nursed that ire reading horror stories on the Reddit home improvement subs: users with handles like JanusHam99 and RealJoeHourz lamenting their contractors' empty promises, the bait-and-switch inherent to any estimate for a job.

*We're sheep*, HanzoHands posted, with a JPEG of his kitchen ceiling bowing under the weight of a flooded bathroom. *All they do is fleece us. They'll take your skin too, if you let them.*

Trent considered calling Hector up to ream him a new one. But the house was pretty much perfect, wasn't it? This . . . this was a thumbprint on an otherwise flawless diamond.

Trent could fix the crack himself. How hard could it be?

So, here he was in the closet with the laptop perched on one of the shelves.

*The Handyman Method*, the name of the YouTube channel. The man in the forest-green overalls had introduced himself only as Hank. Trent couldn't recall the exact sequence of clicks that had led him here. There were a lot of slick videos to surf through out there. Sunny couples promising you could make your dream home come true, *together*! Stiff white guys who spoke in monotone, staring out at the world with a grimace of contempt.

Hank's channel had a whopping two subscribers. There were no auto-ads. The video Trent clicked on—"Patch That Crack, Hank!"—had a grand total of three views.

*"You're looking at a standard crack in a standard home,"* Hank said. *"A home in Anytown, USA. Much like your own home, maybe. A safe place for a man to raise his family."*

The view panned to a crack sawing up a closet wall; for a moment Trent mistook it for the crack in his own wall, though of course it wasn't.

*"You want to avoid laying the patch on too thick or else you'll get a sloppy seam."*

A roguish wink from Hank. Trent felt the first stirrings of affection. Here was a guy who wanted to *help*. If Hank could assist just one troubled soul to replace an ornery toilet flapper, he would die a happy man.

*"Keep those lines clean, sport."*

"You bet, Hank-o," Trent replied, laying in filler with a brand-new joint knife.

Trent was immediately comfortable with Hank; the video was the equivalent of slipping into a comfy wool sweater. But he'd felt self-conscious—an impostor, frankly—earlier that afternoon at Home Depot. He'd gone with a list for the crack repair; it gave him an excuse to be out of the house while Rita dealt with the movers. Wandering the aisles, he'd realized how little he knew about the things that ran under or through the surfaces of his home, delivering electricity and heat. This realization had made Trent's own competencies—he was a lawyer, or at least had been—seem pathetic. What use was intimate knowledge of the corporate tax code when your furnace crapped out or your water tank shit the bed?

His fellow customers made Trent uneasy too. Men who made aggressive eye contact and had tape measures clipped unironically to their belts. Beef-gutted Billy Bobs speaking in code:

*Hey, Gene, you got a seven-eighths skirted flim-flammer compatible with my threaded two-'n'-a-quarter-inch flop-bibber?*

He came home with a few bags' worth of home repair items. The movers had already finished by then. It left Trent mildly depressed, that the entirety of his life could be so swiftly and brusquely dumped off. As though he was some no-account hermit crab—

"How's it going?"

Trent's skin seized as Rita stepped into the closet unannounced with a glass of lemonade. Not looking directly at the laptop, she asked: "Who's this fine fellow?"

"My new buddy, Hank." Trent paused the video. "What's our kiddo up to?"

"Reading in his room."

"He should come help me out." Irritation caused Trent's shoulders to hunch reflexively. "He might learn a thing or two."

Rita folded her arms. "Some father-son bonding, uh?"

"What's he reading, those talking dragon books?"

"What's wrong with that? They build empathy."

Oh, whee. More empathy, just what that boy needed. Might as well crush estrogen pills into his cereal milk.

Rita said: "Why don't you take a break for dinner?"

Trent didn't want to quit. The crack grated on him. It looked like a . . . a *mouth*. A twisted, jeering sideways leer.

*Who, li'l ole me?* the crack lisped. *Let me hang around, pal. Heck, if you let me stay long enough, I'll invite a few buddies.*

Trent shut the laptop with a hard snap. "Dinner, you bet."

It ended up being improvised. Most evening meals required a working range, and Rita made an ugly discovery as she twisted the burner knob, holding her palm over the element. . . .

"No heat."

"Shift aside, babe." Trent blew on his fingers. "I've got the magic touch."

Evidently that was not the case. The stove—a burnished steel Miele, its clean German lines more suited to a sports car—was stone-dead.

"Did you ding-dongs forget to hook up the damn gas line?" he asked Hector once he'd gotten the dodgy liaison on the blower.

"Gas? M'man, that range is electric."

"What? No, it's—ah, *Christ*."

"What can I tell you? Could be the wiring."

Hector promised to send over a guy to check things out. "Do not futz with the wires in the meantime," he warned, as if he suspected Trent might possess the instincts of a chipmunk and go nibbling around inside the fuse box.

"I'm not an infant," Trent replied bitterly. "Just get your guy over here. And tell him to bring a few rolls of goddamn sod."

At least the fridge was in working order, and well-stocked from a grocery run earlier that day. So, sandwiches it would be.

Trent found himself alone in the kitchen with Milo while Rita unpacked moving boxes upstairs.

"Dad, are you ever going back to work?" Milo asked from his perch on the island stool.

Trent hadn't much liked his job. He suspected his moral fiber might be too stern to advance in the legal field, and his underperformance (as a few of the senior partners labeled it) was the result of him not being willing to play dirty games . . . which was immeasurably easier to live with than the alternative: that even if he was a no-good dirty dog, he'd still be a shitty lawyer.

"*If* I go back, kiddo, it'll be when I'm ready."

Milo braced his elbows on the island topper. Trent bit back the urge to tell him to sit up straight. He was leaving elbow smudges on the mahogany.

"It's just that Jason Dinkins—" Milo started.

That would be Milo's best friend back at his old school. His *only* friend, Trent had long suspected.

"—well, it was Jason's dad, actually . . . Jason's dad said that you're a hero."

Something flared brightly inside of Trent, making him momentarily nauseated.

The *Incident*, as it was known in legal-speak, had occurred at Trent's law firm, Harrison and Tate. The same firm where Rita had recently been made partner amid much fanfare. H&T had preferred to keep The Incident hush-hush. Trent provided testimony, patiently walking the police through the events of that fateful afternoon. The consensus was that he'd done not only the right thing, but, yes, the *heroic* thing.

Milo squinted at him closely. "What did you do? Neither you or Mom really say."

Kids caught on to things. If this move represented a *true* fresh beginning, the air ought to be cleared, right?

"Well . . . what I can say is that a man in our office was looking to hurt people."

Milo leaned forward. "A bad man?"

"At the time, I guess so. He wasn't *evil*-bad, but he'd gotten sick up here." Trent tapped his temple. "He worked with me and your mom. Until one day, the bosses told him he couldn't come to work anymore. He was fired for something called gross incompetency."

Nothing Trent had said so far was a lie. He'd been very careful about that.

"Gross incompetency. What does that mean, Dad?"

"He wasn't doing the job that the company was paying him for. Not well, anyway."

"What was his name?"

"Carson Aikles." Trent pushed the sandwich plate across to his son and glanced at the stairs; he couldn't hear Rita up there, but he didn't know how well voices might travel in the house. "Don't tell your mom I told you this."

Milo nodded solemnly. "What did Mr. Aikles do?"

Trent found himself warming to the tale. His son's rapt stare was what did it.

"There's a term, it's not much used anymore. It's called 'going postal.'"

"Postal?"

"It's when someone gets mad at the place they work, usually about being fired . . . they go berserk. I guess mailmen used to do it sometimes."

"*Mailmen?* What's so bad about delivering letters?"

"You got me. But that's exactly what Carson Aikles did."

"He went postal," Milo said reverently.

"Carson Aikles decided the best way to express his anger was with a hammer. He brought it to the office and started hitting things with it. Windows, furniture. And then . . ." Trent let out a breath. "Milo, he hit at least one person with that hammer."

"Wait, did he hammer *you*, Daddy? Is that why you're a hero?"

He wished Milo would stop using that fucking word.

"*Hammer* me? Oh, well, his hammer . . ." Trent cleared his throat rawly. ". . . it hit me, you bet it did. See this spot on my forehead? See how it's kind of . . ."

"Flat!" Milo said. "Yeah. Like a coin. I never noticed that before."

"Hoo-boy, did it ever *sting*. But you can't let something like that stop you, not when public safety's involved, so I, um . . ."

Rita said: "Your father tackled him through a plate-glass office window."

Rita had sneaked down all cat-stealthy, standing at the foot of the stairs with a moving box in her arms.

"Smashed a bunch of glass, it was a real mess," she said, setting the box down. "But the sad man went down, Milo honey, and he stayed down."

"Did you see Dad do that to Mr. Aikles, Mom?" Milo asked her.

"No, I wasn't there. Nobody saw it, in fact. Everyone ran away from the danger, as most people would. All but your father."

The firm had tendered indefinite paid leave, at a reduced wage. *Call it a hero's pension*, were the HR delegate's exact words. Old Man Tate promised to bring Trent back gradually, just to make sure he wasn't suffering any adverse physical or psychological effects.

Trent spanked his hands. "Okay, dinner's made. I'm off to deal with that crack."

Rita said, "Eat with us, why don't you? The crack's not going anywhere."

"It might be getting bigger! Just let me deal with this stupid thing and then you and I can toss the baseball around before it gets dark, okay, Milo?"

"Cool," the boy agreed.

Upstairs, the crack lurked. When Trent opened the laptop from sleep and hit play on the video, Handyman Hank resumed his instruction.

*"It takes a steady hand to lay that compound in. Lay off the coffee for now, tiger."*

Trent scooped filler onto his joint knife. But by the time he reached the wide neck at the top of the crack, no matter how much compound he loaded onto the blade, he couldn't plug the damn thing. Slurry kept slipping into the vent; he could hear it slopping down inside the wall like chunky raindrops.

Trent set the joint knife down. Curious, he pushed his fingers into the crack. They met no resistance—no studs or plastic sheeting bulging against the pressure of fiberglass insulation.

Trent's fingers disappeared to the knuckles inside the crack. His chest, bathed in a sudden shock of sweat, pressed against the wall. His heart slapped in his ears.

Turning his head, his ear now flush to the wall, Trent could hear the various engines of the house behind the plaster: the air conditioning purring and the fridge thrumming and something else, some endless ripping note like the tear of silk sheets. . . .

His whole hand was inside the wall. The very sight seemed impossible, as if he'd sunk his flesh into a black hole hidden within the fabric of everyday existence. . . . It vanished all the way to his wrist, to the blue veins bunched under his skin.

Something brushed his fingertips. A rapid fluttering, soft as batted eyelashes.

Trent jerked his hand out and fell backward, letting out a bullish bleat.

Rita was there within seconds, as if she'd been squatting like a linebacker in the bedroom. "Hey! Are you okay?"

She set a mothering hand to Trent's forehead. He roughly shoved her fingers away.

"I'm fine! I must've brushed a nail head inside the wall. It's nothing."

"We could call Hector."

"What? Why? The man's as useless as tits on a bull. Please, just go finish your supper."

Once she was gone, Trent inspected his fingers. A welt had sprung up on his left pointer: a swollen anthill with a molten corona. It throbbed with a painless, out-of-body heat.

He stared at the crack. He ought to shine a light inside the wall, see what the heck—

The laptop sprang to life. The video—wait, had he even paused it?—resumed, Hank's boisterous brogue filling the closet.

*"Y'know, taping a big ole crack makes filling it a breeze."*

Trent paused the video and sneaked downstairs to the mud-room for a flashlight. A roll of mesh tape poked from one of the Home Depot bags he'd left beside the shoe-rack. Trent couldn't recall buying the tape . . . but anyway, there it was—just what he needed, exactly when he needed it.

He went upstairs with the flashlight and the tape in its shopping bag. Back in the walk-in closet, he shone the flash-light beam into the crack. It was more a slit now. The filler had half-hardened, a pebbly ridge that resembled a dog's gums. He could see nothing inside the wall but endlessly cycling dust. . . .

Trent reached into the wall again, his teeth gritted so hard his skull pounded. . . . His fingers closed around something hooked on one of those protruding nails. He dragged it out through the crack; clumps of filler rained down to the carpet.

A soda can. More rust than metal, and a brand he'd never heard of: Bubble Up. A wire hook—the type used to hang ornaments on Christmas trees—was threaded through the pull-tab.

His fingers slid around the back of the can and slipped into an unexpected emptiness; he rotated the can. . . .

A square had been cut in the back. Something was inside.

A tiny ribcage, a sparrow or a mouse, with some kind of

chrysalis threaded through the pin-like bones. Something had pushed itself halfway out of the papery bolus; the stillborn thing was pink, or had been in the moments it was alive, but was now the dry color of sidewalk chalk. It was suspended inside the can on threads of the same dull pink, which held it in place like a fly in a spider's web. . . .

Trent gawked for a beat before dropping the can. The fall jolted the little horror out of the can—it hit the carpet and crumbled into pieces.

Confused rage bristled at Trent's temples. What the fuck *was* that, and what was it doing inside his house? Trent had heard stories about workmen leaving things in walls, but that was usually fast-food wrappers or orange rinds or even something for luck, a secretly stashed tchotchke or whatever.

"Dunsany," he seethed. "Hector and the rest of those bastards—"

*People've been crisscrossing this great land of ours for centuries.*

The voice belonged to Hank. Trent's head snapped to the laptop to make sure the video was paused, that was how real Hank sounded. . . . It *was* paused. Trent's subconscious must have co-opted Hank's voice, that was all, seeking the clear-cut rationality of it.

*People set down roots, build something, stay awhile, then move on. Or maybe Mother Nature moves them on with a flood, a fire, a tornado. Things get left behind, right?*

Somehow it made sense. Trent's anger dimmed.

*To think you're the first one who's ever lived on this patch of soil, well, that's the folly of vanity, partner.*

Trent rolled the Home Depot bag over his hand and picked up the can and the remains, then turned the bag inside out and knotted it, sealing everything within.

That done, he restarted the video. Hank stepped instantly into the frame, eyes twinkling, with a roll of mesh tape.

Trent got to work. The world faded, the house, even the closet . . . the crack sucked Trent into the darkness inside his new house . . .

When he came back to himself, the crack was gone.

*"Give yourself a pat on the back,* compadre,*"* Hank said. *"I betcha feel about ten feet tall right now."*

The unmarred wall filled Trent with a pride that embarrassed him in its potency.

*"Now, I ain't here to tell you to like and subscribe."* Hank wagged his finger. *"We aren't about groveling. But come on back for more home repair tips whenever you need 'em!"*

It was past midnight by the time Trent stepped from the closet. Funny how time worked when you were sunk down in a job. He picked up the bag holding the soda can and crept downstairs.

Rita was asleep on the sofa. He shook her gently. She came to with a jerk, her fists balled.

"Whoa! It's just me, baby."

She stared at him, her eyes reflecting bovine incomprehension. "Trent . . . you scared me."

"You can head up to bed now."

Once she'd retreated up the stairs, Trent buried the Home Depot bag in the garbage, stuffing it down at the bottom. He didn't want Rita to see. It would put unnecessary thoughts in her head.

As he padded upstairs, one of the steps emitted a shrill *scrrreee!* Dang. He'd have to take a look at it tomorrow.

Milo was sawing logs in his room. Trent had promised they'd toss the ball around, hadn't he? He sat on Milo's mattress, careful not to wake him. Milo had already decorated the walls: a drawing of Billy the Bulldozer, another of Pikachu. Morty lay in his tank at the foot of Milo's bed.

Trent brushed Milo's hair away from his ear. An earbud was jammed in it. A glow wept from under the covers.

Peeling the blankets back, Trent discovered an iPad.

"My boy," he *tsked* softly.

A YouTube clip was playing on the iPad.

*Little Boy Blue.*

Trent watched a felt-limbed, Muppet-y creature crawl out of a wooden box. The thing had a toolbelt strung around its furry blue waist. It capered and jigged, hammer waving in one hand and lug wrench in the other. Dialogue seeped tinnily from the earbuds.

*"C'mon, Junior Blues, let's DIG!"*

Trent removed the buds from Milo's ears. Shut off the device and tucked it under the bed.

As he stepped into the hallway, Trent was swarmed with a sudden impulse to flee.

It came and went like a starburst, leaving no afterimage. By the next heartbeat, he had a hard time believing he'd felt the desire so strongly . . . but he had, and it reminded him of the only other time in his life he'd felt the same way.

He'd been a college sophomore, staggering home from a house party on a freezing February night. He was almost blackout drunk, as if walking into the folds of a dark veil that parted just enough to permit his next step, and the next. . . . Then came the sensation of a stiff wind hitting him from behind, making that blackness total. He came to on the sidewalk with the hair at the back of his head matted with blood. Later, he'd figure he'd been a victim of "the knockout game": an evil prank where the perpetrators sneak up and club their target into unconsciousness.

As dehumanizing as that truth would be, the alternative his drunken mind had conjured up was far worse: Trent was sure he'd been attacked by a monster, one that was still lurking out there in the dark, waiting to play an even crueler trick.

The sensation in his new home was a bracing echo of that long-ago night: a disconnected high-hat terror and the overwhelming impulse to run, run fast, and never look back.

This feeling was there, thick in the hallway with him.

Then, just as quickly, it passed.

"We need to monitor that boy's internet usage," he whispered as he slid into bed beside Rita.

His wife made a sleep-slurred snort that Trent took as a yes.

# 3

"CAN'T HAVE THAT COMPUTER sucking at your brain all the time, bud."

"It's a tablet," Milo said to his dad.

"I know that. Point is, it's good to get outside. Stretch those legs. Keep yourself lean and mean."

The sun hung directly above. Milo watched his father brace his hands on his hips, surrounded by the pieces of a playset scattered around what he called "the backyard," even though there was no fence to tell where it ended.

"There'll be a basketball team at your new school, but we'll need to work on your ball handling before tryouts. You don't want to keep dribbling the ball off your foot and Coach planting you on the bench, like last year."

Dad made one of his *just kidding* laughs, the kind with no real kidding in it.

This wasn't any kind of playset you'd find at Walmart. No bright neon plastic, no foam, no safety stickers. Dad had bought it off a website called Herc's Salvage Wholesale. The playset had showed up that morning, unpacked by two unsmiling men. With its wood beams and posts it looked like a sunken ship, the metal slide and monkey bars winking in the sun.

Dad stood surrounded by heaps of raw material. Tools lay scattered around; more hung from the toolbelt strung around his hips.

"This is gonna take some elbow grease, Milo my boy." Dad mimed squeezing an oilcan into his elbow.

Just him and Dad today. Mom was at work, like always. Milo watched his father slide a long screw through a hole in a thick beam, then try to force it through a hole in a connecting plank. Dad kicked at the screw until it popped through, ripping wood out. Grunting, he twisted on a bolt the size of a baby's fist.

Dad came over, sitting next to Milo on one of the delivery boxes and taking a swig from an orange canteen.

"Things may seem weird right now," he said. "New house, new school in a few months, new friends to make. And if you don't wanna play basketball, that's a-okay. Whatever you want to do, I'm going to support you, all right?" Milo tried not to wince as Dad gave his knee a slap. "Something on your mind? Talk to me, buddy."

There were lots of things Milo *could* talk about. Like, the other night he was looking up at the sky and found himself wondering: *What do the planets in our solar system taste like?*

He figured the closest one, Venus, would taste like a lime Sour Patch Kid. He did Mars next (cinnamon hearts), Saturn (Buckley's cough syrup), Jupiter (like licking wet cement) . . . but if Milo told his dad any of that, he'd get *The Look*.

The Look was Dad's new way of saying Milo had done something weird without putting it into words. Milo hadn't understood what The Look meant at first, but once he made the connection it made him go all shrivelly inside, like a Styrofoam cup tossed in a fire. Now Milo dreaded The Look, and missed being able to tell his father the things that really mattered to him.

"Nah, Daddy. Nothing."

"Good to hear it," Dad said, only half-listening. "Hey, you see these little plastic caps here? They're for the legs of the slide. Why don't you snap them on for me?"

Milo tried to do as he was told. Really, he did. But he couldn't fit the ends into the slide's legs; the plastic caps jammed in the hollow metal stalks, poking out. When his father came over to inspect his work, the breath pushed from between his lips in a hard hiss.

"You know what, forget it."

Dad handed Milo his phone. "I found this new app, okay? What you do is, you take a photo of a flower, any flower, and the app tells you what kind it is."

Dad pointed to the woods, the trees scaling toward the sky.

"Why don't you go exploring? Take some photos—or hey, pick some wildflowers for your mom. She'd love that. Just, nothing poisonous . . . and don't go too far."

Milo understood this wasn't an offer, it was a command. *Get lost, son.*

He slunk off across the open field. When he looked back, his father was a distant stickman isolated in the dirt. He seemed too far away, as if Milo were staring at him through the wrong end of a telescope.

Reaching the wall of trees, Milo stepped into the dusky bower. Branches bit at his arms immediately, as if they'd been waiting to scratch him. The trees, packed tight as sardines in a tin, felt smothering. With each step, the sky disappeared as the pines gripped each other overhead.

He came upon a single purple flower. He took a photo using the app.

*Snow Glory*, the app pinged.

"Cool," Milo said, not really meaning it.

He glumly walked on. Weeds poked at his ankles, their little barbs biting through his socks. Milo imagined poison ivy rubbing into his skin, his legs turning a bright, swollen red.

The trees thinned into a clearing. Milo tripped on snarled tree roots and pitched headlong into the dirt. He got up, inspecting the fresh scrape on his elbow. . . .

Something lay in the open grass.

At first glance, he saw a shed or a shack, half-rotted back to the earth. But that was simply the initial form his mind imposed—and not even because it resembled those things, but simply because one might find a shack or a shed out here. That would be logical, wouldn't it?

Whatever this was, some part of Milo's mind instantly understood it was *not* logical. And when a human mind—even one as flexible as a child's—is confronted with something illogical, its initial reaction is to logic-ify it, pressing it into some sane arrangement.

Whatever this illogical shape was, it appeared to bubble out of the earth in a crude dome.

As soon as Milo saw it—*really* saw it—his breath went haywire.

*It's a nest . . . no, it's a cocoon.*

But Milo knew enough about nature, about animals and plants and bugs, to realize it couldn't possibly be. He couldn't comprehend an insect big enough to build a cocoon like that around itself . . . let alone imagine what might crack out once it had pupated.

Against every good instinct, Milo found himself creeping closer.

Could it *be* a nest . . . or a beaver lodge? It kind of looked like an igloo made out of sticks, or those decorative wicker balls found in ceramic bowls on coffee tables—well, *half* of a wicker ball. It was as big around as his old Mr. Turtle pool, its curved slats covered in a chalky, spidering fungus. There was a slit near the top of the dome: a clenched mouth of bleached wood, banded wires, and jags of rusted aluminum jutting like bad teeth. The thing gave off a lonely graveyard feeling.

Without quite realizing how, Milo had gotten close enough to touch it. He reached out for one curled plywood rib wrapped in oxidized wire. A white film came off on his fingertips. The wood was spongy and greasy, like the bacon fat his mom drained into old soup cans—if he pushed harder, his fingers might squish right through into its dark innards.

He wiped the white gummy stuff on his shorts. It didn't come off. He was worried that the whiteness might start crawling down his fingers. . . .

He touched the wood again (*why?*) and let out an involuntary moan. Soil crumbled at the dome's edges, sending up a rattle from someplace far below. Milo had a flash of his third-grade science class—the avocado pit on Mr. Simpkins's desk skewered with toothpicks and balanced on top of a glass of water. . . .

Pink-eyed bugs crawled over the dome. It . . . it *hummed*. Low and persistent, pushing into the soles of his shoes. It struck Milo that if his father were here right now, he wouldn't hear that sound . . . his adult ears wouldn't be able to register that hum, and this made Milo feel even more alone.

What if whatever might be living in there (was something alive in there?) knew how to disguise itself from everyone except those that it *wanted* to see it, lurking below the surface with only a tiny bit poking out like the nostrils of a crocodile in an Amazonian river—?

His father's phone went off, sending a jangle up Milo's spine. He clawed it out of his pocket and dropped it on the ground.

*"Hey, kids, it's time to go exploring!"*

It was Little Boy Blue. The character from his new favorite YouTube series . . . Blue stared up from the phone's screen on the dead pine needles, its eyes were bright and aware.

It waved a teensy telescope. *"Let's see what's inside, boys and girls!"*

Blue's eyes bugged out of its felt face. Milo felt like stepping on the phone and smushing it into the dirt, but he didn't . . . *couldn't*. Blue seemed bigger than the phone it was imprisoned within; Milo had the stupid impression that Blue could step out of the phone anytime it wanted, swelling hideously to lay its hands on him—hands that would be horridly soft and swollen like lard packed inside a hot water bottle.

In a cold and deathless voice, Blue said: *"Do it."*

. . . Milo's mind felt struck like a tuning fork; an impression came to him out of nowhere. A gift was waiting for him inside that nest. A new bike? Yeah, he saw it clearly. A weirdly old one, with a banana seat and an orange buggy-whip antenna . . .

34

Could something like that happen out here? The earth offering up whatever you dreamed?

Milo pushed his right pointer finger into the blackness past the sticks. Sinking to his knees, he pressed his eye to a thin crack in the dome. . . . He sensed his finger but he couldn't see it in there, his digit wriggling like a worm on a hook. . . .

Blue made a grunt of encouragement. *"Mmm, good, so nice."*

Milo caught sight of something inside, down under the level of the earth.

A pair of small eyes, black and shining and dead—

—a hot wire wrapped around his finger.

Milo jerked it out, shoving himself back and crab-assing away. He gathered his feet and retreated even further. A line of blood wrapped around his fingertip like a red thread.

His attention was drawn to the phone. Blue jiggled inside the screen, its body lengthening strangely and whanging side to side like one of those coil doorstops—

"Here you are."

The voice belonged to his father, who came striding through the trees.

"What in God's name is this thing?"

Dad seemed puzzled . . . no, more than just puzzled. An edge of bewilderment, maybe even stark worry. He circled the structure, tools tinkling musically on his belt. Milo stuck his finger in his mouth, sucking on it.

Dad pulled the crowbar from his toolbelt. His eyes held a dreamy cast.

"Let's see what's inside this thing, shall we?"

"I don't think there's anything in there but bugs."

"Oh, come on. Where's your spirit of adventure?"

Milo clung to his father's free arm. "Don't do it. Please."

"Relax, Milo." A flash of The Look. "If it's full of wasps or something, we will book it so fast out of here, I promise you."

The crowbar sank between the slats. A wet crunch as the attachments pulled free.

Milo pictured senseless creatures emerging to yank his father down, things with eyes made of buttons, eyes made of keyboard letters, kaleidoscope eyes of dead flowers and squirming maggots, eyes that sparked and hissed when they saw the light, all desperately hungry.

Another wet crunch. Silence.

When Milo looked, he saw some splintered slats on the ground and that strange gummy film streaked across his father's clothes.

"Woo," Dad said. "That came apart like butter."

His father dropped the crowbar and peered inside the nest.

"What in the name of—"

Dad pulled more slats free, more hesitantly now. He tore off most of the dome-like top, the old clapboard and rusted siding. His efforts revealed a shallow cup, the look of a clamshell that bellied down into the earth.

"That's not right," was all Dad said.

Milo joined him. They both stared down at the faces . . . *sort of* faces.

Crushed humanlike figures lay inside the shell. Four of them. Made of sticks and tubing, wrapped in mud and scraps of cloth. One wore a helmet. Another had dead leaves for hair. The third had black button eyes—*That was the one who looked at me*, Milo thought, instantly certain. *The one that grabbed me.*

The final one was half-formed, threads trailing off into nothing, limbs missing, neck distended. It appeared to have been eaten: chunks torn from its stomach, its head and feet.

"They look like oversized dolls," Dad said in a hollow voice. Dolls, sure. Toys.

"Is it some kind of an altar?" his father mused.

The only altar Milo had ever heard of was the one people got married at, and what lay below the dirt was nothing like that.

At one end of this molting, rotten pod, Milo saw two names carved into the frail wood of a lost floorboard.

*PHINNEAS & FINNEGAN*

Dad got down on his knees and fished the smallest figurine out of its home. It had old pennies for eyes. Dad's hand clenched, his forearm flexing. White dust spurted out of the thing, flouring his wet, slack bottom lip; with a moan of revulsion, he threw it back.

The impact must have been enough to rupture some vital linchpin, because with a grating shudder the entire nest came apart, falling into some unguessable emptiness—

Wrapping an arm around Milo's waist, Dad hauled him away, squeezing so tight Milo couldn't draw breath. Dad's face had gone waxy with shock.

"Stay right there, bud," he said. "Don't move a goddamn muscle, okay?"

Once he'd gotten Milo's promise, he crawled to the edge and glanced down. "Jesus."

Even from his vantage, Milo could tell the hole had to go down a long way. The nest had only been held in place by dead roots and the pressure of the earth.

A wind pushed up from someplace below, lifting the sweaty fringe of his father's hair.

"It was sitting on a sinkhole or something," Dad said.

"How deep is it?"

It took a while for an answer to come. "Deep."

Forcing himself, Milo edged closer until he could see for himself. The hole went down about thirty feet before it hit a gooseneck. The figures were splayed brokenly down there, staring up at Milo with empty eyes.

Milo pictured the nest grinding through the earth for decades, centuries even, pushing itself toward the surface like a cancerous growth while its ungodly cargo tumbled around like shirts in a dryer. . . .

"I don't want you out here anymore. Okay, buddy?" his father said.

His dad's confused, doomed face sparked anger in Milo's chest.

"You shouldn't have opened it, Dad! It was *private*! It wasn't for us."

Dad's reply was throaty and strangled. "Don't you *dare* talk to me like that."

Down the hole, Milo swore he could hear the dolls—no, they weren't dolls, they were something else, they were *things*—he swore he heard them shucking and grinding. They were crawling up to find him, weren't they? Slowly and patiently, writhing toward the surface, the dim forest light shining like a beacon for them. Guided by the perfume of his skin.

His father grabbed him roughly, shaking him. "You don't talk to your father like that, boy. That's not how things are going to go out here."

Milo turned and fled through the trees. Dad had no clue. He hadn't seen those eyes locking on to Milo's own from the darkness, pleading with him to join them. That thing hadn't been a fort or a wigwam or a nest. It was someone's garbage, but it was still alive, still hungry.

Dad should have left it alone and half-buried, forgotten.

Milo's feet tore through the forest, headed toward the open air and the parched dirt that was supposed to be a lawn. He burst out of the trees, breathing heavily.

The house was straight ahead. He wanted to catch his breath but his legs said no. His lungs burned, the same cold spiders of dread returning to choke him. He passed the playset in its disarray, almost tore through the sliding patio door at the back of the house.

Milo took the stairs two at a time, hurtling up higher and higher until he reached his room. He lay down on the floor with the window open, listening for the forest to follow him. There was no sound except his own.

Slowly he let himself forget the shapes inside that cursed shell, his father's insistence on opening it, the clear chuckle of the dirt beneath as if they were all in on this joke together . . . a practical joke, the kind where someone always got hurt.

"I didn't know," he apologized, though for what he couldn't say. "We didn't know."

As his heart rate slowed, Milo rooted out his tablet from under the bed. He ran his fingers over the screen and found Little Boy Blue looking back at him. There was no telescope, no forest, no demands to do anything other than watch and learn.

*"Today we're going to explore what it means to be a mammal, kids!"*

Milo had already seen this one, but it felt good to have the facts confirmed.

*"Humans. Rats. Whales. You know what they all have in common?"*

The voice soothed him, even if he knew it wasn't real. Just another man like his dad, pretending to be a kid.

# 4

**WHEN THE SENSORS CAUGHT** Trent's movement, the glass doors slid open with a satisfying *vish*.

"Keep up, sport." He beckoned Milo. "Big plans today, big plans."

He grabbed a cart from the corral—making sure to test the wheels first; he couldn't abide a wonky wheel—and guided it onward. Ahh, that signature Home Depot aroma: one part bicycle-chain oil, one part vulcanized rubber, one part *je ne sais quoi*.

A pallet of birdseed sat by the tiki torches. Ten bucks! Trent had no need for seed, didn't particularly like or admire birds, but the twenty-kilo sack presented an irresistible challenge. Flexing his hammies, he dragged one to the edge of the pile, jerking side to side.

"Dad, you okay with that?"

"Your old man can handle it," he said to Milo with a hint of warning in his voice.

He slung the sack over his shoulder like a limbless corpse. Knees buckling, Trent staggered to the cart and flopped it in. "On we go."

God, he loved this place. Some might say: *Whoa, Trent, you bought a brand-new house. The builder's on the hook for those repairs.* To such people he would quote the advice of one Bob Vila, sage of the socket set: *A man tends to his own.*

Plus, who said anything was *wrong* with his house? It was that—and Handyman Hank was a big advocate of this—a safe house marked a man's expression of love for the people under its roof.

"Hey, bud," Trent said, turning to Milo. "How about grabbing me a pack of Tuck Tape? Aisle six—make sure it's the green stuff."

Handyman Hank used the green exclusively. Milo departed on his mission, a good kid, listened to his dad. Trent piloted the cart past woodscrews, glazing points, pipe clamps. How many visits this week? His third—wait, fourth?

He was comparison shopping for respirator masks when he overheard two men in the next aisle. Peeking through the shelves, he spied a pair of headless chests in the fastener section.

"—had that slut lubed up with WD-Forty and I'm torquing like hell. That whore, I tell ya, she was on but tight. I threaded 'er and *that's* when the problems started!" Chest One chortled.

Chest Two replied: "Those rusted hex bolts can be real cunts, uh?"

Trent was no stranger to such terms, having overheard them during previous visits. *This bracket's a real slut, this whore of a drippy flange, that cunting light sconce.* Trent's least favorite was *cooze*: *ooze* with a *c* slapped at the front—

"Sir, may I help you?"

Why, if it wasn't one of the Depot's friendly Orange Aprons. The man looked about eighty, perhaps out on a day pass from his retirement villa.

"I know my way around, pops," Trent said, flipping a six-pack of respirators into his cart.

He made his way to the power tool section, easing around a heavyset gent crouched to inspect the sandpapers. The rear of the fellow's Carhartt trousers sagged alarmingly, displaying a good two inches of humid buttcrack.

Trent wrapped his fingers around the hilt of a Black & Decker sander. Light as a friggin' toy! The Makita belt sander, though, now *there* was the real McCoy. He tried a few practice-sands, running it along an imaginary two-by-four. The sample sanders were moored to yard-long wires. *They really ought to make the wires retractable,* he thought, *like dog leashes.* He'd make that suggestion to an Apron.

His gaze locked on the Metabo RBE 15-180. The $1,389 sticker made it the priciest sander by a wide margin, but all of a sudden he needed it in his hands, *now,* so he picked it up.

"That's a damn fine piece of machinery." The sandpaper aficionado with the buttcrack issue was grinning at Trent. "Got a big project, buddy?"

"You could say so. Got a deck that's itching to be redone." The lie flowed effortlessly out of Trent's mouth. "The little lady and I bought a real fixer-upper. The previous owner was—"

—*a slutting coooooze,* these words nearly dribbling over his lips—

". . . horseshit. Horseshit at home repair."

The guy cleared his throat. "You know that sander's a specialty model, right? For copper pipe. Seven-inch, nine-and-a-quarter."

43

Beads of sweat popped pregnantly on Trent's forehead. Who was this guy, anyway? Shaggy, big-gutted asshole smiling his smile, trying to squash Trent's good vibes . . .

"Oh, this? Different project . . . pipes, yeah. Nine-inchers." He caught himself diddling the sander's flywheel like some horny teenager playing pocket pool. "A few ten-inchers too."

"I didn't think they made copper tube in ten-inch. You had them made custom, huh?"

Trent's head throbbed. "You bet. Nine-inch is for pussies."

"Uh-huh." The guy nodded to Trent's cart. "You're leaking bird food."

There was indeed a growing pile of seed on the floor. Trent grabbed one of the boxed sanders and tossed it on top of the seed, then gripped the bar of his cart and set sail.

"Have a good one, bud," the guy blabbered.

Trent hissed under his breath: "Tight lines, you fat prick."

Trent grabbed a set of masonry drill bits, a claw-end recoil-less hammer, a three-pack of work gloves—he rubbed the gloves against his cheek, the calming rasp of split leather against his stubble—leaving little hillocks of birdseed wherever he stopped to browse.

Where the hell was Milo with his green fucking tape?

Trent bumped the cart down the lumber aisle, between dead horizontal forests. The aisle spat him out at the contractors' register. Trent shuffled foot to foot. The line here *was* a lot shorter. . . . He was purchasing plenty of professional-grade equipment, wasn't he?

He slipped in behind a wrinkled gentleman chaperoning a dolly of roofing shingles. With his thumb-tip, Trent lovingly rubbed the end of the three-quarter-inch rebar strut he'd put into his cart without any clear purpose or even memory of—

"Hey, bud, you're in the wrong line."

Trent turned to face the man behind him. One of *Those Guys*. They all had the same look: wide-shouldered, flannel-clad behemoths with windburned faces, the pinpricks of open pores spackling their cheeks.

"You're over thataway, chief." The guy hooked one thumb toward the plebe checkouts.

Another habit of their breed. Denying you the courtesy of a name. Always *bud, chief, pal, guy, captain, champ, boss, buddy-guy-chief*.

"No, I'm where I belong." Trent faced the cashier again, concentrating on her beeping the items with her *Star Trek* phaser.

"You got a card, Sarge?"

Trent turned back, his jaw set off-kilter. "A credit card? Do I need one to be in this line?"

The guy held up an orange card that, though foreign to Trent, exerted an immediate and almost sexual appeal.

"This one. For contractors, who stand in this line, while you Saturday guys stand in *that* line."

*Saturday* guy? What was this asshole on? It was a friggin' Thursday.

"I'll get one from the cashier," Trent said. He couldn't take his eyes off the seductive orange plastic rectangle in the man's hand.

"Don't work that way. Gotta apply. Show your union ticket, guild licenses, all that."

The guy nudged out one of his clodhopping boots and gave

Trent's cart a little push. More shocked than outraged, Trent jerked the cart back to him.

"*Don't* touch my shit."

A voice farther back in line said: "Go easy, Kelly."

How about that for life's little coincidences: the voice belonged to Asscrack Al. Kelly glanced back and noted, "He's wasting *my* time, Ned. Christ, I've got that job over on Easton, y'know, with the—"

"The duplex?"

"—yeah, I'm on the clock and we got assface here holding us up, and I mean, seriously, fuck *that*—"

Kelly the Contractor spun on Trent, a flush fingering up the hide-like skin of his neck. "I'm trying to keep it classy here, boss. But I'm in here five times a day, seven days a week. I got no time for you weekend warriors."

Shouldering Trent aside, Kelly grabbed the cart and gave it a good shove. It shot off spraying birdseed to collide with a display of garden rakes.

Trent stepped up to Kelly, whose flaring nostrils were the only part of him to move—

"Don't do it, hoss," came Asscrack Al's grim warning. "Unless you know some wild karate shit, they're gonna be scraping you off this floor."

"Daddy . . . ?"

Milo stood at the head of aisle twelve with a three-pack of green Tuck Tape. Spotting him, Kelly immediately softened. "Shit, I didn't know he had his kid with him," he remarked to the others in line.

Trent's heart jackrabbited. The shelves warped and wobbled. He stalked over to Milo and grabbed his arm.

"Dad, *owww.*"

Trent pointed one trembling finger at the prick. "I bet you wipe your ass with a corncob, you fucking Piltdown."

After paying at the jabroni checkout, Trent wheeled his cart out to the parking lot.

"Dad, what did that man say to you?"

"Nothing of any intellect," Trent snapped, adrenaline still spiking through him. "He's a fucking douchebag idiot."

Milo's head jerked up at him, his expression stricken. A contrail of guilt streaked through Trent. He was a grown god-damn man. A lawyer (well, he used to be) who earned (used to earn) six figures . . . well, nearly six. The way he'd acted in there, in front of his boy . . . what *was* that? Surely not the behavior of an evolved human being.

"Milo, I'm sorry. It's just sometimes two grown men have a disagreement, okay?"

Trent tossed the injured sack of birdseed into the Sienna, found the split in the packaging, and patched it with a strip of do-everything Tuck Tape. Out of the corner of his eye, he saw Asscrack Al ambling over. Trent's jaw crimped. *Here we go.*

"I come in peace, man."

Trent slammed the trunk. "Yeah? Well, your friend's a real piece of work."

"Ah, don't mind him," Asscrack said. "He's a first-class"—bugging his eyes out at Milo—"*buttface.*"

This earned a big laugh from Milo. The guy stuck out his callused hand and tousled Milo's hair with it. He offered the same hand to Trent, and for some terrible reason he shook it.

"Keep your stick on the ice, man," Al remarked, moseying off.

# 5

**AS IT TURNED OUT,** Handyman Hank's channel was a cornucopia for the Y-chromosome set. There were a *lot* of videos. Way more than Trent initially assumed. Which was weird, because when Trent first stumbled on Hank's feed, he could've sworn there weren't that many at all. In fact, there might only have been *one*: "Patch That Crack, Hank!"

But it turned out there were hundreds, perhaps *thousands*. How could Hank film so much content so quickly, unless he was creating around the clock? When Trent tried to bend his brain around this phenomenon, his eyelids fluttered and his breath bottomed out—some kind of psychic brownout that interrupted the power grid of his brain.

The more Trent investigated Hank's channel—which he did a dozen or more times a day—the more he saw that Hank was presenting a how-to guide on manliness. A certain *kind* of man, who did things the Old-Fashioned Way.

*"Most men never use a straight razor,"* Hank said presently. *"Hell, they'd probably slit their stupid throats."*

Milo was asleep, the house quiet aside from an inconstant gurgle coming through the vents. Trent was in the bathroom, his face foamed up in the mirror. His razor was from the Beard Club: $18.99 via mail-direct, including a handsome faux-leather case. The case had a loop to hang it off a belt, but really, what kind of maniac walked around with a straight razor on his belt?

His laptop was perched on the toilet tank. On-screen, Hank dragged a straight razor down a leather strop in practiced strokes: *shing, shing* was the honing sound it made.

*"Gotta be sharp enough to cut the hairs off a flea's nutsack, old hoss."*

Grinning—his teeth variously gray or dark like a mouthful of TV static—Hank positioned the razor next to his ear. *"Back in the war, COs used to make the grunts dry-shave as punishment if they caught 'em dog-fucking. But me, I love a dry shave."*

Hank drew the razor down his cheek, making the *scritch* of snapped stems.

*"I love my humps wet and my shaves bone-dry. You tuning in on my frequency?"*

"You bet," Trent said, awkwardly scraping his own face.

*"Now, some fellas walk their razor south for a bit of, ahem, downstairs groomery. Ole Hank'd tell you the only ones who're bald down there are newborns and pervos, but hell, I have heard that some tactical pruning can make your ole John look bigger. Not that I've ever seen the need."* Hank repositioned the apparatus between his own legs, shifting it from left to right like a shot put. *"Just make sure your little fella doesn't end up looking like a naked mole rat."*

Trent hooked a thumb under the waistband of his boxers—

come to think of it, things *were* a bit brambly down there. Corollary to this, it dawned on him that he hadn't had sex with Rita since moving in, making it, what, a solid month now? They were *waaaay* late christening this joint, weren't they?

Why *hadn't* they done the deed yet? Jeez, Trent just had so many projects on the go. But whose fault was that? Dunsany, Hector Hannah, that whole crew of Fuck-a-Roo Freddies.

Not to say the fixes were anything *big*, just regular home repair stuff. Like that squeaky stair, which he'd fixed by filling the gap between the tread and the riser with a seam of powdered graphite. And the other day he'd noticed one of the cumulus globes in the chandelier had gone the brown of a dead tooth. He'd bought a sixteen-foot Louisville stepladder ($1,105.21) at the Depot and ascended high into the main living area. At that elevation, he discovered the globe was full of bloated crickets—nearly locusts, size-wise—with pink-tinged compound eyes. All dead. There was a shard punched out of the glass cloud; that's how the bugs must have gotten in . . . or the mama bug had, anyway, to lay her eggs.

He'd unclipped the globe, taken it to the basement, and flooded it with bleach; the insects dissolved, sluicing down the laundry tub drain in a chunky slurry. He'd buried the globe in the trash, same as he'd done with that old soda can. Rita would be better off not knowing . . .

. . . but late at night, while his family slept, Trent retrieved the globe and put it on a shelf in the basement, hiding it behind a box of laundry detergent.

Currently, Trent came to a snap decision: he'd give his short-n-curlies a trim so his little soldier could breathe more freely.

The electric clippers were under the sink. He shut the laptop.

There was no need for Hank to watch, was there? He straddled the toilet so the hair would fall into the bowl.

He ran the clippers below his belly button and down, down, taking a thatch off his testicles and instantly regretting it: some things looked vulnerable and weird without hair, such as Irish setters and balls. He guided the clippers down his shaft, getting the pesky hairs where they met his—

Needling pain.

"Fuck!"

The clippers splashed into the toilet, buzzing and sparking—

"Fuck *me*!"

He leapt up, jerked the plug out of the socket, then surveyed the damage. At the base of his unit, where the skin went all shar-pei-y . . . the clippers had broken the skin. Blood rilled down the weld-mark of his testicles, a drop falling to tint the water of the toilet bowl.

He dabbed the cut with some toilet paper and then slapped a dime-sized fabric bandage on it. Shame crawled over him like stinging ants.

Trent forced himself to look in the mirror. He curled his lip at the pudgy, sallow nonentity staring back at him.

"Tell me, Trent, why do you suck?"

He hadn't always sucked, had he? He'd been a letterman tennis player in high school, captained the debate squad, and later made the dean's list in college. He couldn't track the exact decline, seeing as it was more a blind cliff he'd toppled off.

Though he'd never confess to it, the Carson Aikles affair at work had come as a blessing: when it happened, Trent had been floundering. Minor gaffes had morphed into major ones: he'd flubbed the McGlashan file, misplacing a single zero, no biggie, but then he'd done it again, *worse*, on the Corkins affidavit. The senior partners started poking through his backlog for errors—and sure enough, they were lurking. His confidence took a massive nose-dive . . . as Rita, meanwhile, was a total dynamo, H&T's rising superstar.

A nickname had started to circulate in the halls: *Sonny and Cher*, a reference so antiquated it could only have come from Old Man Tate himself.

The Incident allowed Trent to leave the firm with his dignity somewhat intact. The idea was for him to go back when he was ready. But the sad fact was that day might never come.

The bedroom was dark when he stepped into it, but Trent could see Rita's shape in the moonlight falling through the window.

"Come to bed, hubby."

He eased under the covers. Rita slid into him instantly, her hands all over him. He wanted to shove her off—a heady stew of shame, love, and vexation swarming him—but he also wanted *her* too, more than he could remember desiring anyone.

"Hey, Reets, fair warning that I kinda . . . screwed up."

"Oh no."

He didn't care for that *oh no*. It was the tone of someone who suspected him of a colossal stupidity he hadn't yet admitted to.

"Listen, I was"—big exhale—"uh, *personal grooming* and . . ."

"What did you do, Trent?"

"I nicked myself, *okay*? Not a big deal. Don't get Dr. Sanjay Gupta on the line."

Her immediate laughter raised his hackles. "But why?"

"You used to do it, remember? Your landing strip, wasn't that what you called it? I was just trying to be, you know, gentlemanly."

Her hand slid under his boxers. She was still laughing, the sound of it grating on his nerve endings—his stomach clenched as her fingertips moved southward to find the Band-Aid.

"Poor Trenty. Does it hurt?"

"Nope. I'm iron."

"You're getting there." Her fingers manacled him. "Does that feel satisfactory?"

"Yes, nurse."

She tucked tighter to him, chin pressed to his clean-shaven throat. Her heart thudded against his skin with force enough to echo inside his own chest.

It happened so quickly. They set upon each other with an intimate hunger. Trent had an overwhelming sense of thirst; he was dying of dehydration in an endless desert and Rita was a wellspring—he uncorked her and drank deep. There was something out-of-body to it, something fiery and ignitable, as if they were two children playing with a beaker of nitroglycerin.

As he scaled toward climax, Trent had the cold certainty of being watched: the walls sprouting unblinking eyes that stared at his and his wife's bodies. Instead of making him wilt under their gaze, the exhibitionism served to broaden Trent's shoulders and arms, adding new thickness and muscularity. . . . Rita did things that shocked him, perverse whorehouse techniques Trent had no idea she knew, let alone where she might have refined them, a mystery that excited and unnerved him in equal measure.

His passion mounted to a point of painful tension and he levered his body on top of hers. Under his ramming strokes, Rita went glossy, her body rippling like wax only to become something cold and inflexible with a hungry face . . .

. . . and finally, awfully, she transformed into that prick at Home Depot.

Into Asscrack Al.

The contractor's grease-stained hands gripped Trent's elbows and pinned him in place, Al's boiled-ham face topping his wife's sweat-slicked breasts, that bastard reaching up to tousle Trent's hair the way he'd done to Milo in the parking lot, Al breathing, "I'm a first-class *buttface*, ain't I?" and so Trent wrapped his hands around Al's throat, cutting off Al's fucking air supply, putting a crimp in the mainline (*I'll pop your head off like a dandelion, how about* that, *buttface*), and then the bedroom appeared to fill with fleshless effigies resembling scarecrows with their stuffing tugged away by the wind, scarecrows that had somehow crawled up through the pipework of Trent's perfect house; they shucked in some obscene dance, their joints screaming like unoiled hinges.

When Trent looked back down, Rita's face was her own again but her eyes were dark as onyx and her mouth widened in a shock orgasm, her chin tilted to the ceiling on cabled tendons, as a moronic and unmanly thought—*My wife is fucking me!*—rocketed through Trent's head, only to be forgotten the instant his own release thundered through him.

Groaning, he slumped off her. Rita's exhales came whistlingly, like a sick dog's.

"Did I— Rita, did I hurt you?"

"I'm okay. It's fine."

"You know I don't go in for rough stuff. I'd never—"

"I asked for it."

"Did you? You . . . you like that?"

"Sometimes."

Trent got up, ashamed for reasons he couldn't put a finger on. He padded into the en suite bathroom, flicked on the lights. He squeezed toothpaste on his brush; a bitter curd had built up along his gumline, some weird excretion his body had pumped out during sex. . . . *It's fear,* spoke a small voice in his head. *It's the curdle of fright.* Stupid thought.

He spit a bitter wad of foam down the drain hole. A punky smell drifted out of that dark metal eye: the stink of a rotten, abscessed tooth.

One of the pot lights fritzed and went out; the dead bulb fell from its mount, dangling on the electrical wire like an avulsed eyeball.

# 6

**HOURS AFTER SEX,** Rita lay beside her husband willing her hands to unclench.

Sex could be emotional for her. It had been with some men she'd dated before Trent. Those encounters had been marked by a joyful abandon, because by the time Rita slipped between the sheets with those men, she'd known they could not be *the* man. Those fellows would never know how close they'd come to annihilation, their lives like so much space junk hovering at the gravitational rim of a black hole—

*Stop thinking that way, daughter! It's soft, and that's not how I raised you.*

Her mother's saccharine and falsely chipper voice in Rita's head.

*This will soon be over. Then you can start again fresh.*

Rita had lain motionless in bed since it had ended. Jaw tense, teeth grinding away like bricks. Trent slept still as a corpse, though he'd once yelped "Hank!" in a schoolboy's voice.

She could feel the change inside her already.

Her mother had approached her task differently. She'd . . . she'd *cheated*, in Rita's view. Rita had been conceived at the Cozy Inn Bed and Breakfast in Niagara Falls, years before her mother made the pilgrimage. But Rita had decided her own daughter would know precious little of this time at the house—but the only way to ensure that was to make sure the spark of her life was kindled under this roof.

As for Milo . . . Rita wished like hell there was some other way, but some obligations are inherited the moment you first suck breath.

Rita hadn't been prepared for the . . . the *wilding* of their intercourse. How she'd thrashed and clawed, locked her legs around Trent's waist and pumped him into her, accepting his thrusts (themselves more lustful than anything he'd brought to their bed before) and pulling him deeper, snaring his bottom lip in her teeth and *holding* him in place, whimpering and making him do the same as his hands wrapped around her throat—

Which was when she'd felt it under the bed.

It had arrived with the hiss of a sharply taken breath. She had the impression of it swelling out of the floorboards under the mattress: a living growth, huge and gelatinous and demanding. . . . Without seeing, she could tell it was moving to the rhythms of her own body, each gyration and thrust, a mocking mimicry that made her skin shriek. . . .

She lay in bed now, these impressions churning uneasily in her mind, until she caught the soft sound of footsteps out in the hall.

"Mom?"

She turned to her side, pretending to stir. "Milo, baby . . . something the matter?"

"It's Morty."

She slung herself out of bed, instantly alert, pulling her robe on. Trent didn't wake. Rita followed her son into the hall, cinching the sash around her waist.

"Don't turn on the light," Milo said as they reached his room. "It hurts Morty's eyes."

The moon streaming through the blinds was strong enough for Rita to see the turtle resting in its aquarium in an inch of stagnant, malarial-smelling water.

Milo picked the turtle up. Morty gave out a frail wheeze.

"What's wrong with him, Mom?"

Rita took her son's pet in her hands. In the moonlight falling through the window, she could see that the turtle's legs were furred with a colonizing pinkness. It looked like someone had glued clumps of pink insulation to them. This mold or fungus, this *wrongness*, was visible when Morty poked its head out of its shell: there was a fuzzy pink collar around its neck like a costume boa.

Turning Morty upside down, balancing its shell on her palm, Rita touched the hole in its stomach plate: a crusted crater ringed by that hungering pink. The turtle made a pained wheeze.

"Let's take Morty outside."

They put on their boots and walked out onto the porch. Rita carried the turtle in a shoebox hunted out of Milo's closet. She and Milo walked toward the trees.

As a law student, Rita had studied the trial of one Boris Petrovic, Slobodan Milošević's head of intelligence during the 1990s Bosnian conflict. "Head torturer" was the more honest job description, which Petrovic cheerily admitted. One thing he said had stuck with Rita: *There is a point an interrogee reaches after which he can no longer be found.* A euphemism for how a victim of torture can endure such an intensity of suffering that they come to an event horizon—beyond which they become unreachable. Nothing can get to them. Not acid, electrocution, dismemberment. Not even the dismemberment of their loved ones.

Rita wondered if it might not be a good thing to reach that point, at least in certain situations. A glittery realm past all care. She figured it must come as a relief.

"How do you feel, Milo?"

He looked up at her, his face a question mark.

"Are you sleeping okay? No bad dreams?"

Milo said: "I don't remember my dreams out here."

They reached the edge of the forest. The trees stood in tight-packed ranks. No moonlight penetrated the canopy. Rita lifted Morty out of the shoebox. She felt movement under its shell. Something that was inside the turtle but not a natural part of it.

"We could let Morty go."

"I thought that's what you were going to say."

She caught the edge of reproach in her son's voice. "Well, why not? If he's sick, maybe being in the wild is best. Let him find some turtle friends out here."

That look from her son—was it a *sneer?*

"Animals don't have friends, Mom. Animals *eat* each other. If we let Morty go, something will get him."

Wind wicked under the hem of her robe, icing her. "What if I told you that if Morty could talk, he might ask you to let him go? As a good pet owner, would you do that?"

Her boy appeared to consider it. Not for long.

"He'll be okay. I know how to fix him."

"Oh?" Keeping her tone mild.

"I found a video online. 'How to Fix Your Turtle.'"

"Okay, but . . . do you think you can trust the internet, Milo?"

Milo's chin jutted. She was staring at a pocket-sized version of Trent. "Sure, if you're smart. Morty will be just fine. I'm sorry I asked you. It was stupid of me."

"No, I'm glad you did."

Milo took the turtle from her and put it back in the shoebox. He turned and headed back toward the house.

"Milo?"

Her son turned to face her. His eyes were chips of ice.

"If you start to feel bad . . . start to have thoughts that you're not sure where they came from . . . you tell me, okay? Promise me."

Milo's face softened. He was her boy in that moment, the sweet boy he'd always been. "Okay. Are you coming, Mom?"

# PART II

# JULY

# 7

RITA COULD ALMOST TOLERATE the house when it was empty.

It was five past noon. Trent was off on a quest to secure just the right tool to tackle an upcoming project. With him gone and Milo playing outside, Rita could almost imagine she was somewhere else. She could ignore the land outside (and under) the spotless bay windows, the earth scraped down like a raw wound barely beginning to heal. . . .

Old memories were like land mines: dormant, forgotten, but forever deadly.

She stood in the kitchen, peeling a mandarin orange for Milo's lunch.

When Rita saw its outline tucked behind the potted cat palm, her hand clenched. The mandarin crumpled as her thumb punched through its flesh.

"Shit."

She dropped the crushed orange in the sink. Crossed the

open area, wiping her hands on a dishcloth, halting where the walls met in a trough of darkness.

The contraption sat behind the browning, listless leaves of the cat palm. She stared down at it: a shoebox with a cardboard satellite dish affixed to the top. The dish spun, paused, spun again, as if picking up signals. It stopped, pointing at Rita.

She picked the thing up. It was dry and light like the skeleton of a rat, the cardboard warm from the mechanisms at work within. Turning it over, she carefully opened the flap cut in the bottom. The inside was a knitwork of Tinkertoys, Lego bricks, wire and fishing line, a toilet paper roll, a circuit board, more. The parts meshed with a calibration that would spark envy in the heart of a NASA engineer.

She took the contraption up the stairs to the second-floor landing. Reaching Milo's room, she discovered the doorknob wouldn't turn. Tucking the box under her armpit, she twisted the knob hard enough to send tendons cabling up her forearm—it relented so suddenly that her wrist buckled, the bones grinding.

"Oh, you sonofawhore . . ."

Stepping inside, she beheld more junkyard than bedroom. Detritus was spread across every inch of floor; what wasn't colonizing the ground was crammed into Tupperware bins. Rita recognized Milo's old toys: the Tinkertoys, the magnet and robotics kits, the busted pocket calculator with its rubberized number keys sprayed on the floor like teeth. . . .

Rita felt the miasma of her son's new obsessions as a sticky film on her skin.

She set the contraption on Milo's bed. Other inventions were lined against the walls or tucked lovingly under the desk. Boxes and cylinders, vibrating or blinking or winding on armatures. Her son's room ticked like a watchmaker's shop.

She spared a glance at Morty in its aquarium. The pinkness had migrated up the turtle's legs, crawling over its shell in fuzzy fingers. . . .

Its presence invaded the room with a sly inrush that vibrated the air molecules in her ears. At the outside edge of her vision, down by the bed, tucked just under the shadowy overhang of the mattress, Rita caught a frail bloom of light.

Milo's tablet. It was under the bed. And it had activated on its own.

*"Today's lesson is all about privacy, Junior Blues."*

Rita willed herself to be calm. It couldn't hurt her . . . no, it *could*, but it wouldn't.

*"Mommies and daddies should respect their children's private spaces. They must honor their imagination stations."*

She couldn't see it fully. Only hear its disembodied voice, and glimpse that rancid glow under the mattress leaching across the carpet until it almost touched her feet. If it did touch, she'd probably scream. She could picture its awful face—it was supposed to be felt or Muppet-skin, but to Rita it always looked diseased, like reindeer moss furring the jowls of an abandoned corpse in the woods . . . those horrible sucking eyes . . .

She looked out the window instead. The thing under the bed tittered, a cold reptilian note, as if that was precisely what it wanted.

Rita stood frozen as a dot formed out of the cloudless sky. As she watched, the dot resolved into the shape of a bird. It flew across the yellow dirt on a broken line, its wings flapping unnaturally. . . .

*"Mommies need to learn how to behave."*

The bird was flying right at her—

*"Mommies can be real nosy cunts, kiddos."*

—it slammed into the window, leaving a fishhook of blood on the glass.

*"Blammo!"* the voice under the bed cried.

Then it was gone, with that same dreadful outrush.

Rita bent over at the knees, releasing the air knotted up behind her ribs. Finally she straightened and stepped from the bedroom. She was halfway down the stairs when Milo's door swung shut. The latch caught with a soft *click*.

Rita padded across the living area and went out the back patio door. She found the bird on the ground beneath Milo's bedroom window. It spun paralytically, clawing itself around in an agonized circle using one wing. Its black eyes were floured in the ever-present golden dust.

Rita picked the bird up. Its heart beat against her palm with the pounding of a tiny hammer. She gripped its body in one hand and encircled its head with the thumb and forefinger of the other. Those two digits cinched into a noose.

Her hands rotated remorselessly in alternate directions.

Rita carried the little body inside. She wrapped it in paper towels and took it to the garage, laying it carefully in the organics bin. She went back inside, returning to the kitchen.

*—thud—*

The house made noises. Rita was used to hearing them at night: a sly crackling within the walls, or scrabbling sounds she tried to tell herself were the vents shaking off the builder's dust.

*—thud—*

That sound was coming from someplace outside. Was someone knocking on the door?

But when she opened the front door, no deliveryman was waiting on the front step. She opened the door wider, scanning the trackless dirt for a departing truck—

A pile of rags lay on the stoop. Reflexively, she knelt to touch them—and recoiled. An old rain barrel smell assaulted her nose. She lifted the crumpled pile. Not rags, but an unraveling figurine the size of a fat toddler. It smiled at her with teeth carved into the old foam head, brown and greasy.

"Milo!"

She stepped outside as a waft of throaty, vaguely mocking breath pushed from the vents.

"Milo, where are you? Time for lunch!"

Rita walked as quickly as she could, calling out her son's name, praying that the figurine was all he'd found.

⁓

Fear was useful. That was what Little Boy Blue always told Milo. Fear kept you from getting hurt.

But fear was also just another tool. *You can't let fear control you, Junior Blues!* You had to harness it, use it like anything else in your toolkit.

The shovel belonged to his dad, but Milo figured he could use it. Dad never said it *had* to stay in the garage, did he? Plus, the voice on the phone had told Milo to dig. Plus-*plus*, Milo was tired of that awful playset. Every time he climbed it, he got a splinter. At night he felt the spots where he'd been pierced and wondered if the playset got off on driving bits of itself into his skin. Milo thought it might.

Using the shovel, Milo had uncovered a new nest. His own little secret—well, his and Blue's. A nest not much different from the one he and Dad had stumbled on out in the woods, except this one was a whole lot closer, buried at the side of the house.

To be honest, Milo hadn't *wanted* to uncover the nest. He hadn't wanted to dig a hole at all, really. But he couldn't help himself after having that dream.

How many nights ago had he dreamt it? Was it four by now, or five?—in it, Milo had found himself in the shadow of the house with the chilly air coiling around his bare ankles, holding his tablet. Blue shone out of it, because by then Blue had learned how to invade his dreams. Milo couldn't get away from Blue, even if he desperately wanted to. Blue's eyes shone from the tablet like two cancerous wet plum pits. Blue's mouth ripped its moldering felt face apart to show off rows of blunt yellow teeth. . . .

There was a phone in Milo's dream, too. It rested on a column of moon-glossed marble like the phone the butler answers in a fancy mansion. It was ringing. A tinny, old-fashioned ring, the kind that could only be made by a bell-and-clapper inside the Bakelite housing.

Milo picked up the dream-phone. A voice said: *"X marks the spot, you dirty little shit."*

Milo had awoken with the *overwhelming* urge to do what that voice said.

To dig.

He'd started the very morning after he'd dreamt it. But before digging, he'd built the same phone from his dream.

Milo hadn't wanted to do that either, but he found himself doing a lot of things out here that he hated, wishing he could stop himself. He lacked the capacity to describe the thrust of these urges—why was he doing these things, what *drove him* to? All he could summon was this image of iron filings getting dragged around by a magnet. The filings had no choice. The magnet was strong, and in charge. Powerless, the filings went where the magnet wanted them to go.

Milo built it using the skeleton of an old phone, what Blue called a rotary dial . . . where had Milo even found the thing? He vaguely remembered unscrewing the receiver, snipping wires and adding parts, tightening them with the jeweler's screwdrivers his father left unused in the garage. . . . When it was built, it didn't look anything like the phone in his dream. Yet it *felt* the same.

Deep down, Milo suspected the phone shouldn't work. He was certain that anywhere else on earth, it *wouldn't* work. That if he showed it to the man at the cell phone kiosk in the mall, the guy would stifle a smile and say, *Oh, little man, isn't that cute?*

It only worked out here. But here was the only place it needed to work.

Milo was shocked when the phone rang, shocked the way anyone would be when a fragment of their dream followed them into the waking world.

*"Come find me."*

The voice that drooled out of the receiver was cold and leprous. Milo imagined some ancient tongue dry as a ginger root, pocked with softly pulsating boils. His skin had broken out in gooseflesh right there in the shadow of the house, next to the thrumming AC unit.

So yeah, he hadn't *wanted* to dig. Who wanted to seek out the owner of that voice? But an iron filing couldn't help but wriggle like a worm when the magnet moved.

He used the shovel to rough out a grid on the ground near

the house. He dug down methodically, creating levels in the earth: effectively a dirt staircase leading down.

As he'd dug, Milo's mind had wandered . . . thinking about the coming school year, a new school with a real track and an indoor swimming pool. Nobody knew old Milo. He'd be reborn. But that rebirth started there in the ever-deepening hole, so deep that his palms tore and leaked blood down the shovel. That was okay, though—that was part of doing the job right, being willing to get dirty.

His parents didn't bother Milo as he dug his hole. In fact, neither of them even noticed. Mom was at the office, and Dad . . . a day or two ago he'd wandered near Milo's excavation site, even called Milo's name in a brittle tone. Milo poked his head above the dirt line to see his father's face twitching as if a live current were flooding through it; then Dad's head had cocked as if he'd heard a voice from the house and he honest-to-God said, "Oh, fiddle-faddle," and went back inside.

Over two long afternoons, Milo had gouged steps into the dirt, ten and twelve and thirteen, down to where the sunlight turned grainy. . . . The wind whipped, carrying dirt away, leaving no evidence of his work. Milo became part of the earth, a creature of dirt and stone, until his shovel blade scraped against something.

"X marks the spot," Milo had said, hollow-voiced.

The nest had cracked apart at his gentlest touch—it broke *eagerly*, wishing to reveal its treasures. Milo crawled inside, tucking his head to fit. He'd run his hands over the inner bands of wood, all etched with little circles, interlocking like a crude fence. It hadn't smelled like the other nest he'd found with Dad—there was less rot here. It wasn't as old as that one either.

He felt what could only be described as a vacancy underneath the nest. Cool and bitter air—*sepulchral*, the word leaping unprompted into his mind from some spooky YouTube video he must've watched—purred between the cracks of the curved wood. This thing's journey must have started someplace far below. It was pushing itself toward the sunlight, leaving a tunnel underneath it, same as that other nest. . . . Holding his breath, Milo had felt a queasy rotation, as though the nest was still in restless motion.

There were figures inside this nest too. These were bigger, almost like the mannequins you'd see in a store.

A mother. A father. Three kids. Maybe they were triplets.

The father's fingers were shoved deep into its discolored eye sockets.

Milo had considered taking a few of them inside the house and arranging them in his room. That would show his dad he wasn't a scaredy-cat . . . but he couldn't bear the thought of it.

Milo had steered clear of the farthest corner of this second nest, the place that hung in crusted darkness like an old scab . . . the area that hissed like a bike tire that never emptied.

Milo had spent all of yesterday down under the earth with the beetles and worms and those strange figures, his new friends. . . . It was nearly dark by the time he'd slogged up the dirt staircase, feeling as exhausted as if he'd run a marathon.

He'd covered the hole with a big square of plywood. He wasn't embarrassed about his discovery—he just hadn't felt like sharing it with anyone.

Today, this very morning, he'd pulled the plywood aside again. He had his Maglite and his backpack. He reseated the plywood overhead, flicked on the Maglite, and went down the steps to the nest.

As he crawled inside, the broken ribs of wood raked his spine like fleshless fingers. This far underground the only sound was the slow tick of the earth. Reaching into his backpack, Milo pulled out his newest invention. He didn't know how it worked. He didn't even recall building it, which was increasingly the case: he'd start the YouTube video, and as soon as Little Boy Blue appeared, Milo's brain fuzzed out to static. . . . He'd come to sometime later with the new thing, whatever it was, resting in his lap.

This one was thick and brown and it buzzed unpleasantly in his hands like a huge blind cicada.

As soon as he positioned his invention on the floor of the nest, it sent out a painful pulse, like needles stabbing his fingers. Tiny legs hooked from its base, anchoring it to the floor. It purred softly as he watched, mesmerized. . . .

*Knock knock.* That sound came from someplace above.

Milo grabbed the Maglite and backpack. The invention skittered toward his sneakers. He pushed himself away—the nest made ominous crackles as the wood under his legs threatened to give way, sending him crashing into the yawning dark below.

Little Boy Blue's advice rang in Milo's ears: *Fear is a useful tool, Junior Blues!*

Leaving the nasty invention, Milo crawled out of the nest and started up the stairs—

The plywood cover peeled back. Sunlight flooded in.

~~

Rita stared down at her son, his face smudged in dirt. He was dragging himself up the stairs that he must have carved into the earth. The same smell from the porch drifted up out of the hole after him, a cloud of stagnant water and dead flies.

"Milo, *what* the hell are you doing down there?"

"I don't know, Mommy."

Her son looked so old, exposed in the brilliant sunshine.

Rita went to him, taking ginger steps down the dirt stairs—she could see the cracked-open husk below, splintered wood poking like fangs, and the shock dawned: Milo had been sitting *inside* that fucking thing in the dark, hunched in there like some nocturnal bug.

Wrapping her arms around her boy, Rita hauled him up to level ground.

"Are you okay, baby?" She could see the blisters on his hands; some had popped and bled.

"I've been digging," he said meekly.

"Okay," she said, the word ribbiting out of her. "Okay, okay, okay, but you're okay, right?"

Guilt crashed over her in a staggering wave. She should have been more attentive, seen what he was up to out here . . . but something had stealthily put Milo in her blind spot, hadn't it?

She brandished the figurine she'd found on the front stoop. "Did you drag this up from down there? Did you leave it for me?"

Milo's head shook, neck-snapping swings. "Nuh-uh. I didn't put that there."

Rita dropped the figurine and kicked it away. In as calm a tone as she could manage, she said: "I'm not angry, I swear. Just tell me. What were you doing down there?"

He looked at her wretchedly. "He . . . phoned me. Told me to dig."

Arctic cold pelted through her. "Who phoned you?"

Milo shook his head, refusing to meet her eyes.

"*Milo*. Was someone contacting you?"

No response.

"Did someone send a message on your iPad? You must never answer those."

He sawed his wrist across his nose. "Wasn't on my iPad . . . it was a phone. One I built."

"Okay. You built a phone." Rita's words were so light that they seemed to rise, each syllable filled with helium. "You need to show me it, okay?"

The sun didn't shine on the northern side of the house. Milo led her to the bushes Trent had planted to conceal the air-conditioning unit from their nonexistent neighbors. He got down and pulled a partially melted telephone receiver out of the brush, adorned with metal washers and bits of insulation that had been stapled onto it.

"This . . . is the phone?"

Milo shrugged, bashful. "Sometimes it rings."

He handed it to her. Half of an old landline set. Its weight was warm and repulsive, the plastic a bilious olive-green. Instead of connecting to a phone jack, the old-style coily phone cord was buried in the dirt under the AC unit.

"Who calls you, Milo?"

*Who could?* said a cold, knowing voice in her head. *Or what?*

"Blue does sometimes," Milo said. "To tell me stuff only he knows. Like where to find frogs in the dark. How to skip a stone with your eyes closed. What dogs think."

"And to dig," Rita said.

Milo said, "No, the other voice told me that."

The receiver pealed in Rita's hand. A shriek from a strangled larynx, or maybe just the inner wires singing.

With every fiber of her being protesting, she lifted the receiver to her ear. Milo watched expectantly, like some explorer who had brought his mad secret into her world.

*"Stupid fucking bitch, you coulda warned me."*

The voice thrummed up out of the earth.

*"It's so dark down here,"* the voice hissed through the wire, spitting in her ear. *"You'd never believe the darkness."*

Rita's fingers tightened around the mutated receiver.

*"Nothing to say, darling?"*

Wrapping her hand around the cord, Rita tried to tear the phone from the ground, severing the obscene connection—but the cord came endlessly from the dirt, flexible and springy, like the scarves from some Catskills magician's sleeve. The cord ran hotter the more she pulled out, grooving a fiery line across her palm.

*"Shoulda taken all your heads clean off! Chop-chop-CHOP!"*

Dirt spat as yard after yard of cord unspooled in her hands. She couldn't stop the moan from bubbling out of her throat—there came a high, singing snap, and then the cord was flapping out of the earth like a sprung snake, the jack-end lashing her ear as it whipped past. A lunatic screech came through the earpiece, then a bellow that bled to a whine, and then nothing.

She chucked the receiver as far as she could. Her whole body shuddered and she collapsed, as if she'd just removed an organ from her own chest.

Rita wanted to stay where she was, panting on the ground, but she couldn't. She rose to her feet and went over to Milo, pulling his shivering body tight against her own.

"We have to get rid of that phone, okay?"

She felt his chin nod into her shoulder.

"Promise me you won't take orders from anyone but me from now on, okay?"

"Even Dad?"

"I guess you may as well listen to your dad." *For now.* "But only us, all right? I don't want you thinking these . . . video guys are your friends. They aren't."

Milo said: "Blue's not real."

She didn't correct him.

# 8

THE SABAN FAMILY SIENNA idled in the Home Depot lot. Trent's fingers gripped the steering wheel, twisting until the rubberized vinyl squeaked.

Men stepped inside empty-handed and exited pushing carts full of raw possibility. Everything they'd need to shore up their homesteads against the predations of wind and water, and the more insidious threats that hid behind the walls: black mold and rodents and—

"—*bugs*," Trent said throatily. Weevils, ants, and those whispery little centipedes that were 99 percent leg.

The men coming out the main doors wore khakis and loafers and sported freshly barbered hair. The men galumphing out of the contractors' exit were thicker, crew-cut down to their pink scalps, skin bunched up at the backs of their necks like a pack of hot dogs.

Those guys were duded up the same as Trent was now. He'd ditched the suburban-dad look for something in keeping with his projects: DeWalt shock-absorbent boots (*Guaranteed Tough®*) and Milwaukee Tool bib overalls. The overalls chafed—he had a touch of jungle rot going on, to be frank—but the clothes felt right on him.

Come to think of it, he probably looked a bit like Handyman Hank. Not to say it was intentional, just the general look of any hard-workin' joe.

Trent wanted to go in, but the unpleasant encounter with Asscrack and his yee-haw goodtime buddy lingered. He desired one of those contractor cards. He'd researched the benefits. Sakrete concrete mix, the thirty-kilo bag, only $5.08 (non-cardmembers paid $18.33, like fish). Wire mesh, five-feet-by-fifty, a steal at $133—they were practically *giving* the stuff away.

"Toilet seats," Trent muttered. "The good ones, Kohler Cachet Quiet-Close, not the piece-a-shit American Standards . . . forty-one seventeen," breathing out the price as a Zen koan.

The contractors bustled out to their trucks with dollies of pressure-treated deck boards, ribbed sheet metal composite, Shop-Vacs, all good stuff. Trent rubbed the double-woven rip-stop polyester over his crotch absentmindedly as the contractors' pickups drove off to erect things, reinforce things, make things safe.

Trent drove away from the Depot moody and anxious. He wended past mini-malls and factory outlets listening to Handyman Hank's podcast, *To Make a House Your Home*.

*"Now, some smooth-brains will tell you double-reinforcing your foundation slab's just wasted effort and a sunk cost. Tell you what, friend: when the bad wolf comes, I'd rather be the piggy who built his house outta bricks."*

His phone shrilled three times in rapid succession. Texts from the wife.

Hard day at the salt mines.

Henderson file, ugh.

Can you make dinner, hubby?

The Henderson file? That was *his* old file! The one he'd screwed up during the discovery phase, preventing a bloodless settlement. As if Rita didn't remember.

*"What a thoughtless bitch,"* Hank might've said. Trent was only half-listening. Surely not.

Helplessness sank its claws into Trent. An insidious metamorphosis was taking place at the peripheries of his consciousness, a sly process of transformation he could only liken to the molting of a dragonfly except in reverse, turning Trent into a hideous shrunken parody: the dinner-maker, the lunchbox-packer, the button-mender and sock-darner.

*Yes, wifey, no, wifey, please may I have my testicles back so my friends don't spot the yawning abyss in my cargo pants, wifey?*

Trent's role was to fix stuff when it broke, to mow the goddamn lawn (well, when they had one)—to get his hands greasy, dirty, bloody, for the love of Christ! The division of labor had gotten all screwed up in his household. If Rita thought he was going to tuck his dick up the crack of his ass and start swanning around with an eggbeater wearing a safflower apron—*Kiss the Cook!*—she was in for a rude surprise.

*"It's a thankless job, being the provider,"* Hank said sagely. *"A role a man takes on by dint of the swing of his hammer and the power in his frame. He has to, because the world would stop working otherwise. And do so selflessly, often without any credit or acceptance. That's the grisly toll. Isn't that right, fellas?"*

"You're good goddamn right," Trent growled, hunched over the wheel like a gargoyle.

After an hour of aimless driving, his only companionship the increasingly fulminating brogue of Handyman Hank, Trent found himself in the air-conditioned confines of Sarkasian's Chevrolet Buick GMC.

"Got your eyes on the Denali, uh? Ooh, ain't she a beaut."

Trent snapped back to the here-and-now to find himself standing near a man in a cowboy hat and bolo tie with his arms crossed companionably on the Denali's hood. The man's hands sat level to his eyes, partly because the truck rested high on its shocks but more because the man was embarrassingly short.

"I'm just looking."

"Oh sure, get yourself an eyeful." The Lilliputian salesman unfurled from the hood. "You can look all you want, but touching? That'll put you back a few bucks." A smile, a proffered hand. "Rick Sarkasian, owner-slash-operator. I drive one of these bad hombres myself."

Trent almost scoffed. What did this little feller need a workingman's truck for—ferrying his purebred Pomeranians around?

Sarkasian nodded out the showroom window. "That what you're driving now?"

The Sienna sat in the shadow of the lot's pickups. He and Rita had bought it not long after Milo came along. Trent hadn't protested the sensible purchase at the time, but he'd since come to hate the minivan. Who wanted to be seen driving around in a big beige tampon?

"Why not take her for a spin?" Sarkasian slapped the Denali's hood. "Driving is believing."

Sarkasian rode shotgun as Trent nosed the Denali into traffic. The truck was so *wide*—an ocean separated Trent from Sarkasian—so *tall*. He felt like Zeus staring down from Olympus. He had to fight the urge to tromp the gas and blow through every red light. Why *should* he stop? He could smash every puny car on the road to iron shavings and keep on trucking.

"How's it on gas?"

Sarkasian just chuckled.

By the time they rounded back into the lot, Trent's euphoria was peaking. "I'll take it."

"Ding-dang right you will!" Sarkasian slung his hat off and gave Trent a whack on the shoulder with the brim. "Let's go make it official."

Trent was in the sales office inspecting the framed photos—mostly golf or equestrian sports, and in none was Sarkasian wearing a cowboy hat—when the salesman returned. Trent intuited an alteration in Sarkasian's demeanor as he settled behind the desk.

"So, Mr. Saban . . . we ran your credit and, uh . . . I'll try not to be indelicate here." The good ole boy shtick was gone. "You wouldn't take one of my trucks out for a spin if you couldn't afford it, would you, now? You wouldn't waste anyone's time, I'm sure?"

Trent cleared his throat. "I'm unclear as to what you mean."

"Mr. Saban, are you currently employed?"

"Not as such, no."

"What was the date of your most recent employment? I recognize that's sensitive information, but for the sake of our financing terms, I do need to know."

"There was an incident at my place of business." Trent ran his fingertip along the edge of Sarkasian's desk. "They call it stress leave . . . *enforced*. Not my choice."

"Mr. Saban, look. Maureen over in financing, she punches the numbers in and the system spits out a yes or a no. Now, I've made a generous trade-in offer, but still, the system's saying what it's saying." His tongue flirted with the tip of his eyetooth. "So, we have two options. One, you get a guarantor. Two, I can have one of my junior sales reps take you over to the resale lot and find something more fitted for your price range."

Trent mumbled something.

"What was that, Mr. Saban?"

"I said, '*Call my wife.*'"

# 9

IT WAS EIGHT O'CLOCK by the time Trent pulled his new Denali into the driveway. He'd been driving somewhat purposelessly for hours, hogging the center line and daring anyone to honk at him. After that, he'd made a much-needed stop at Home Depot.

Trent swung down from the cab, licked his thumb, and rubbed a speck of dirt off the driver's-side whitewall. The Sienna was parked at the curb—or where the curb would be once a paving crew eventually laid down a damn street. Distorted fury arrowed up Trent's spine.

Inside, Rita was making dinner. The sight of his wife peeling carrots over the kitchen sink soothed Trent. A lady in the street and a freak with the sheet-pan . . . wasn't that one of Hank's lines? Hah, who else? That Hank, such a roguish sense of humor.

Trent latched his arms around her waist. "Whatcha got cookin', good-lookin'?"

She said, "You're late. I texted a dozen times."

"Technology." Trent chuckled. "Quick question: What's the minivan doing out there?"

He didn't want to spark a fight, but the sight of it in the driveway galled him. The Denali *fit*. The new house *fit*. The Sienna was like a camel turd on a wedding cake.

"We ought to have a second car," Rita said. "I called Royal Towing and had them bring it from the dealership."

Trent unwound his arms from her waist and sat heavily at the table. He waited for her to ask about the truck; when she didn't, he said: "You know I'm good for it, right?"

He hated sounding like a thirteen-year-old who'd cadged seventy-five cents off his buddy for a pack of gum.

"You like it, though?" she said lightly. "You're a truck guy now?"

The veiled insult—if it was that—he let pass. "I really do need one, Reets. I've got a lot of projects on the go. . . . I got one of those Home Depot cards too." He pulled it out of his pocket to show her, but she wasn't looking. "I get all sorts of perks."

In truth, his inveiglement into the Mysteries of the Card had been a huge bummer. Turned out you didn't need guild licenses or certificates. The Pro Xtra card was available for a yearly fee; all you had to do was ask . . . which brought up the prospect of *another* card, the Titanium Premium: a secret upper echelon with the promise of otherworldly bargains—bags of Sakrete for a nickel, unlimited nails—offered via veiled *wink-wink* to true initiates.

The rake of Rita's peeler against carrot flesh set Trent's teeth on edge. He slumped at the table, feeling boneless and small.

"I wish you'd support me a bit more."

The peeler clattered into the sink. She pivoted and came over to the table, sitting hard.

"Support you in what, pray tell? The truck? I mean, do I think anyone needs heated cup holders? I figure if you drive a truck, you could handle a mouthful of lukewarm coffee."

"See? Shit like that. Poking little holes. In me, in everything I try to do lately."

"I don't have a problem with the truck."

"Oh, you have problems, though!" he flared, his voice snapping off the vaulted ceiling with such force that the chandelier globes tinkled.

"What kinds of problems do you think I have, Trent?"

"You have a problem with this house. Us moving here. Me dragging us out because—"

*—this is the only place we could afford to live.*

Except that wasn't true, was it? Rita already made enough that they could have bought a house somewhere else. In the city, even. The mortgage might have been tight for the first term, but within five years—hell, maybe only three—Rita would be making plenty to cover it, plus any extracurricular classes Milo wanted to take, plus biyearly trips to Disney World with her deadbeat husband in tow. . . .

Next, a powerful impulse went blazing through Trent. His head jerked up so rapidly that dizziness swarmed him. He stood, stiff-spined, sending the chair toppling over.

"I've got to take care of the hose spigot . . . it's leaky."

He went outside, stretching his limbs under what was left of the sun. The spigot had dripped the last time he'd used it to spray the dust off the patio. The constant drip represented dollars leaking out of his (or his wife's) pocket. This could be addressed with a little care.

Another homeowner would have bought a whack of washers and doodads, but all Trent needed was a roll of Teflon tape. He wrenched the top off the faucet, pulled out the stem and loose bonnet. If Rita came out, she'd see him holding part of their house in his hand. She'd see how needed he was, and value that in him.

He created his own bonnet packing with the tape, compressing it and twisting the knob back into place without stripping the threads. The faucet sat secure in the wall, just beautiful. He twisted the tap. The water flowed. No drip. Professional. It made him happy, these repairs. Small but essential, and the joy he felt in accomplishing them was evidence of a change taking place in him, one he was fully committed to embracing.

"You get it taken care of?" Rita asked, finding him in the yard after the sun had set.

He was going to show her, but was distracted by the sudden bloom of light over the night rise. They watched it resolve into the beam of two headlights coming steadily toward them.

"If that's Hector at this hour, I swear I'm going to split his wig, Rita."

A glossy sedan pulled up beside the Sienna. A man and a woman got out. Both were corporately dressed. The woman carried a briefcase.

"Mr. Saban," the man said. "I'm Ted Delsom. My associate is Anna Flint. We're with Hollis-Cooper Security, acting on behalf of your current employer, Harrison and Tate. May we beg a few minutes of your time?"

Rita said, "I'm with H-and-T. Senior partner."

The gentleman, Delsom, said, "We're aware of that, Mrs. Saban."

"What's this in reference to?"

Anna Flint's eyes were pinned on Trent. "It's better we talk inside, if that's all right."

"It's not all right, actually."

Trent held one hand up. "Rita, let's not be impolite."

Once Milo had been sent up to his room and the adults were seated at the kitchen table, the woman, Flint, snapped open her briefcase and took out a tablet device. Her and Delsom's attitudes weren't hostile, but *brisk*. Definitely brisk.

Delsom said, "Just to confirm, Mr. Saban, you're still on the H-and-T payroll, yes?"

Rita spoke first. "You already know he is, correct?"

"At a reduced salary." Trent had to work not to fidget. "Trauma leave."

"That is, in compensation," Delsom went on, "for mental and physical pain and suffering related to the incident where your coworker Carson Aikles—"

"Went berserk with a hammer," Trent said coldly. "You're not going to make me rehash it, are you? There's a deposition file an inch thick."

Flint turned the tablet to face him. "Mr. Saban, another of your coworkers, Ashley Greco. She had the office next to yours, correct?"

A sudden sweat sprang out on Trent's chest. He felt slimy with it, as if he'd rubbed himself with sliced okra.

"Unbeknownst to anyone, Ms. Greco had a nanny cam in

her office," Flint rattled on. "She was convinced the cleaning staff was stealing her petty cash. The installation of such devices is a privacy issue—a big no-no, as Ms. Greco well knew. Which is why she sat on this evidence for as long as she did."

Flint tapped the tablet screen. It sprang to life: a black-and-white image of Greco's office. The angle played from behind her desk. The timer on the nanny cam ran at 11:02:13, which would've been right around the time when . . .

. . . and yes, here he came, right on cue.

In the kitchen of his new home, Trent watched the recorded version of himself duck into Greco's unoccupied office. A sense of disorientation gripped him as he watched the little three-inch-tall black-and-white Trent on the tablet screen cringe and try to scurry under Greco's desk, but of course the same thing happened on the screen as had happened that day: Trent was too big to fit under her desk, so his back poked above it like the hump of a breaching whale—

Trent watched this unfold, uncomprehending. He was reliving a repressed memory, forced to reckon with it springing out of his memory banks like a delirious skeleton, jambling and bambling on the pillowcase of his brain:

*I'm back, Trent! Hee-hee-hee, remember me? REMEMBER ME?*

—next came that sunny lunatic Carson Aikles, straight down the hall toward Greco's office. The nanny cam caught him barnstorming toward her window, slashing the air in front of his face with his hammer. . . . The camera shivered as Carson Aikles did exactly what Trent knew he was going to do: Carson ran straight into the plate-glass barrier fronting Greco's office, knocking himself unconscious.

"Turn this off," Rita said from some alternate dimension.

The image ran static for fifteen seconds before Trent slunk out of the office and over to Carson's supine body. . . . Tiny black-and-white Trent glanced around, assuring himself he was alone . . . straddled Carson Aikles, sitting on the man's chest. . . . Trent punched Aikles. Once, then again, quite a bit harder. Trent then stood up, heaving, fixing his hair back in place.

Trent sat openmouthed in his kitchen, both knowing what was to come and not knowing too, like a film he'd watched years ago whose plot was too convoluted to remember.

Grabbing the hammer, Trent sat back on top of Aikles. He raised it over his head and brought it down at Aikles's head, checking his stroke an inch short of the man's skull. Trent sat on Carson for what felt like a long time, turning the hammer over in his hands. Finally he rotated the nail-pounding end to his own face, let the hammer fall to his belly button . . . then brought it up swiftly, *bam*, into his own forehead.

He slumped off Aikles and lay on the floor, dazed. He staggered up. The nanny cam even managed to capture the gray, quarter-sized welt on his forehead. Trent picked up the hammer and backtracked down the hall. Rearing back like a baseball pitcher, he hurled the hammer at the plate-glass office window. The glass shattered in a cold starspray. Trent's shoulders joggled as he laughed like some overadrenalized teenage vandal.

The video stopped on that pathetic image. Flint shut the tablet off.

"This runs contrary to the events you depicted at the deposition, Mr. Saban."

Trent cleared his throat. "Somewhat, yes."

Rita sat with her head down, breathing like a woman trapped

at the bottom of a sour gas well. When Trent opened his mouth again, she gripped his wrist. Her nails dug in.

"As your potential attorney in this matter, I advise you not to speak."

"This can be resolved painlessly, Mr. Saban," Delsom promised. "Amicably, even."

He drew some papers out of his attaché case. Five minutes later, Delsom and Flint were back in their glossy sedan.

Trent went upstairs and undressed for a shower in a numb stupor. Water chuckled from the showerhead as he scrubbed, but the filth was embedded under his skin. It would take acid, some kind of emulsifying sulfurous compound used to strip marine paint off boats. . . .

Later, he slid under the covers. Rita was a ramrod, her eyes locked on the ceiling. A cold trench lay between them, so deep Trent wondered whether he'd ever find its bottom.

"Milo doesn't need to know."

It was Rita who said so, not him.

"Okay . . . Did *you* know, Rita?"

". . . Of course not."

"Old Man Tate didn't come to you first? Ask if you couldn't smooth those waters and prevent the necessity of the goon platoon?"

They lay for a while, not touching.

"If he did, Rita, then that was some kind of performance you put on down there."

"It wasn't any kind of performance. My embarrassment was a hundred percent real."

Leaning close to her ear, Trent rasped: "I don't believe you."

She jerked away as if she was being forced to share the bed with a gigantic perspirant slug. She turned onto her side, going over like a dead log in a river's current; a string of shapeless syllables slipped from her mouth. . . .

"What did you say?"

"Nothing." Flat, toneless.

"No, you did. I heard you."

"What did I say, then? Go on, tell me."

A feeling of suffocation swarmed him, a sense of being alone and somehow *duped*, as if he'd married a changeling whose true face had lain hidden from him for all these years.

"You said, 'Maybe something-something what's coming to you.'"

Except even that was a lie, because he'd heard her exactly. The acoustics of the house had amplified her words.

*Maybe you deserve what's coming to you.*

"What's coming to me, Rita?" Trent wanted to know—he had to stop himself from ripping the knowledge out of his wife, starting at the base of her spine.

"Go to sleep, Trent."

He should send Carson Aikles a thank-you note. It wouldn't be read, so kind of a wasted effort: Aikles had committed suicide at the funny farm. Hanged himself with an extension cord—he'd have used a double-insulated 12-gauge cord if he was smart; those things were super durable. One of the associates at H&T whom Trent remained chummy with said that Aikles's head had swelled up like a grisly blue balloon.

Trent ought to lay a bouquet of posies on Carson's headstone, at least. He'd provided Trent with an escape hatch from the cycle of failure he'd been gummed up in. All it took was Trent sensing his opportunity and embracing it.

*It takes a certain kind of strength to hit yourself with a hammer,* he thought before drifting into a troubled sleep. *The strength to step off the path you'd put yourself on, becoming a brand-new man.* Perhaps Rita would see that in time, perhaps not.

# 10

*"WHAT IS THE* PURPOSE *of today's man? Brothers, ask yourselves. No wars to fight, no borders to invade. It's all been done by the men who came before. But that* need *still burns, doesn't it?"*

Handyman Hank spoke from Trent's laptop, opened on the coffee table.

*"What does our stalwart brother do? Moves out to the edge of a great unknown wilderness—that's what your old pal Hank would do. Puts himself to the last true test, away from the bullshit of cities and the brigade of assholes who'd love nothing more than to make you their footstool. Make no mistake, the lot of the modern man is a* hard *lot."*

Trent made a grunt of agreement as he hefted the new sixty-inch LCD flat-screen, leaning back awkwardly and putting the entire weight of the TV on his L5 lumbar disc.

*"We men are beset, predated upon on all sides!"*

"Preach," Trent hissed through gritted teeth as he blindly angled the TV toward its mount—

"Hon, how's it going?"

Trent's face wrenched up in fury. He staggered to the couch, dropping the TV on the cushions. He paused *The Handyman Method* and forced himself to face Rita.

"Aren't you a stealthy wife, sneaking up on me."

Rita crossed her arms, pasted a bullshit-sweet expression on her face. "What are you watching?"

"'Hank's How To.'"

"How to what?"

"What's it look like? 'How to Mount Your TV on the Wall.'"

"I'm off to the office. Won't be home until late."

"That's just Jim Dandy with me."

"Milo's up in his room. I told him to keep himself inside until I get home. Make sure he doesn't wander, okay?"

"*Jah*, Commander."

Trent kept his head down until Rita left the house. They'd barely spoken since H&T's emissaries had shown up late last week. He resented her intrusions. She wouldn't appreciate him hovering over her shoulder in her office, would she?

He restarted the video.

"*A man needs time with his projects,*" Hank went on. "*And women . . . they don't always get that, do they? Not saying my wife's a nag, but she does have too great a fondness for sugar cubes.*" An earthy chuckle. "*Now, with that wall mount you're gonna brace the T-joint with . . .*"

Once the TV was mounted, the spotless LCD screen gave Trent's reflection back to him. He turned admiringly in its blank gaze. He'd lost weight. Must be all this clean country living. He'd become rugged, *durable*, more the strapping lad he'd been back in law school before Rita skulked into his life. . . .

*"Fuck."*

His finger. The left pointer. It'd been bugging him since he woke up. Every bump or jostle sent a throbbing fang of pain down to his wrist. It was the same finger—this realization landed with a dull thud—he'd hurt reaching into the crack in the closet wall on their second day in the house.

Using the thumb and pointer of his right hand, he applied pressure to the injured digit—his mouth opened in a silent scream as bayonet-bright agony zagged to his elbow. Syrupy yellow pus leaked from under the nail, giving off a gangrenous tang.

"I should see a doctor," Trent said tonelessly.

*Like hell*, Hank said in his head. *It's nothing a little meatball surgery can't fix.*

Trent plodded down to his workbench in the basement, the pegboard above it hung with tools lovingly outlined in Sharpie.

Standing at the bench under the basement bulb, he wrapped duct tape around the base of his pointer to cut off the blood supply. The fingertip went purple—a brief but manageable flare of pain—then white as the blood leached out.

With his fingers starfished on the bench, he selected the needle-nose pliers. The air through the vents rose to an appreciative purr as he dug the tip of the pliers under his fingernail.

The pain was monstrous; he could see the metal tip of the pliers under the milkiness of his nail, dug in like a sliver. He brought the pliers' jaws together on the nail and pried upward—

His fingernail tore free with a gluey suction and a warm sense of relief, like the top blowing off a pressure cooker. The nail detached from the nail bed all in one piece, like a press-on nail, trailing snot-like webs of pus. It was a lot longer than he'd guessed, the way the roots of an excised tooth will shock you with their length.

"*There*," Trent gritted through clenched teeth. "There you go, you fucker."

His fingernail fell from the pliers and hit the concrete floor. The flesh of his nail bed was red and pulpy like a skinned salamander. Trent squinted. . . .

Something was glinting in there.

Regripping the pliers, he probed the mealy tissue.

"Ohhh, you bitching bastard you . . ."

He rooted the jaws inside his fingertip, twisting and pulling. The pliers seemed to sink deeper than his finger should've allowed; they ought to be digging into the workbench now. . . .

He gripped something solid, but not bone. Carefully, eyes bulging, he drew it out.

When he levered open the pliers, it fell to the bench with a dull *tink*. The tip of his finger now had a caverned, deflated look. Bits of tissue were gummed in the pliers' jaws.

Trent took whatever had been inside him over to the laundry tub. He twisted the taps and rinsed it off, being careful not to drop it—he didn't want it going down the drain.

He gazed at it in his cupped palm. A piece of glass.

Trent stared at it with mesmerized bewilderment. How the hell had it gotten in—?

Something twigged in his hindbrain. He reached up to the shelf above the tub, pushing aside the box of laundry detergent. . . . The chandelier globe was still hidden there. The one he'd replaced because it had been full of those pink-eyed bugs.

With a species of disbelief, he took it down. Turning the

globe over in his hands, his ruined finger leaving bloody streaks on the glass, he located the missing keyhole he'd assumed the bugs had gotten in through.

He rotated the wet shard of glass until it slotted into the hole as neatly as a puzzle piece.

This piece of glass . . . a piece from his chandelier . . . he'd pulled it out of his—

*"You ought to put a dressing on that owie of yours, Trent."*

Trent's focus, his apprehension, the groundswell of existential terror gathering in the dark spaces of his brain . . . it all dissolved, turning to smoke, vaporizing.

He tilted his head toward the intake vent running through the rib-beams above him. Hank. Trent could swear that was his voice drifting out of the slotted grate cover.

*"It's not what you think it is, Trent,"* Hank whispered from the vent, his voice honey-soft. *"It's not worth thinking about—it'll only distract you from your purpose."*

"Right," Trent breathed. "It's just a weird coincidence."

*"And life's full of those, isn't it?"*

Trent ran water in the laundry tub, rinsing the shard of glass down the drain. He carried the chandelier globe upstairs. Opening the patio doors, he heaved it as far as he could. The globe arced over the deck and detonated on the hard-packed dirt.

By the time Trent shut the sliding patio door, the whole episode began to feel trivial. By the time he'd slapped a fabric Band-Aid over his finger—which looked skinny and somehow formless at its tip now, like a withered fiddlehead—he'd pretty much forgotten it entirely.

Where the fuck was Milo?

He wasn't in his room. Which, to put it mildly, was a god-damn disaster zone.

*Better clean this shit up, buster,* Trent thought, *or it'll be my boot up your ass.*

He peered out Milo's window, his eyes goatish with irritation. Kid wasn't out on the playset either. He hadn't used it much at all, in fact. Trent had spent good money for the thing only to have Milo treat it as if it had been spritzed with Ebola.

Trent stalked outdoors. Wind whipped across the wasteland, slapping grit against the siding. Trent's hands clenched into fists, relaxed, became fists again.

*Oh, my fine young son, if you don't give that playset some atten-tion, I'm gonna beat you black and blue.*

"You and me, buddy." The anger coiled up from his heels, pushing into his veins and making him tremble. "Until the sun sets. Until the *fucking SUN—*"

Stopping dead in the bile-colored dirt, Trent slapped himself. A blow hard enough to rock his head to one side. His eyes stung as he fought to reclaim his thoughts, which spun on reckless and violent orbits.

"I'm not going to hurt my son, not for any reason." Trent's voice was choked, barely there. "Why would I do that—?"

—something lunged at him then. It came from behind like a sneak-thief, from the brick and eaves of the house but more predominantly from below, from the dust and the cold earth.

*The beet . . . the beet,* jefe . . .

As a university senior, Trent had gone to Cancun with a group of buddies. Around the fifth day, stir-crazy and beer-bloated, he'd taken a solitary excursion off the resort. The cheapest day trip was horseback riding. The bus dropped him and a dozen other sun-blistered tourists at a clapboard barn. Trent's horse, a swaybacked scoundrel named Loco, kept angling off the path to graze on the weeds. Trent tried nudging Loco, tried cajoling Loco, but Loco did as Loco wanted—that was, until one of the gauchos rounded back.

The gaucho was over sixty, a tanned strip of rawhide. He dismounted his horse and gestured for Trent to get off Loco. "I show you trick, *jefe.*"

The gaucho took hold of Loco's head—the horse's eyes rolled wildly while in this man's grip—and peeled the horse's lips back.

"You see this?" The gaucho pointed. "Is the bit."

*The beet.* That's how Trent heard it. *The beet*, jefe.

Trent spotted a grooved bar of metal in the horse's mouth—in the soft spot between Loco's molars and incisors. The metal was roughed up like the face of a chisel.

"Next time he do bad, you do this."

Gripping Loco's reins, the gaucho gave a yank; the bit drew against the soft spot between Loco's teeth, putting pressure on the bone. The horse issued a thin, shocked snort that made Trent think of how a person might breathe with a knife pressed to their throat.

The next time Loco stopped to crop the weeds, Trent dutifully tugged the reins and felt the bit do its ugly work, the pain tremoring right through the horse's flesh. . . .

. . . *the beet . . . the beet . . .*

This was the feeling now, though Trent couldn't contextualize it as such. Whatever came at him in the shadow of his house, it was as if a bit had been threaded into Trent's mouth, slotted into the sensitive groove behind his teeth. . . . Except that wasn't quite right either, because this bit was *inside* his head. Skewered straight through one ear and out the other, spiked through his gray matter, and with it came a control so absolute and yet so subtle that Trent was unable to distinguish his own motivations from any outside force.

"Where's that fucking boy of mine?" Trent snarled, packed full of rage again.

He stalked around the side of the house. The garage door yawned open, dust scrolling inside. The floor was colonized by Trent's recent purchases, the lion's share still unopened.

"Milo?"

He shoved aside the candy-apple tool caddy and a mammoth bale of bubble wrap—he spotted the crown of his son's head, tufting up behind a stack of all-season tires.

"What are you doing in here without my permission?"

Milo didn't register Trent's presence. Was Trent being *ignored*? Milo knelt by the wall, fiddling with something. . . . Trent's rage peaked, a trumpet-blast down his nerve endings.

He grabbed Milo, jerking him around to face him—Trent's palm was open, ready to slap the ever-loving shit out of the disobedient, ungrateful little—

"Dad . . . ?"

At the sight of Milo's frightened face, the *beet* disintegrated. The rage sluiced away like water out a storm drain, leaving Trent breathless.

"Are you okay, Dad?"

Trent steadied himself on the garage wall. "Fine, buddy. . . . Just, I couldn't find you. I was worried."

Milo was wearing the Junior Handyman toolbelt Trent had picked up at the friendly Depot for a mere $34.99. His son had replaced the plastic hammer and wrench with real ones. The belt sagged around his hip bones, which jutted like ears. They'd both lost weight lately.

Milo had carved out a spot in the cramped garage. Trent got his first good look at what his son had been up to.

"What *is* that?"

Milo looked away bashfully. "Just something I made."

Trent sat down next to his son. "Wait, you *made* this? Milo, that's amazing."

His awe was genuine. Milo had cobbled together a device using K'Nex rods, a miniature Tesla ball, three stacked circuit boards, and the Amazon Alexa.

"What does it do?"

"It listens?" Milo said uncertainly.

"To what?"

"I don't know . . . the idea just came to me. Well, no, Little Boy Blue helped."

"Blue? Wait, the puppet thing on YouTube?"

"Blue says you can listen to the earth. There's a lot of interesting stuff down there."

"I see. So . . . how does it work?"

Milo held up the Makita drill. "I have to make a hole in the wall first."

"You shouldn't use the drill without me, sport. A small hole's fine. Let me do it."

Trent took the drill and cored a hole in the garage wall six inches from the floor. "That good enough?"

Milo bit the inside of his cheek. "Mom said I shouldn't play with phones anymore."

"Phones?"

"But this is different, right, Dad?"

"Yeah, you bet." *Fuck tight-ass Mom and her rules, buddy. This is Cool Dad you're dealing with.* "This isn't anything like a friggin' phone, is it?"

Milo grinned and said: "Okay, hand me that wire, then."

Trent had purchased the fifty-foot spool of copper wire for some project, he couldn't remember which. Milo stripped wire off the spool, feeding the length into the hole.

"So okay, this wall, right?" Milo knocked on it. "There's a space behind it, yeah? Maybe eight inches? And then the mudroom wall. The space between the garage and mudroom goes down to the basement."

Trent had no idea how Milo knew that, but he wasn't wrong. "Absolutely correct, my son, but everything stops at the basement's concrete foundation pad. That's what the whole house rests on, and that thing's a good two feet thick."

Milo clipped a red wire to the copper wire. The red wire was connected to the Alexa, the copper wire playing through a noose-like clip on the red.

Milo unwound more copper wire and pushed it through the hole in the wall, playing off eight or nine feet—it made a silky rasp against the drilled hole, down, down. . . . It would touch the basement pad at any moment. . . .

Milo turned his invention on by activating the Alexa. Trent half expected it to fizzle out in a sad zigzag of sparks. But it came on immediately, quilling the hairs on Trent's arms. The Tesla ball strobed with moody purple skeins.

*"How can I help you today, Milo?"*

"Just listen, Alexa. Thanks."

Milo kept feeding wire in. The hole accepted it. Ten, twelve, fifteen feet . . .

"The wire must have snagged on a nail, Milo. It can't go down any lower than the basement—that concrete pad, remember?"

Tension collected in Trent's chest. He wanted Milo to stop, but why? Exploration was key to a child's development. . . .

The first voice was so faint it was almost not there.

Somehow Trent was able to *feel* it traveling up from below: less an audio signal transmitted invisibly through a wire than a poisonous gas bubble bulging up a rubber tube.

". . . *whsshsh eat my damned meal in peace shhhhwhisss . . .*"

Trent's heart—the living muscle—went cold. Milo made eye contact, his breath coming in sharp little pops as his hands kept peeling wire. . . .

The wire went down twenty, must be twenty-five feet at this point. There couldn't be anything *down* there. Nothing but dirt and stone and blind earthworms.

"You've snarled it." Trent swallowed; his Adam's apple clicked. "Just reel it back in, okay? No use snapping it off inside the wall and wasting good wire."

The next voice was louder than the first—a shrill, rage-filled screech. The Alexa shot out a burst of raw static and then:

"—*shhhwHAAA now do it now or I'll smack you into next week Shshwhubbawhuuu*—"

It wasn't the electronic feminine Alexa voice. These voices belonged to men.

*Milo's invention must've picked up a pirate radio station.* This was Trent's harried thought. The mica and other minerals in the ground amplified the signal, trapping it in the copper wire. There was no other answer.

The plastic was beginning to show as the wire reached the end of the spool. Milo kept feeding and feeding, his face blank and somehow mindless, the hole in the wall now looking to Trent like a tiny screaming mouth.

"It's talking, Daddy," Milo gibbered. "The earth. It's telling us something. You hear it, right?"

The instinct reared up to hit his son. Smack the shit out of him.

"No, it's some atmospheric anomaly."

The Alexa burst to life:

*"BITCH I'LL RIP YOUR TITS OFF—"*

The Tesla ball throbbed with nervous bloody light.

"Switch it off, Milo."

Milo did as he was told, but the Alexa stayed on.

*"YOUR FACES TEAR THEM OFF AND SEE THE REAL YOU—"*

This couldn't be pirate radio. This was a broadcast from a criminal psychiatric ward, the inmates grabbing hold of the mic.

"Milo, turn it off!"

"I'm *trying!*"

The spool jerked out of Milo's hands. The last five feet peeled off in a blur as something in the wall gripped the wire and yanked—the spool slammed the drywall, wire stretched to the snapping point until it did, *tock!*, skating down inside the wall with a satiny hiss.

Trent pulled Milo protectively to him. They stared at the hole, *into* it, waiting for something to come out of it—or *look* at them from inside the wall with its sour, diseased eye.

Nothing peered back.

Trent mopped sweat off his forehead. Shakily, he rose to his feet. "You okay, buddy?"

"I think so."

"I'm going to check the basement."

"I don't know if that's a good idea, Dad."

"I'm sure it's fine."

"Can I come?"

"Absolutely not."

Trent's boots thudded down the basement steps. His hand searched for the light cord in the cool darkness—his heart rate accelerated like a dragster, 70 to 160 beats in an eyeblink.

His fingers snared the cord and popped the light on.

Nothing was out of place. He walked up to the wall behind which the wire had snaked down. Ran his fingertips along the drywall. . . . A soft hum like the beat of a moth's wings, but it was just the A/C thrumming through the floor and up the wall. Totally normal.

That horrible voice battered inside his head like a fly in a baby food jar.

*bitch ill rip your tits off*

The anger in it. Unhinged, nearly inarticulate—less like a human and more some animal that had been locked up in a lightless cage, poked and teased and mistreated until its rage became a form of insanity. It scared him. More than the spool jerking out of his son's hands, more than anything else . . .

It came again, that presence from earlier. Not a lunge this time, no, it didn't have to be now. Only a breath, soft, an echo of whatever had touched him before . . . The *beet* slid in much easier now—the initial intrusion had left a hole—and even as Trent's pulse blipped at a nervy flutter, even as he tugged his earlobe as if he'd gotten pool water trapped in there, a calmness washed through him.

"It was an animal," he said dully.

That made perfect sense, didn't it? The woods weren't far off. The walls of his house were warm and safe and probably full of bugs and other vittles for furry uninvited guests.

He set his ear to the wall . . . *there*. A sly scrape and skitter. Could be squirrels or possums, even a raccoon. Those bastards could squeeze through a hole the size of a soup can lid.

"I hope you're happy in there with a mouthful of my copper wire," he said. "You're gonna need to find a new home soon."

Small fingers in his head were busy tearing the incident in the garage into shreds and scattering them to the four winds. . . . It probably *was* a radio signal of some kind. The house was in the middle of nowhere, metal-beamed and sturdy—Trent imagined his house as a crisscrossing metal antenna, the kind that topped the roofs of old radio stations.

"Ninety-seven point seven Saban FM." He chuckled. "Home of the hits."

Something new caught his eye. The casement window, looking onto the parched dirt of the backyard. When he unlatched the window and slid it open, clods of soil fell onto his boots.

The bottom edge of the window rested below ground level. Not by much, maybe only a few centimeters.

That wasn't right. Couldn't be.

When he got back to the garage, Milo was gone. Trent picked up the abandoned drill and found a wooden dowel on a shelf.

He walked the perimeter of the house hunting for holes chewed by wildlife. He didn't find any obvious intrusions. When he got to the casement window, he drilled a hole in the exterior wall down at the dirt line.

He stuck the dowel in the hole horizontally, touching the dirt, leaving three inches poking out. The rage he felt now was genuine, unaided by any external force.

"If my house is sinking, Hector Hannah, bet your ass I'm gonna skin you alive."

# 11

IN THE DRIFTLESS SPACE between sleep and waking, Rita heard the screams. But they could be a figment of her dreaming mind. That's what her dreams had usually been, almost as far back as she could remember: just blackness, full of screaming.

She sat bolt upright in bed. The dividing line between dream and reality cleaved cleanly.

The screams were in the house with her.

She slung out of bed and down the hall, knowing even then that it was too late. She'd fallen asleep or been lulled into slumber, her guard let down—humans *had* to sleep, but not all things did. Some things could be up at any hour, restless, lurking, waiting on their chance.

Light bled under Milo's door. The screams were coming from the other side. Rita twisted the knob but it wouldn't give.

"Milo! Open the door!"

Her son's screams reached a pitch that broadcast a horror beyond comprehension. Rita's knees went to jelly—did she really *want* to see what was going on in there?—but that was her baby on the other side of the door. She slammed her shoulder into the wood, felt it splinter.

*"Milo! Open the goddamn door! Now!"*

After an endless beat, the door opened on its own. Milo sat on the floor in his candy-cane pajamas. His face was a scalded, bloaty red.

*"Mommy!* It's Morty!"

The bedroom light was off. The glow came from two sources: a desk lamp trained on Morty's tank, and Milo's tablet, which was playing a YouTube video.

Rita sank down next to the tank . . . but wait, it wasn't Morty's tank, was it? In the murk she'd made the mistake of thinking so—but there was the turtle tank, over in its regular corner spot. Morty was sitting in a clear plastic tub.

Something was clipped to the side that looked like a sous vide cooker or an aquarium aerator, but wasn't either. The water, the liquid, the *broth* the turtle sat in bubbled away like a jet tub.

Morty was almost completely encased in that colonizing pink. The turtle looked like a blush-colored sandcastle, with crystallized stalagmites rising off the top of its shell.

Under the bubbling, Rita heard another sound: the high, drilling shriek of a teakettle made of skin and shell.

Rita glanced at the tablet. Little Boy Blue pranced around on the screen, waving an Erlenmeyer flask in one felted hand.

*"Experimenting is fun, kids! You can fix anything!"* Blue shrieked.

The turtle's body jittered in the foam as if raw voltage was flowing through the liquid, as if someone had dropped a tiny electric toaster in Morty's water.

"Help him, Mommy!"

"What did you do?" She grabbed Milo, shook him. His body radiated an unnatural, overcooked heat. "What in God's name did you *do*?"

"I tried!" Milo yelped. "Blue said to make a recipe that would fix Morty—"

She hissed, "Don't listen to that thing! It doesn't want to help you!"

*"Mommies aren't always right, boys and girls!"* Blue chirped.

The turtle kept making that insane, horrific squeal, the sound of a dog's jaws grinding on an India rubber ball.

"What did you put in the water, Milo?"

"Blue's top-secret super recipe!"

She didn't have gloves or anything to stop whatever was in that tub from stripping the skin right off her fingers—but instinctively, Rita understood that wouldn't happen. It might be nothing more than water tinted with food coloring. The important point was that *Milo* believed in its properties. That was all the activation something like that needed.

Pushing her fear aside, she reached into the tub and grabbed Morty.

*"Be careful, kids!"* Blue tee-heed. *"Don't take the cake out of the oven too early!"*

As soon as she lifted the turtle from the bath, the cakey pink began to crumble away. It came off in crackling plates like sandstone, revealing the turtle's pink-tinged stomach plating and the stubbed-cigar legs. Rita turned Morty over gently, balancing it in her palm as she picked the crust off.

"Is he going to be okay, Mommy?"

"I don't know. Maybe, maybe he'll be fine—"

The turtle began to shriek in her hand. *Louder,* if that was at all possible.

Rita and Milo looked on in horror as Morty's legs began to shrivel like twigs in a fire, turning first the bloodless gray of freezer-burned meat and then a mushy black as they atrophied and began to suck inside the shell in pathetic jerking spasms.

"No," Rita breathed. "No, no, no please no—"

Cracks shot through the turtle's stomach plate. Pinkness squeezed against the cracks and then foamed through with a pressurized pissing sound—Rita conjured the image of mashed potatoes squeezing through the gaps of a disembodied set of teeth—and the smell was ungodly, the smell of flyblown meat, and she felt the cracks snarling across the shell in her hand, tracing a blistering web on her palm—

*"Uh-oh spaghetti-o!"*

—the liquefied remains of Morty began to burp from its leg holes, the legs all gone now and stomach-wrenching pink yolk pumping out, warm and shucked-oyster-y on her fingers.

"Mommy, do something!"

"I'm trying, Jesus, I'm trying, I can't—"

All she could do was hold Morty, it was all that was left *to* do, hold the turtle and hope it understood that its dying moments were spent cradled by something that had at least *tried*.

"I can't fucking *DO ANYTHING,* Milo, don't you *see that*?"

She turned away and saw Trent. He stood in the doorway. Hair tousled, eyes puffy and lethargic with sleep.

*"DO SOMETHING!"* she screamed, holding the turtle out to him.

"Whu?" her husband said.

In its final moments, the turtle's head strained against the lacework of pink threads clustered over its head-hole. The threads sliced into its skin like cheese wires, but Morty kept pushing against them mindlessly and in doing so cut himself apart—his head exited the shell as segmented shiny strings that elongated as the turtle kept pushing, pushing—

*Stop,* Rita thought, *oh please, you poor little thing, just stop.* She glanced at Milo and saw her boy's world folding in on itself as the wet tatters of his pet's head drooled into his mother's cupped palm.

*"If at first you don't succeed,"* Little Boy Blue crowed. *"Try, try again."*

The tablet screen faded to black. Lunar silence filled the house, running down the hallways and infesting the empty rooms.

Robotically, Rita cranked her head downward at the shell in her hands, where the cold, pinkish, snot-like mush of the turtle clung between her fingers like the webbing on a duck's feet—then over to Milo, who swayed unsteadily with the blood knocked out of his face, his lips peeled back in a disbelieving snarl because this *was* unbelievable, it simply shouldn't happen, and anywhere else on earth, anywhere but these 8,500 square feet landlocked out in the dust, it surely *wouldn't* happen, but here, now, absolutely anything could happen, anything at all—and that limitless sense of possibility sent fear crazing through Rita's innards as her gaze skated finally to her husband, whose mouth yawned open, his eyes piggish in their inability or unwillingness to comprehend; he was no help at all, he had no idea what he was in the jaws of, and Rita's isolation was such that she could feel her loss of control as a physical thing: the steering wheel slipping through her fingers as if coated in bear grease, as the vehicle they were all in veered dangerously close to the moon-silvered guardrail and the dark delta beyond—

Rita willed her hands to stop trembling. Gently, reverently, she put the shell down.

"We should have let Morty go when we had the chance," she said.

They buried the turtle in a DeWalt radiating miter saw box.

It was past 3 a.m. by then. The wind moaned through the forest pines, raising gooseflesh on Rita's calves. She cinched her robe tighter. Hugged Milo closer.

The house brooded while Trent dug the hole. The windows stared like sightless eyes, the sockets stuffed with mocking blackness. He used the posthole digger he'd bought at Home Depot.

"Sixty-seven bucks," Trent felt compelled to inform them. "Regular one thirty-three."

"You're a man who knows a bargain when he sees it, Trent."

Her husband bit his lip. "Sorry . . . don't know why I said that."

When the hole was finished, Rita lowered Morty into it. They could fashion a memorial tomorrow. A tombstone topped with a tongue-depressor cross. It wouldn't last—nothing did—but it would teach Milo about the value of life, and of mourning.

Rita asked Milo if he'd like to say anything. Some kind words for Morty. His mute slackness worried her.

"Anything?" she prompted.

He peered up at her, dressed in his pj's and a pair of rubber galoshes. His face appeared to crumble, coming apart the way Morty had. A racking sob tore out of his chest.

"I didn't mean to!" His voice blistered across the emptiness. "All I wanted to do was stop him hurting, Mom!" Milo sank to his knees, hugging himself. "I'm so sorry I'm so sorry I'm stupid a stupid idiot—"

Rita hunched next to him. "No, it's not your fault. You tried your best, Milo."

"I killed Morty, Mom . . . I'm a murderer."

Her son's words hit her like a fist. "No. *No*. You stop that right now. You did nothing wrong." She shot a glance at Trent. "Tell him, for Christ's sake."

Trent mumbled, "These things happen, big guy. Morty was . . . he was old."

*Great save, hubby,* Rita thought bitterly. *Our son's turtle dissolved due to old age.*

Milo slept with her that night. Once she'd gotten him tucked under the covers, she backtracked, finding Trent in Milo's room. She watched from the hallway shadows as Trent straightened up Milo's plastic tubs and boxes, the detritus of his experiments.

What was it she'd said to her husband the night he came home with the Denali? *You're a truck guy now?* How unfair she'd been. *Of course* Trent was a truck guy now. The farcical truck, the tools, the inarticulate silences where he stared off into some spectral horizon . . . they *all* became truck guys, didn't they? And before trucks existed, well, Rita figured they must have sauntered down to the farrier and bought the sturdiest slab of horseflesh they could afford. All of them walking the same path to becoming the same man, no different than if they'd rolled off an assembly line.

Trent scooped up the tacky pink stew that was once their son's pet with rubber-gloved hands and slopped it into a Hefty sack. He worked obliviously, a machine with a pulse . . . but while scrubbing the hardwood he paused, staring at the scrub-brush bristles twined with shreds of pink.

"I don't understand. How can an animal . . . how could it die like this?" he asked himself.

He seemed perched on the precipice of a staggering discovery—Rita wished so badly it might dawn on him, with no real belief it would . . . and surely, the moment passed. He went back to scrubbing. When all traces of Morty had been erased, Trent made Milo's bed, smoothed the covers down, and sat.

"You remember, Rita, the day that turtle found us?"

How long had he known she was there, watching him?

"It was one afternoon in High Park, remember?" he went on. "We walked Milo through the petting zoo. The pair of capybaras had escaped."

"Oh yeah, right. Those big rodents."

Trent nodded. "They were mates. Bonnie and Clyde, on the lam. I loved that idea . . . just, escaping your cage."

Their eyes met. Hard to say what flickered between them.

"Anyway, you packed that picnic. We spread the blanket near that pond with the mallards and the chrysanthemum flowers, which Milo used to call *slowers*, remember?"

"And *soupcase* instead of *suitcase*."

"Right!" Trent seemed to fly back into himself. "A case just for your soup. We were eating our sandwiches when Morty waddled up the shore, onto Milo's plate, and stuck his nose in the potato salad."

Rita could still feel Morty coming apart in her hands. The sense of some inner principle or logic dissolving.

"Morty was a good little dude. And that was a good day." Trent looked so lost on his son's bed, a child himself. "I miss those times, really, I do."

What could she tell him? That there would be more like them ahead? Why disrespect him further with a lie?

She tried not to hate him, at least. Tried not to despise his stupid, sleepy ineffective face when she'd held the dying turtle out to him.

"You're a good husband, Trent. A good dad."

"If you say so." He puffed air, lifting the fringe of his hair. "You go on to bed. Milo needs you tonight."

She didn't argue with him, and walked back to the master bedroom, getting in under the covers with Milo. His body hummed hotly.

She awoke to a soft bluish light trailing down the hallway. She did not bother checking the source. She could picture Trent on their son's bed, laptop open on his stomach, his slack, untroubled face bathed in its glow.

# 12

DARKNESS ROLLED IN. The lights of the closest development glimmered along the curve of the earth, a chain of phosphorescent deep-sea life. But that light didn't touch them out here, no more than the starlight did.

The isolation filled Trent with a pioneering spirit: Saban the Bold, dominating at the edge of civilization! He stood outside, under the slope of the garage roof. Milo was there too, with his Junior Handyman toolbelt.

Hank made it a happy trio. His face ballooned in the Mac-Book balanced on a kitchen chair on the flagstones.

"Soffits? So What?" The title of the video. Part Two of Hank's *Outdoor Defense* series.

Trent switched on his EverBrite headlamp and angled his chin to illuminate the hole in the soffit, barely visible under the eaves.

*"Now, some contractors'll tell you,"* Handyman Hank started, *"he's gotta tear the whole thing out, just to be safe. Once he's done that*

*and found nothing, he'll make you pay him double to put it back up again. Nice racket, don't you think? You bet, reeeal nice racket."*

Trent positioned a ladder against the side of the house. "I want you to hold tight, okay, Milo?"

Trent climbed the ladder until he swayed fifteen feet up. The ladder's metal shoes gritted on the flagstone below, running a quiver up the rungs through the shockproof soles of his boots.

"I said *tight*, didn't I?"

"Sorry, Dad."

The hole in the eaves was too small for a raccoon or a squirrel to have made. Too small for anything much other than a mouse or maybe a barn swallow.

*"It'll take balls to reach in there. Big gold-plated cojones."* The night amplified Hank's voice. *"Feel around in there, see if anything's made a home."*

*Just do it,* Trent commanded himself. *You can't back down now, with your boy watching.*

*"—attack that damn hole, now."*

Pinching his fingers together, making a bird's beak of them, Trent stuffed his hand into the hole. He felt nothing at first, just cool air . . . then his fingers touched a struggling warmth. It was as if he'd grabbed a misplaced bodily organ.

He got a grip and pulled whatever it was out to inspect under the lamp's light.

*"You may be surprised what you find,"* Hank said jovially.

These little fucking trespassers in his cathedral. The home where he intended to teach his boy how to be a man.

*"It ain't gonna bite you, is it?"* Hank said. *"Hell, chances are it doesn't even have teeth, Trent . . . not yet."*

"Daddy, did the man just say your name?"

"Shut up." Trent hurled the thing down to the flagstones. "When I get down, *you're* dealing with it, buster."

Trent set a mesh screen over the hole, slamming in staples to hold it. The rest of those things could starve in there.

Trent clambered down the ladder. Milo was crouched, observing the thing as it writhed on the stones like a hairless rat . . . except it had no limbs, only wriggling stubs. No eyes either, only dimples where they should be.

"Is it a bug?" Milo asked.

"Whatever it is, kill it."

Milo straightened. "I thought you'd do that."

"Didn't you hear me up there?" Trent's finger menacingly tick-tocked. "You didn't hear me tell you to deal with it, bud?"

Milo stared down at his boots.

"You think we're keeping this thing as a *pet*?"

Milo said, "No, but . . ."

"But what?"

The pink grublike thing squirmed on the flagstones, now squeaking like a wet beach ball.

"*Do it*, son. Use that hammer in your toolbelt or your boot or your fist. I don't care."

Milo was such a weak specimen, wasn't he? Moony-eyed and dreamy. Trent saw that clearly now, a fact that both shamed him and made him ill.

"*You've got to steer him down the right path,*" Hank said—from the video, inside Trent's head, it was all the same. "*That's your fatherly obligation, and fathering ain't always easy.*"

The thing was now nosing at the boy's boot, emitting those pitiful squeaks.

"Kill it, Sarge."

Milo's face crumpled. He let out a croaking sob.

"*Kill* it, or I'm going to make you *eat* it."

Milo's head jerked up. He could see his father just might be serious.

"I've never killed anything." His chest hitched. "Just buh-buh-bugs on accident."

"Ohhh, I don't think that's true, is it? Who killed Morty last week, Milo? Was it the *wind*?"

His son was struck dumb for a second. Then every muscle in his body tensed to the point of rupture, and he screamed in a voice of wounded rage:

"That was a fuh-fuh-*fucking ACCIDENT!*"

Trent's boot lifted up and came crunching down. The thing bulged like a balloon before peeling open like bad fruit, its shapeless insides splattering the bricks. Trent lifted his boot to inspect its remains, stuck to his tread. A few rusted roofing tacks fell from its wrinkled-condom carcass.

"Take that off." Trent pointed at Milo's toolbelt, his voice hoarse with fury. "Right this instant. You don't deserve to wear it."

Milo did as he was told, a disgraced general stripped of his bars. Trent tore the belt out of his hands.

"Are we done? Can I go inside now?" Milo said, squaring his shoulders at Trent.

*He's a defiant little bastard, ain't he?*

Trent snatched Milo by the elbow and marched him around the side of the house, past the forgotten sack of bird feed that bulged grotesquely, the seed fruiting inside the humid plastic, swollen grains sprouting through rips in the plastic like crippled fingers.

"Daddy, you're hurting me."

What Milo really wanted to say was *Daddy, you're scaring me.* Fuckin-A right. Sometimes it paid to be scared of your old man. Should've thought about that before trying to be Mister Big Shot.

When they reached the criminally underused playset, Trent gave Milo a hard shove that sent him sprawling. Christ, the boy was all mealy inside, couldn't even stand on his own God-given feet.

"Get up."

When Milo just lay there in a pile of mute confusion, Trent's fingers twisted in his son's shirtfront and dragged him up. Some part of Trent saw the scene through Milo's eyes: a boy alone in the dark with a father who appeared to have gone dangerously insane.

"You want to call for Mommy, Milo?" he said in a mocking voice.

Milo's eyes were wide and fearful but not looking away. A flicker of backbone. "Mommy's never home."

The playset scaled up to a flybridge jutting off the main mass. Trent had never seen a similar feature on any other playground. Positioning himself under it, he tossed Milo's toolbelt up . . . hooked it over the end of the beam his very first try.

"Now, go get it."

Milo stood there sniveling, his nose plugged and shoulders hitching. In the shadow of the house Milo's face became that of Carson Aikles . . . Carson's ignorant wrath and a belief that his problems could be solved with a hammer . . . the next moment Trent was looking at his own face topping his son's body, tucked under Ashley Greco's desk like a mole in a burrow—

Cocking his hand back and swinging sidearm, Trent slapped Milo in the face about as hard as he dared.

The impact didn't just send Milo down—it sent him *flying*. He crashed back to earth in pieces like a tower of toy blocks.

*Get his ass up!*

But before Trent could act, Milo scrambled up on his own. The slapped side of his face flamed an angry bee-stung red, but a mingling of fear and fury flared in his eyes.

"Are you scared, buddy?"

Milo nodded, a machinelike movement. *"Yes."*

"That's great. That's the world telling you you're still alive. Now, go. Get your property down like I told you."

*"Fine."*

Milo climbed carefully, testing each foothold to see if it would bear his weight. The playset creaked, swaying in the night like a half-rotted tree. Trent suddenly wanted to tell Milo to come down and forget it—forget *all* of it—wishing he could erase the last ten minutes from his son's mind.

"If I fall, I deserve it," Trent heard Milo say way up there. "For killing Morty."

Milo made it to the highest platform, twenty feet in the air. The flybridge jutted from it like a narwhal's tusk. His head swiveled, looking up at the sky. "You see that star up there, Dad? It's Sirius, the Dog Star."

He wobbled dangerously, his breath catching with an audible hitch. "The brightest star in our galaxy, and know what?" Milo gave Trent a sad, hopeful smile from what could've been a million miles away. "I think it must taste like peppermint. What do you think about that?"

There are times in life where one senses on a cellular level, a wire in the blood: *So much rides on this.* This heartbeat, this breath. Infrequently, these moments are big, but more often they're small. Still, everything balances there. Everything.

Trent hesitated. *Felt* it.

He gave his son a look.

"I think that's pretty stupid. Stars don't taste like anything. Stars are just hot gas."

Milo nodded as though this answer confirmed a fact he'd long come to grips with. He got down on his hands and knees and began to crawl onto the narrow plank.

The idiocy of the scene hit Trent with a dull thud—but weren't so many tests, especially ones of manhood, kind of stupid when you rubbed down to the nub of it?

"Forget it, Milo," Trent called. "Come down. I'll climb up and get it myself in the morn—"

The flybridge split with a rending shriek. Trent watched his son's body jolt down at an unforgiving slant as the beam holding him split apart in a firework of rotten splinters—

*"Milo!"*

Trent turned to catch Rita in midstride, coming around the side of the house with her briefcase in hand.

Milo fell silently, not screaming or calling out, his posture curled and somehow larval . . . His body hit the ground with a sound like doom.

Trent reached him first. He rolled Milo over, made sick by the boneless drag of his torso. Bloody bubbles foamed from his mouth—the bubbling meant he was breathing, but his chest had a crumpled appearance, and that scared Trent very badly.

"Milo, buddy, come on come on *come on.*"

Milo sucked in a breath and jerked up like a vampire from its coffin. He coughed out a tooth.

"Bud, you okay?"

Milo jumped up to his feet like an adrenalized toy. He walked a wobbly circle, patting his chest like he was on fire.

"Oth boy," he lisped, the air whistling past his lost tooth, "oth boy oth boy oth—"

Oh Christ, okay, okay, he was alive. Nothing looked broken, none of his limbs were bent or hanging loosely—

Trent fished his son's tooth out of the dirt. Rita was over with Milo. She got him to stop moving so she could inspect him. Other than the knocked-out incisor, he seemed okay.

She wheeled on Trent. "You stupid fucking *asshole*."

Trent dropped his eyes, the guilt pulsing through him—

*How is this on you? It's her fault that you've got a marshmallow for a son, isn't it?*

Trent let his eyes come up to meet Rita's gaze. "He's *fine*."

"How the hell would you know?"

"Look at him. Walking and talking. You're okay, aren't you, big guy?"

Milo didn't say anything. He'd tucked in close to his mother's side.

"Rita, for God's sake, it's just a tooth."

"*Just a tooth?* That's not something that grows back, Trent. Most things don't! Not teeth, not fingers or toes or arms or legs!"

*Keep your tone, m'man. Hysterics are for womenfolk.*

"He would have been fine if he'd just done as I told him."

"Climb that death trap, you mean? I wish I'd burned the fucking thing!"

Trent laughed, *ho-ho-ho*. "You just don't get it. Sometimes a boy's got to lose a part of himself in order to grow. It's the toll you gotta pay." He wanted to make Rita see, but how could a cobra explain itself to a mollusk? "You simply don't understand how hard it is."

She stared at him in mulish disbelief. "How *hard*?"

"It is . . . to . . . be"—punctuating each word with a fist slammed into his open palm—"a . . . fucking . . . *man*."

Something came into Rita's eyes. She pushed Milo behind her. Untucked her blouse from her skirt and began to unbutton it from the bottom up. There was nothing sexy about the display.

"Remember this, Trent?" Thumbing her skirt lower, her fingers flirted with the lopsided grin of the C-section scar spanning from hip to hip. "Remember what you saw in the delivery room? My insides slopped in a steel tray like the ones that hold tater tots in the junior high cafeteria—those were pretty much your exact words, weren't they?"

It all returned in a rush. Rita's exposed organs in the delivery room and his thought: *How are they going to get those back* into *her?* Rita moving across the hospital room the night after Milo was born, pulling herself on her *toes*, inching them forward as she dragged herself to the toilet.

"So, please, keep telling me how hard it is to be whatever it is you are. Why don't you try being a *real* fucking man for once in your life?"

"Why don't we go up to the bedroom?" The words oozed over his lips cleansed of all seduction. "I'll show you what kind of man I am."

"Oh God, you don't even know anymore." She turned away. "You're not yourself."

*Did that uppity bitch just turn her back on you?*

"I can't deal with you like this, Trent. Unstable, flying off the handle."

"I'm as stable as a board." He squeezed Milo's tooth so hard that it left a dent in his palm. "You're the one who's unstable."

Rita gathered their son to her hip. "Milo and I are spending some time away, starting tonight."

"Oh no. No, you're not."

She kept walking. "Try to stop me, *hubby*."

*Well, she's* asking, *right? Lots of ways to stop a woman. I've made some videos.*

". . . Please, Rita. Wait a sec."

Trent jolted back into himself: the sensation of a space capsule reentering earth's orbit. His head throbbed with feelings he couldn't bring into words because saying them out loud would lay bare some privately festering wound.

*I can't do it, baby. I thought I could, but I can't exist in the shadow of your excellence.*

Trent didn't dare say this. It shamed him too much. Plus, Hank might hear.

. . . but Trent could sense Hank inside his head now: this nauseating feeling of two trains running side by side, his consciousness on one rail and Hank's hulking on the other, the air between them stale and ancient.

*You keep growing bigger every day, Rita,* he thought. *Meanwhile, I'm shrinking. Soon you won't be able to see me . . . then one day you'll step on me, maybe accidentally but maybe not. Then you'll find someone new.*

"I love you, Rita." This much he could manage. "And I love you, Milo, so much. I'm sorry, but can't you see that I need something to call my own?" Trent spread his arms to the house. "This. I need this."

As soon as the words were spoken, the house ground heavily on its foundations. It sounded like a moan of disgust.

"Why don't we go away for a while?" he said optimistically. "Just a few days . . . get a hotel room in the city, catch a ball game. A quick sabbatical. What's the harm?"

Rita turned, her gaze locking on their home for a moment. When she faced him again, he could swear that a glittering fear had invaded her eyes.

She walked over to him. Braced her hands on his shoulders.

"You should stay."

Something ticked up from the ground, implacable and restless: the sensation of suction-cup mouths sprouting from the dirt and battening onto him as leeches do. . . . Rita was right, for a change. He ought to stay. He didn't *want* to leave. In fact, the prospect made him sick.

"You'd rather stay put, wouldn't you?" Rita's voice held him mesmerically.

"This place would fall apart without me," he agreed.

"For sure it would. You stay. The house needs you."

Trent was gripped by an urge to dash away from his wife, Milo, Hank, all of it . . . sprint just as fast as he could, shedding his clothes as he went, ripping off his suffocating costume—the scaly workman's chambray chewing at his skin—running until his lungs burst and his thoughts became orderly once more. . . .

She kissed his cheek. "Just a few days, then we'll come back."

Ten minutes later, Trent stood clutching his son's tooth as the Sienna backed out of the drive, its taillights flaring into the dark.

Letting his lungs inflate like two bellows, Trent forced everything out.

The night ate his screams. The night ate everything.

# 13

THE AFTERNOON FOUND TRENT pacing his garage like a caged bear. Hector Hannah was on his way, and Trent was going to tear that fraud a fresh asshole.

His wife and son had scampered off three nights ago. Rita hadn't bothered to provide a timeline for their return. Fine, screw it. Trent was better off alone. He could focus on his projects, unfettered by clingers.

As Hank said: *The happy man is the man who finds repose in solitude.*

Yesterday Rita called from the hotel they'd ratted up in with news that the dentist had screwed an acrylic tooth into Milo's mouth. She had to pay through the nose on account of the emergency scheduling, but she could afford it.

"You okay, buddy?" he asked when she put Milo on. "Your choppers feeling better?"

A mumbled "Mm-hmm, fine."

"That was a real stupid thing I did. When you get back, things will be different, I promise. You still love me?"

". . . yeah, mmm love you."

After Milo hung up, Trent sat in the kitchen with the hurt moving through him. That was the thing about your kids: they still loved you, well past the point they ought to quit. . . .

—Rita had stolen his son! The *bitch*. Snatched Milo up like a doll, like *property*, and traipsed off. A boy without his father was like a plant without sunlight: it would wither, its fruit turning mealy and sour. Fatherless boys grew up to be sex pests and compulsive masturbators; Trent had read as much on the internet. Would he let Milo grow up to be a seedy trench-coat type, a depraved whack-off artist who spied on outdoor yoga classes from the shrubs? He'd die first!

Things would be different when they got back, oh yes indeedy. But today was his to seize, full of fresh challenges!

Trent thumbed a button on the garage wall. The automatic door clattered up to let in the brilliant sunshine.

*"Here's a question, bright boys: When did men stop wearing hats?"*

Handyman Hank spoke from the laptop perched on stacked sacks of potting soil.

*"Hats used to make a statement. Wearing a flat cap meant you walked the high steel. A porkpie told everyone you worked with your hands. A boater? You might be a sportsman, but then again you could be a little light in the loafers, if you catch my drift and I'm sure you do . . . gotta tread careful with a boater."*

With the house now deserted, Hank was on more or less constantly, one video looping seamlessly to the next.

Trent crouched at the edge of the garage, the dividing line

where it met the driveway's interlocking brick. That familiar anger tightened within him, hot wires winding around his spinal cord.

There was now a . . . *drop*. The floor of the garage currently sat *beneath* the driveway. No cracks or dust, nothing to indicate stress. But the garage—the entire frigging cement floor—had dropped nearly an inch like the world's slowest and shittiest elevator.

And it wasn't just the garage, oh no. Yesterday Trent had checked on the dowel he'd stuck in the foundation near the basement window. He found it snapped, and the hole he'd drilled in the brick had disappeared below the dirt.

Fucking Hector Hannah! Fucking Dunsany Estates!

What kind of house had those nefarious pricks sold his family? A *lemon*! A brand-new, fancy-dancy, dyed-in-the-wool, cash-sucking *LEMON!*

A *sinking* lemon.

Trent ran his fingers along the tiny cliff that had developed across the garage's threshold. No moisture, only the slightest breath of cave-like air. There would be hell to pay, bank on it.

He straightened as Hector's truck came blistering across the dimensionless yellow dirt. The pickup slowed on its approach. Trent smiled. Hector must have spotted the new Denali.

"You like that, uh?"

Hector parked at the nonexistent curb, though there was plenty of room in the driveway. Trent's Denali sat a good half a foot taller than Hector's dinky-toy Ford Maverick, so obviously the liaison wanted to avoid getting caught in a dick-measuring contest.

Trent's anger shimmered brightly as Hector ambled over into the garage . . . quite the *ambler*, was ole Hec.

"That the EcoBoost package?" Trent said with a nod at the Maverick. "Yeah, that's about right for you."

Hector didn't bother taking his sunglasses off. When those twin tinted mirrors caught Trent's MacBook in their reflection—where Hank had gone silent for the moment—Trent swore Hector's face blanched.

"What's all the hubbub, Trent?"

"Hunker down with me here, Hec."

Hector waited for Trent to kneel before remarking: "I can see what we're looking at from here."

"Then you can see," Trent grated, "that our garage is sinking? You see that from up there?"

Hector kicked the little cliff with his boot. "It's settled a smidge." He hooked his thumbs into his belt loops. "Look, I told you about coming early, didn't I? You're in a flap—that's why I drove out. Didn't have to. You know that, right? You read the fine print. You're an adult."

*Oh, so that's how you're gonna play this, Hector, you stinking wet-brain?* "Where do *you* live, Hector?"

Hector looked off evasively. Trent pounced.

"I'm gonna guess Oak Bridges? That fine development ours is gonna edge up on when all's said and done? That's not too far. Four, five miles? We're practically neighbors. Rita and I should come over." Off the liaison's stony silence: "Bring a casserole."

"Where is Rita, anyways?" Hector rocked on his heels, flashing a sunny grin. "Look, I'm not trying to give you a hard time here, okay? Are you giving me a hard time, Trent?"

"If your house was sinking on my watch, would *you* ride *my* ass?"

"If it was a crack in the foundation, we'd be on it quick as quick. We are vigilant. I promise you that, all right, but—"

In a fey, mocking lilt: "Oh, you *pwooomiss,* do you?"

"—*but* we cannot redo every little thing. Give it a year or so and then . . ."

Hector prattled on. Trent's outrage—a lidded pot set on a low simmer—began to bubble dangerously.

"My. House. Is. *Sinking.*" Every staccato word capped by a hissing little rage-hat.

"Says you." Hector stepped from the garage, a rat off a sinking barge. "I say it's *settling.* Therefore, so does Dunsany Estates."

What could Trent do? He was Everyman Homeowner at the whim and mercy of Shitbag Contractor, aided and abetted by Shitbag's devilish sidekick, Fine-Fucking-Print.

"Houses are unpredictable," Hec said airily. "It's all about the dirt."

The sheer inanity of the phrase—*It's all about the DIRT*—lit the fuse on the powder keg of TNT nestled in Trent's chest—and, *ooohh,* how combustible that keg had become lately: beads of nitroglycerin sweated down its stave-joints, just *itching* to ignite.

The pruning shears rested in the toolkit. Trent grabbed them. The raw, unforgivable power of the tool flooded into his fingertips.

Grabbing a handful of Hector's *Hee Haw Jamboree* shirt, Trent shouldered him bodily against the garage door rollers. Hector squawked like a startled parrot. The thin metal crimped under the liaison's bread-dough body.

Trent's fingers manacled Hec's throat, pinning him to the

rollers. Hector went *"Horrfff!"* as the air barfed out of him. The look of soul-deep fear on the man's face made Trent's chest swell; he could feel the buttons of his own work shirt straining—in a moment they'd pop right off, *ping! ping!*, as his hairy, thickly muscled chest surged out.

Thumbing the locking lever, Trent popped the pruner's jaws open.

"Tell me, Hec." The blades angled into the split between Hector's legs; Trent rooted the jaws deeper, into the obliging softness of the liaison's little fellas. "What d'you think's gonna happen if my son's bed falls through the rotted floor and he breaks his neck?" He applied more pressure. Hector squeaked. "Think I'll give a shit about the fine print then?"

"Trent, man, I swear—" Hector's words came out in terror-hiccups, his spineless corpus grinding into the buckling rollers, but there was no place to flee.

"Do you know how easy it would be to unman you right now?" Trent's grip pulsed on the pruner's handles; a few microns of pressure was all it would take. "After I cut them off, I could dig a hole in the yard and plant them. But what the hell would grow? Some sterile flopped-over *stalk*."

Sweat sheeted down Hector's face, carrying his hair with it. Trent cackled as Hector's toupee—"I knew it!"—slid garishly down his forehead at a sloppy tilt, drifting over his left eye.

Trent gave the pruners one final tweak—Hector squealed like a fatted hog—before shoving the little man away.

"Git on, little dogie!" he shouted with a laugh as Hector stumbled down the drive. "Get in your sewing-machine-engine truck and beat it!"

"You're a maniac!"

"And you've got fucking arms like car antennas!" Trent brayed, pointing the pruners meaningfully at Hector. "If you don't fix my house, I'll find out where you live! I used to be a lawyer—you know how many dirty cops I know? Don't you test me, you little ninny!"

After Hector was gone, a crippling wave of exhaustion forced Trent to rest against the side of the house. His mind spun on confused orbits, his skin ice-cold in the bright sunshine.

It was as if a stranger had seized control of his operating system for a minute there . . . but there was no denying the energy surging through Trent's system. This sense that his skin was going to split apart at any moment and something new would push through, something vulcanized and chromed and roped in livid knots of muscle.

Would Hector tattle on him? Reasonable to assume, knowing Hec. So what? His word against Trent's. What proof did he have? A little rip in the crotch of his Wranglers. He could've gotten that playing a game of overly aggressive pocket pool, the bald-headed soy boy.

Trent wandered back into the garage in a joyful daze. The door lowered balkily, the runners now dimpled from Hector's wide behind. The rubberized flap at the bottom didn't even touch the goddamn floor, on account of that cliff.

An idea popped into his head. Trent rummaged through the boxes heaped in the garage.

". . . there you are."

The concrete drill was a Bosch, the brand most trusted by pros. Twelve-amp keyless rotary hammer. The bit was thirty-six inches, the longest Home Depot stocked.

He lugged the drill downstairs with an orange coil of extension cord looped over his shoulder. The laptop was tucked under his other arm.

The basement hung under long shadows. He keenly felt his aloneness: a man living among half-completed cages crowding his sunsets and sunrises, well aware that the first man sent out into the cold didn't always come back.

He opened the laptop. It didn't take long to find the right video:

"Let's Drill a Hole in Your Floor, Dumbshit!!!"

The titles of *The Handyman Method*'s videos had become flatly insulting, but this had happened so gradually that Trent had barely registered it.

He unwound the extension cord and plugged it into a socket. He thumbed the trackpad to start the video.

On-screen, Hank stood in a basement that looked jarringly similar to Trent's own. The Handyman's green shirt was plastered wetly to his chest. Trent could almost smell the brackish undernote. The big man sauntered over to a bare patch of floor and picked up something huge.

*"You're looking at a DeWalt CustomPro brushless rotary hammer drill."* Hank hefted the monstrous tool with ease. *"Hell, with this bad boy I could drill clean through to North Korea and kick the Supreme Leader in his fat commie ass."*

The DeWalt made the Bosch seem like a toy. Its drill bit looked about a mile long. But after his encounter with Hector, Trent was pleased to find himself unbothered by this disparity.

"It's not the length of the tool, Hankie, my boy," he said, revving the Bosch, "it's how you wield it."

The Handyman looked up from his drill and stared right at Trent. A savage grin cleaved his face. *"Come on, then, He-Man—"*

—*T-Man*—

"—*let's drill ourselves a motherfuckin' hole!*"

Trent pulled the trigger. The Bosch filled his arms with thunder. It pulsed against his groin as the bit corkscrewed into the concrete.

He drilled down a foot into the concrete basement pad . . . foot and a half . . . a gray anthill formed around the hole. . . .

On the laptop, Handyman Hank straddled his DeWalt like a man riding a show pony, his grin now a demented rictus.

Two feet . . . the heat off the drill broiled Trent's chin, blue sparks spitting inside the housing, which had gotten too hot to touch. . . .

"*Remember to wear your safety goggles, fellas!*" Hank screamed, froth leaping from his jaws like a rabid dog.

There came a guttural *pop!* as the bit cored into an abrupt emptiness. Trent had his entire weight on the drill. Unbalanced, he dropped to his knees. The drill chuck whirred, its teeth gnashing at the inseam of Trent's overalls a hairsbreadth shy of chewing up the meat of his inner thighs—

Trent's finger *sproinged* off the trigger.

When he looked, the laptop screen was black. Hank was gone, his instruction concluded.

After removing the drill bit, Trent stared into the hole he'd made. From it breathed the same cave-like air he'd smelled up in the garage. Had the drill punched into some kind of a vault, an empty gas pocket? He'd call Hector and lay into him: *There's a sinkhole under the house, asshole! Where's that in the fine print?*

Trent tromped up to the garage and came down with a weighted plumb line. He fed the lead bob and string through the hole.

The bob and line went down three feet, four . . . then five and six and seven and eight, meeting no resistance until the line finally went slack at eleven and a half feet.

"What in the name of all Christ—"

Hank's voice twisted across the basement floor.

*"It feels good to exert your will, doesn't it?"*

Trent's eyes became heavy—it was as if fishing weights had been fastened to them. His eyelids dropped, gummed in concrete dust . . . *the beet,* jefe, *the beet . . .*

Trent's head swung slowly to his laptop. The screen was still dark. Hank wasn't speaking from it now. Hank's voice came from everywhere. Hank's voice was everything.

*"The world is full of shitheels who'll try to tear a good man down. Competitors waiting to cut your Achilles when you're weak . . . sneaky bitches spiriting your children off in the dead of night, ain't that the sad truth?"*

The basement light flickered overhead. Speechlessly, Trent watched the filament fade inside the bulb as if it was wired to a dimmer switch going down, down. . . .

*"The only stimulus people like that respond to is force. And you have the power, tiger."*

The basement was now pitch-black. Not a drop of light filtered through the windows. Just Trent and Hank and that sly grinding of teeth in the walls . . .

Something was moving in the dark. Not in the walls. There, in the basement with him.

The clumsy, sludgy slap of feet—a pair of feet belonging to a mason who'd worked on Trent's dream home, just maybe, some swarthy hard-knuckled gent who'd poured the concrete floor alone, late one night, becoming the victim of a workplace accident when he tripped into the hardening cement and floundered to his death like a woolly mammoth in a tar pit. . . . Of course Dunsany had covered it up, construction had continued apace while the man's carcass decayed under the house, but Trent's foolish drilling had set the remains free as some kind of putrid sentient ooze that wept up through the drill-hole to reconstitute itself in the dark, forming arms and legs and a grotesque carnival-freak head that was nothing but a huge bolus of rot that swayed atop the neck like a sunflower on its stalk— that *thing* was in the basement now, its feet squelching on the floor as it stumbled closer to Trent, its eyes two festering pearl onions, filth squeezing through the eyelets of a pair of moldering work boots threaded with the blackened soup of its toes. . . .

The working stiff's bloated lips pushed noxious fumes right next to Trent's ear.

. . . or were those Hank's lips?

That breath reeked of decay, wrongness, death.

*"All the shitbirds who did you wrong, T-Man. You know who I'm talking about, don't you? Let's make them pay."*

# PART III

# AUGUST

# 14

—*NEED MY TOOLS*, *I need my tools, my* tools, *need my, my, my* *TOOLS*—

This one thought looped through Trent Saban's mind, un-cluttered by feedback. A man *did* need his tools. To hell with bread, *tools* were the staff of life. How could a man bake bread without an axe to cut down the tree to feed the fire to raise the loaf? And anyway, what sort of man baked?

*"Here's a joke for you, brothers."*

Hank's face shone in the screen of Trent's iPhone, resting in the heated cup holder.

*"Why don't you buy your wife a watch? Because there's a clock on the stove!"*

Trent's laugh held the timbre of a busted ooga horn: "Haa*AA*aaa*Aa*."

Numbness crawled up Trent's arms. He emitted a flavorless burp as he piloted the Denali into the Stockyards shopping area. Dusky now, past seven o'clock. Under normal circumstances he'd be expected home for dinner, but circumstances were far from normal these days.

Rita and Milo had been gone a week. While the cat was away, the mouse would play. Trent would continue making his own hours after Rita slunk back, too—and, *oooh*, she would. Gone was Domestic Trent, ball-clamped hubby. The sooner his wife got that through her thick noggin, the better off they'd all be.

Trent had . . . *evolved*, one might say.

*"You bet your cherry-red ass you have, T-Man."*

The fact that Hank was talking to Trent—and had been doing so for an unquantifiable period of time, roughly coinciding with his family's departure . . . well, Trent knew Hank wasn't *really* talking to him. He'd just watched so many videos that the genial Handyman's presence had sunk into his brain, the way a catchy song chorus did. Trent did find that Hank's presence tended to get waterier the farther he ventured from the house, a radio frequency fading from range . . . but Trent hardly left home anymore.

*"You know the question every milk-livered Modern Man ought to ask his daddy?"*

Hank was piping in loud and clear right now. He'd been on quite a tear about Modern Men in all their rainbowed deficiencies.

*"'Why didn't you teach me how to be a man, Pappy?'"* Hank said, affecting a whiny simper. *"'The way Grandpappy taught you to be a man, and Grandpappy's pappy taught him?'"*

Hank's tone deepened to a muscular baritone. *"'Son, my forefathers and I learned our lessons on factory floors and in the trenches. Your generation? The day you told your mother and me you were going to barista college was the day I realized I'd fathered a walking stool sample.'"*

Trent glanced at the title of this particular video:

"How to Mortar Sheetrock"

The glowing orange Home Depot sign punctured the dusk. Trent steered into the site of his most spectacular humiliation at the hands of Asscrack Al and his goodtime buddies. But that fate had befallen an outmoded version of himself, hadn't it? The newt-like, pre-chrysalis Trent Saban. Trent 2.0 now walked in his skin—and if the updated version wasn't quite diamond-hard, he was sure to Christ getting there.

*"Watch the doors, T-Man."*

Hank's now-frequent nickname for Trent. *T-Man.* Part He-Man, part T-Rex.

And lookee here—if it wasn't ole Asscrack himself, big as life and twice as ugly, sauntering out of the contractor area's garage-style exit.

Voltage forked from Trent's reptile cortex. His fist smacked the horn: *Blat!* Asscrack eyeballed Trent's truck, but couldn't spot him through the tinted windows.

When Trent glanced at the video again, the title had changed:

"How to Murder a Shitbird"

*"Follow him, T-Man."*

Trent pulled out behind Asscrack's pickup. He dogged Al as his truck slowed into a traffic circle. An ancient Datsun slipped in between them, but the Denali was jacked up high enough to see over the little car. Trent let some distance build between them. No use putting a wild hair up Asscrack's caboose.

*"You don't mow another man's lawn,"* Hank said. *"You don't*

*shovel his damn drive. And you sure as hell don't tousle the hair of another man's son."*

Trent's jaw hardened. Damn skippy. You most fucking well did not.

Al veered into an industrial area. A sign read: HOLD IT SELF-STORAGE. Trent hung back as Al's truck turned into the maze of storage lockers.

Trent pulled into a spot near the entrance and turned off the ignition. He would have to follow on foot. He didn't have any weapon aside from his fists . . . oh, and his Beard Club straight razor, which he'd started to carry on his belt. What else was the carrying case for, after all?

He stopped by a dumpster and found a three-foot length of rebar, bent like a hockey stick. It felt good in Trent's hand. Grippy.

He slid around the cinder-block wall into an alleyway of sorts. Storage lockers rowed him on either side. Three hundred feet ahead was Asscrack's truck. The driver's door hung open in the gloom. He couldn't see the man himself, but caught the muffled clink of tools.

"I'm only going to give him a warning," he said to himself.

*"You bet. Rattle his cage, teach him a lesson."*

Trent realized he'd left his phone in the car. Didn't matter. Hank was always there.

He found Asscrack in his storage locker, working under the glow of a utility light. Asscrack's back was to him as he poked through a coffee can full of screws—

Trent said, "Hey, bub."

It wasn't his voice. That brogue belonged to Hank, oozing out of Trent's mouth.

Asscrack turned, startled into a smile.

Trent brought the rebar up.

Asscrack warbled, "Whoa, chief—!"

Trent chopped sideways, the bar cutting the air with a soft *whish*. It crunched into Asscrack's knee, his leg caving in the middle and turning into a gruesome lesser-than symbol.

For a heartbeat they stood there looking at each other, in mutual states of shock. Then the pain hit Asscrack's neural centers and he screamed, lunging for Trent: one of his shovelish hands clamped on, grotty fingernails digging into the meat of Trent's shoulder.

*"We got a live one, T-Man!"*

Asscrack hauled Trent forward until their noses were squashed together. Foam flecked his lips as he muttered, "The fucka—?" Trent swung the rebar again, hitting the same spot. Asscrack's leg gave out with a horrible crunch, his boot still planted as his leg crumpled like a book slamming shut.

Trent followed the man down to the grease-spotted floor. He wormed up Asscrack's chest and sat on him, pinning Al's arms under his knees. Al squirmed, making kittenish mewls.

*"I'm going to teach you how to peel a man's face off. Listen carefully, T-Man."*

*I'm not doing that,* Trent thought. Okay, the guy had touched Milo's hair, yeah, and poked a little fun at him in the sander aisle, but Trent wasn't going to mutilate him, change the guy's body in some way that couldn't be fixed. . . . Yet even as his mind rebelled, his fingers crept down to his belt to release the Beard Club razor.

When he flicked the blade from its sheath, the man began to babble in terror.

*"You got to make a decisive incision from the top of the ear all the way down to the jawline,"* Hank said chipperly. *"There's a tangle of blood vessels 'n' shit under there, so expect a torrent of the red stuff."*

"I don't want a torrent," Trent said clearly. "I don't want to—"

Hank's presence filled Trent's head: he felt the Handyman bubbling from his ears, expanding like some kind of florid and veiny foam.

Asscrack felt like nothing under Trent; his body seemed to be coming apart like a moldy bag of leaves as he wriggled on the cement, incapable of fighting, more like he was trying to burrow into the ground like a grub—

*No, no, no, NO!* Trent was a father, and for all he knew, this guy was one too. He couldn't do this to another living thing, he couldn't peel anything's face off—

Yet there the razor was, winking loathsomely next to the man's ear.

*"Teach this fucker that you don't stick your hoe in another man's onion patch!"*

"Ruffle my boy's hair, will you . . ." Trent rasped.

He drew the razor blade a half-inch down, from the tippy-top of Al's ear—blood fanned from the incision—

With a convulsive jerk, Trent flung the razor. It hit the wall and fell behind some shelves. He heaved himself off Al.

*"Trent! Get back to work!"* Hank thundered.

Clutching his skull, positive it was going to explode in his hands, Trent fled.

He staggered back to the Denali and drove a few miles to

find perhaps the only pay phone in the city. Inside the booth, he dialed 911.

"There's a guy in a storage unit. He's injured. . . . Hold It Self Storage, yes, off Lampley—he needs help. Come quickly."

"Stay on the line while we send emergency assistance—"

Trent hung up and slumped against the plexiglass wall of the booth, shivering.

The phone rang.

Trent didn't dare pick up. He got back into his truck. He'd left the razor and the rebar at the storage locker. The place was surely monitored by security cameras. His fingerprints were all over the place.

The radio snapped on, that all-too-familiar voice booming from the speakers.

*"Hey all you hepcats, it's DJ Hank-tastic spinning the fattest platters and playing aaaaaall your favorite hits!"*

Trent cringed.

*"This is a long-distance dedication to the T-Man from his ole buddy the Handyman, who says he's sad to discover the T-Man's such a fucking limp-dick pussyyyy!"*

The special request, Lesley Gore's "It's My Party (And I'll Cry If I Want To)," blasted through the interior of the Denali. Something tore into Trent's head, coring deep, and then—

"—ent—"

A metallic *thump* shot through the dark. He drifted alone. . . . No, that's only what *it* wanted him to think. He was never alone anymore.

*"Trent."*

A name. *His* name. The realization brought on a paralyzing flurry of panic, the sizzle of electric butterflies—but he knew even then he wouldn't remember the threat: it would sink deep again, lurking in a cubbyhole of his lizard brain—

Trent was in the Denali, stretched over the front seats like a gutshot corpse. Morning sunlight cut around the silhouette of a figure staring in at him.

"R-Rita?"

She opened the door. "Are you okay?"

He felt stiff and crumply, a stick of wicker lawn furniture left out in the snow. He let Rita take his wrist—he had no choice, really, weak as a kitten—and help him from the truck.

He was in the driveway of their new home. Where had he been? How had he gotten here? Fright blitzed through his chest at the realization that he had no earthly clue.

"I'm okay . . . must've been working late."

He ransacked his memory circuits, but the past hours— *days?*—were sunk into a black hole. His overalls were starchy with sweat and his mouth tasted like he'd been chewing on live rodents.

"I wasn't drinking, Rita." He rubbed his face, furred with five-day beard. "I don't know, exactly, but I wasn't boozing."

"That's not what I think you were doing."

The sun glinting off the shingles hurt his eyes. The whole house hurt.

"Have you come back? Both of you?"

Rita said, "Yes, we're here."

The relief was too much to bear. He collapsed into Rita, his arms swallowing her.

"Oh, thank God," he breathed into her hair. "It's going to be different this time, I swear."

"I know, baby." Rita grunted with the effort of keeping him upright. "You've always meant well."

She helped him inside. The house accepted them, its door closing like a mouth.

# 15

**THE NEXT FEW WEEKS** were the best the Saban family would ever spend in the house.

There was nothing remarkable about that span. All three of them slept well and deeply, their dreams untroubled. They made suppers together and ate in the honey-colored evening sunlight lazing through the bay windows.

Trent and Rita also found themselves having more sex than since they were randy law school students. Their bodies fresh to each other, a pair of explorers traveling old routes to thrilling new destinations. More than once, Trent had to slip his hand over Rita's mouth to muffle her cries so they didn't wake Milo.

The repairs Trent made during this period were minor, but as durable as any by a triple-A–rated handyman they could've hired from a professional outfit. His pride was subdued. His fixes would last, yes, but why shouldn't they? Sometimes Hank was there, but more often the Handyman was strangely absent.

Trent's conscious mind didn't register this lack, but the deeper layers of his psyche were relaxed and bright.

The odd night, Trent crept down the hall and slid under the covers with his sleeping son. Trent curled into his boy, imagining how Milo's body and mind would grow over the years. He could not say why he crawled into his boy's bed . . . but it came with the feeling a death-row prisoner must have upon being served his last meal. You had to gorge, didn't you? Eat enough to stay full for that long trip into the dark.

This persistent sense was the only intrusion on the perfection of those weeks. As if Trent was approaching a cataclysm yet to reveal itself. War veterans often talked about "getting short": the closer they were to the end of their hitch, the surer they became of a catastrophic tragedy striking before they could make it home.

*I'm so short I could parachute off a dime, Sarge . . .*

As for Rita, she existed as she had since arriving at the house. As the conductor of a steam engine pounding toward an inevitable impact with another train coming down the same tracks to meet her: a locomotive of incomprehensible dimensions grafted out of bone and meat and dust, ancient and clattering at Rita with its grinning chrome grille—

Otherwise, those weeks were ones of ease, spent in simple joys. The police did not call with uncomfortable questions about unremembered incidents in storage lockers. Trent serenaded Rita in the kitchen, crooning "Endless Love" into a carrot microphone, swanning around the island and sticking the carrot in Milo's face—"Sing along with me, son!"—Milo not knowing the words but willing to try, the three of them dissolving into a fit of laughter, which the walls soaked up greedily, as the walls of that house did.

Some nights Trent lay in bed in a semi-stupor, an oasis between sleep and waking. . . . A man tells himself he needs things in life: a job of merit, wealth, the fear or respect of his peers. What other signposts exist to let him know he can hold his head high?

But you can't have it all, not at once, every duck in a row. Life won't bend that way, and a belief in the possibility is corrosive . . . and all the while, the most precious stuff is sprinkled right at your feet, waiting to be held.

Those weeks passed in a state of domestic ecstasy. Why would that be?

When prey dies in fear, hunters will say the meat tastes bitter.

What of happiness, then? May we speak of the taste of joyful meat?

# 16

**MILO LAY IN BED** thinking how nice it was to watch Mom and Dad kiss. They had kissed more often lately, the way they did when he was really young. After Mom said her good-nights when Dad was coming in to say his, they used to stand in front of Milo's bedroom door and kiss. Only three or four quick smacks, but it made him feel safe, his world steady and—

*click*

Milo went stiff. He pictured a spider in a high corner of his room, making that sound with its legs as it spun its web.

Milo actually liked spiders. They were nature's engineers. Spiders understood it was the work that mattered, not the result. If their work got destroyed, they simply began anew. People could learn a lot from spiders—but he shouldn't be able to *hear* one in his room unless it was huge: a spider the size of a fat dachshund with its limbs gnashing like knitting needles in the dark. . . .

—*click click*—

No, it couldn't be a spider. And that sound was too steady to be a pest like a mouse or a cockroach. He yanked the covers over his head . . . but his father's voice (*You're nearly ten, Milo, it's time to start thinking reasonably*) made him pull them down just enough to show his face.

That sound was in the room with him . . . somewhere on the floor. Or under the bed.

*click . . . click . . .*

Milo was overheating in his pajamas; the sweaty cotton was stuck down the knobs of his spine. Whatever was making the noise, he needed to see it—to *make himself* see.

He needed to grow up and start acting like a man.

If he could just *do* that, strengthen his mind, it'd make his father happy. And when Dad was happy, the house was happy. And when the house was happy, they could *all* be happy.

—*click, click, click*—

Milo let his right hand creep from the safety of the covers and down the mattress. . . . His fingertips brushed the metal bedframe, then lowered into the blackness under the bed—

*CLICK*

He flinched at what sounded like a huge metal eye snapping open.

He'd awoken a cyclopean creature lurking underneath the box spring: a suffocating squid with gummy flesh whose curved beak, the beak of a toucan, was getting ready to snip his fingers off as clean as hedge shears—

Teeth gritted, Milo forced his fingers down to the carpet in search of his iPad. But it wasn't there. For a moment he pawed around in the dark, not finding it, that squid tracking him closely now, debating its chances at snipping his whole hand off at the wrist—

His fingertips brushed the tablet. He yanked it from the floor and brought it under the covers and switched it on. The hardest part was over. Tucking his knees to his chest, he kicked the covers off and leapt out of bed with the iPad shining like a lighthouse beam. . . .

*click click*

". . . Morty?"

A turtle sat in the middle of his room . . . one just like Morty, except Milo was instantly clear it *wasn't* Morty. Not only because Morty was dead, and Mom had explained what dead meant—*when something is gone*, really *gone, it never comes back*. He knew the real part of Morty had gone into the ground . . . or, the more awful truth, it had dribbled between Mom's fingers.

But Milo knew this wasn't Morty because this thing didn't move like Morty or even look like him, not up close . . . but mostly it didn't *feel* like Morty.

The shell belonged to Morty, he could tell that much: it was eaten through in spots, and bits of pink crust still clung to it. But the legs jutting out were made of the cardboard box Morty had been buried in, and its new head appeared to be an old Christmas-light bulb: a gentle yellow that now began to sputter on and off with that clicking noise, a bit like a firefly in early summer.

Guided by the same logic that told him this wasn't his pet, Milo also knew something was alive inside Morty's old shell . . . but in a different way than normal, like how a tumor could be said to be alive: a cancerous growth with the instincts of a hermit crab that enjoyed invading old abandoned things. Or maybe Morty's heart was still inside, sending out a weak signal that made that clicking noise and flickering light.

The turtle skittered forward, moving faster than Real-Morty ever did.

Milo took a big step back, almost falling. "Morty, please. Stop."

It came to a halt in front of him. The Christmas bulb was fully lit now, no flickering. Milo reached down and touched the shell. It was cold and dry under his fingers, unfamiliar. He tried to pick it up, but the thing scrambled back toward the hallway. Not-Morty then lifted its small bulb head, as if summoning Milo to follow.

Milo did so, trailing the turtle as it crawled down the hall. Normally the floors creaked, but they now lay silent under his feet. The chandelier loomed over the living room below.

Not-Morty reached the top stair and pitched itself off, *clunking* as it rolled down, over and over . . . Milo peered over the landing and saw that, halfway down the steps, the turtle's body appeared to change, lengthening out somehow, its stubby legs becoming dark crablike stalks.

The shell glided down the last few stairs with a scissory *clickety-clack*. When Milo joined the turtle, he found it flipped over on the tiles, its legs feebly wriggling. Milo put his hand under his pajama shirt and used that to right the shell as fast as he could. He just didn't want to touch Not-Morty. Even through the shirt, its body felt like a bunch of picked scabs packed into the shape of his old pet.

The turtle continued on, Milo following the bright seed of

Not-Morty's lightbulb through the kitchen. It stopped at the closed basement door. The turtle couldn't open it, just knocking its flickering head stupidly against the wood.

Milo knelt to examine it, his fingers not quite touching the wires that disappeared from the end of the bulb into its shell. The turtle's head-bulb snapped, something inside its body making the squeal of a servo. Milo jerked his hand back. That bulb was melting hot.

Not-Morty kept butting the door. Its lightbulb-head fizzled with each bump.

Milo's voice bobbed like a balloon on a string: "Why do you want to go down there?"

The moment he asked, the door opened all on its own.

Not-Morty was knocked aside as the door swung silently on its hinges, the way a nightmare opens its jaws. Nothing stood at the top of the stairs. Milo couldn't even picture what *might* have been waiting for him . . . except he could, sort of. Something made of screws and pipes and baling twine and chunks of cement and rust and dust, so much dust, staring at him with eyes of molten lead.

Not-Morty clicked over to the basement steps. Pink fluid had started to dribble down its cardboard legs.

"No, don't," Milo breathed, though he wouldn't be sorry if he never saw Not-Morty again.

It flung itself over the top step. Milo heard it bump clumsily down the stairs. He tried to back away, but some nasty signal in his brain was prodding him toward the basement, which he could feel exhaling its damp breath in his face . . . his own breath coming in ragged gusts, his arms out as if a car were speeding right at him, its headlights pinning him.

*"Hey, there, Junior Builder, we've got a real big project today."*

Little Boy Blue's voice drifted up the unlit basement steps.

*"We all like to work with tools, but do you know the best thing of all?"* A soft titter from the dark. *"Some of us get lucky enough to be tools."*

Milo's heart was now pistoning in his chest so painfully that his skin jumped.

*"There are lots of tools* you *can be."*

Milo found himself in the basement doorway. *Oh no, no, NO . . .* It was so black that he couldn't even see the top stair. The darkness of deep space unrolled past his bare toes.

*"Digging tools and ripping ones. But the best tool of all is the one we use to find secrets."*

Milo watched his hand reach over to the light switch. The gloom vanished. Helpless to fight the momentum, Milo went down the stairs—not walking so much as drifting, his feet propped on cushiony clouds.

He'd run if he could. Dad wouldn't blame him, he didn't think, wouldn't give him The Look or whatever passed for it these days. He tried to scream, but when his lips parted, all that came out was a papery whistle.

Halfway down the stairs, the basement began to reveal itself through the beams: the mess of his father's unfinished projects, busted lawn furniture. Boxes of holiday decorations: a jangly Halloween skeleton, a string of Christmas lights missing a single bulb, a basket of Easter eggs—

And a different kind of box.

It sat on a bare patch of floor. The appearance of a sailor's chest. A big toy box. Except it looked too ancient for that. . . . Milo struggled to picture the child who'd stash his playthings in such a thing. All that came to him was a wrinkly face topped with scraggly snow-white hair, a pair of yolky-yellow eyes, and a twisted knife-slash of a mouth that blabbered madly—

*"If the boy behaves, he can go in the box."*

It wasn't Little Boy Blue's voice anymore. This one was raw, cloggy, like a person gargling through a throatful of rancid slime.

*"If the boy misbehaves, into the box he goes."*

It was the same voice he'd heard coming through the phone he'd invented. An old, old man who'd witnessed things that human eyes should never see. Things that had driven him a kind of crazy that Milo couldn't even comprehend.

Milo's foot hit the next step. Three more to the basement floor.

"You're not here." His voice shook. "You're . . . you're gone."

*"Oh. Is that what my dear daughter told you?"* A gassy chuckle. *"You'll see, boy. Yeah, you'll see."*

The basement light flickered. Not-Morty lay upside down on the floor, the inside of its lightbulb-head filling with black fluid.

The lid of the box swung open. Milo caught a glimpse of unclean geometries, gears winding and things ticking—

His feet settled on the basement floor. Not-Morty's head exploded with a glassy *pop!*

He could smell the box now: the odor of a rain barrel, the kind that birthed mosquitoes. His skin was cold, and his eyes were bulging: he could feel them beating from his sockets with each crazed *thack* of his heart.

. . . and then he saw it.

It was hunched behind the moving boxes marked KITCHEN and GLASSWARE and HOLIDAYS. Glimmering as pinkly as skinned meat and quaking with an undiagnosable sickness, or *eagerness*, ageless and haunted all over in dust . . .

The basement light cut out.

*"All the boys go into the box."*

Trent woke, his fingers already sliding under the pillow to wrap around the linoleum knife he'd taken to sleeping with.

He slipped out of bed, leaving Rita sawing logs. Padded down the hall to Milo's room. The bed was empty. Milo's tablet lay upside down on the floor, outlined in a blue square. He turned it over . . . a YouTube video. Little Boy Blue, Milo's favorite. The floppy felt-armed puppet capered across the screen. The video title:

"Let's Play Hide-and-Seek!"

Concern rising, Trent went downstairs. He didn't bother flicking on the lights, didn't want to worry Rita by turning the whole house into a beacon. The front door was locked. He peered out the window . . . nothing but starlight playing on the open foundations out there.

"Milo, buddy . . . ?"

Trent went into the polished kitchen area and hunted a flashlight out of the junk drawer, shining the beam over the spotless sink and fridge, everything they'd ever dreamed of all aligned in perfect order—

The basement door was open.

He went to the top step and flicked the light switch. Nothing. Bulb must have burnt out. He shone the flashlight down the stairs, watching dust tumble over and over in the beam.

"Milo—you down there?"

He wouldn't be. Milo never went down there, which was fine by Trent. It was the one place in the house he could hear himself think.

Trent was set to backtrack—had he checked the spare rooms?—when a sly note floated up the stairs from someplace down in the dark. A muffled tick like the winding of a watch.

"Milo?" No response.

Trent's feet made heavy footfalls on the steps. There was a smell, a mildewy mop-bucket odor. The manhole-sized beam of the flashlight cut across the furnace, stacked boxes with their flaps hanging open like tongues, the projects he'd taken a hand to before being diverted by some more pressing task.

He felt around for the light cord hanging near the furnace. You could never find those damn cords when you needed to—his fingers snagged the string, jerked it. The light popped on, flooding the basement . . .

. . . revealing a box he'd never seen before.

It was made of an exotic grain: tigerwood or camphorwood, sleek and glossy. It seemed to be of one piece: no tongue and groove, no visible nail heads. The box was clearly making noise as well, giving off a collection of hums and ticks like a complex timepiece.

Trent stepped back as the box rose on one end, slamming back to the concrete. It was about the size of—

"Milo!"

His hands moved over the box's surface as a cold lather broke over his body, as he searched for a seam, a latch, a button, something, *anything*, but the box was solid as a tree stump. He could now hear Milo screaming in there, a high keening note, but the wood must be cushioned, or else Milo was suffocating because his scream cut out, only those cold mechanical ticks and whirs meeting his ears now—

Footsteps pounded down the stairs. Rita rammed her shoulder into Trent, knocking him aside. Her fingers hunted knowingly over the box until—

The lid sprang open like a grisly jack-in-the box, regurgitating their son onto the floor. Milo's face was a ghastly blue, his lips distended, his body a limp bag of skin.

"Help him, Rita!"

He would never forget the look of poisonous hate she gave him. It burned through him, bit deep and hard into all the ways he'd stumbled, spoke to the unsayable secret he suspected most: that she was ashamed of him, she despised him. . . .

She turned to Milo, thumbing his lip down. His teeth were clenched so tightly that droplets of blood sprang from his gums.

"Shhh, baby, I've got you. Mommy's here."

Milo's heels drummed the concrete, then went still. His breath came raggedly.

Rita flung an acidic glance at Trent. "Did you build this thing?"

"Me? No!" Her accusation shrank him to half his size. "How in God's name would I know where it came from?"

"Christ, Trent. Do you even know *what* you're building anymore?"

Whatever togetherness he'd experienced with Rita over the last few weeks evaporated right there under the basement lights. Trent stared into the overturned box. Its insides beggared logic.

A nonsensical augment of gears and sprockets and pistons, hanks of fur that seemed to dilate from the box's inner ribbing, small glass cubes and what appeared to be . . . were those needles?

He drew closer to Milo, inspecting him. Blood trickled from a puncture at the base of his son's neck. Holes were worn through his pj's at the knees and elbows, the skin abraded.

*He'll be fine, T-Man. It's just a few scratches. Toughen the boy up a little.*

Trent's gaze worked over to the drain hole. Was that Hank's voice burbling up from it, ribbony as smoke?

No, the voice was back where it had been before. Where Hank belonged. In his head.

Rita was watching him closely. "I'm taking Milo to the hospital," she said. "We can all go. We can leave." She paused. "Leave this house."

It wasn't too long ago that Trent had made the same proposal. After that thing with Milo where he lost his tooth, wasn't it? A sabbatical from the house. But that was then; now that same proposition stuck in Trent's brain like a barbed quill. No. No, no, no, he didn't like that idea at all. Hank . . . well, hell, Hank was right. It really *was* only a few scratches, wasn't it?

"Why would we leave, Rita?"

"I can't make you go." An exhausted sigh. "You have to want to."

"You've always been against this. Right from the start."

"Yes." She eyed him dead-on. "You're fucking right."

Abruptly, Trent reached a vanishing point that rendered his wife's behavior nonsensical, even hostile. She was threatening him. Threatening to take their son away again.

Threatening the house.

"You never gave this place a chance. You wanted it to fail. *Me* to fail."

She simply sat with Milo in her arms, lording their closeness over him. He pictured himself as she'd sprung the latch on the box, hovering over her like a dickless lump. . . . A withholding bitch, was Rita. Always had been. A fucking ice queen to her husband, simpering coddleworm to her son.

*You said it, T-Man. Raised a sop who can't even spend a few minutes in a box, for Christ's sake.*

One of his toolkits lay near at hand. The tack hammer was in that one. A sudden inkling came to Trent to—to *do* something to Rita with it. Something that would shut her big mouth, make up for what he didn't have the balls to do to Carson Aikles—

His attention was diverted up the stairs. Someone was there, at the top. A black cutout in the burly shape of a man.

"It's up there right now, isn't it, Trent?" Rita said softly. "It's watching us."

A grin from the shape up the stairs. A cutthroat slit of silver.

*Let her go, tiger. She ain't worth the effort. What woman is? And we've got work to do.*

"I can't just leave, Rita. This house needs me."

He waited for her to bark, to curse him out, to finally reach a hand into his chest and tear him open. She did none of this.

"Of course. You're the boss."

Hank wasn't occupying the stairs by the time they ascended. The house quiet and calm as Trent carried Milo out to the car, settled him in the front seat, and clipped his seat belt on. The boy had slipped into a dreamless-seeming state.

"Drive safe, Rita. I'll see you at the hospital as soon as I can."

Trent watched them go, thinking that he ought to be

worried . . . about what? That sense was distant now, a warning from a far mountaintop. He trudged back inside the waiting house, on back down to the basement.

The box rested on its side. It looked different now, not nearly so solid. Scraps really, held together with staples and snarls of copper wire.

Its innards were complex. He couldn't locate a battery source or a winding knob . . . tubes and wires and tightening coils attached to sprockets, the sort of stuff you'd find inside old automatons. A hank of fur protruded from an inner wall, swollen as an anthill. A tubular wormlike *something* had birthed from its corona: it looked sort of like pus ejecting from a whitehead.

One of the glass cubes was full of gears and winding stems; shreds of pink were stuck to the gear teeth, as if they had ground something up and sent the liquefied remains through the tube projecting from the cube, wrapped round a sewing-machine assembly that would pump the attached needle into—

The puncture in his son's neck.

*It's nothing, T-Man. C'mon. Kids are tough. Parents don't give them enough credit.*

"Kids are tough," Trent croaked.

Not giving the ruined box a backward glance, he plodded up the stairs. To bed, to sleep, jiggedy. He would reexamine the thing tomorrow. If anything was the matter, he'd call Rita.

Before dawn's light threaded across the gritty gray concrete of the basement, the box was gone. But that was okay, because by then Trent had mostly forgotten about it.

# PART IV

# SEPTEMBER

# 17

"WE'LL BE ABLE TO MAKE a clearer diagnosis once further tests come back, Mrs. Saban."

The physician, Dr. Paslov, stood with Rita at Milo's bed. Her son was covered in one of those spun-glass sheets seemingly only found in hospitals, locked in a state that was kissing cousin to catatonia.

"We'll figure it out, never fear," Paslov assured her before stepping out. But wasn't that what doctors always said?

She'd been here for three days . . . no, four. Time scalloped. Rita hadn't expected Trent to join them—she recognized the harbingers—but she'd called anway. When he finally picked up, it was with the wild claim that some airborne fungus had belched from the basement drywall.

"This stuff could be toxic, Rita. It might even be responsible for Milo's state. I need to investigate"—his voice had been overtaken by a silky snakelike hiss—"make it safe by the time you both come home."

A knock at the door. She opened it to find Hector in his aviator sunglasses.

"Rita, my sincerest condolences. May I have a word?"

"Take those damn things off first."

He complied, hooking the sunglasses into his breast pocket. "Good enough?" he said with open hostility. She stepped aside to let him in. He studiously avoided looking at Milo.

"This is the hardest part of my role, Rita," he maundered like some discount funeral home ghoul. "Your family, my family— we've done this dance so many times."

"Don't give me that bullshit. It's never been the same onus," Rita told him. "Your family only builds the tomb."

"And you think that's a cakewalk? You don't know the work that gets done before you show up. Your family never has." Hector walked to the window overlooking the parking lot. "You know one of the builders sawed off his own hands? Not *hand*, okay? *Hands,* plural. He was cutting boards with the table saw. Put the boards aside and ran one arm through at the wrist, then the other, just another day at the office." Big exhale. "Eddie somebody . . . Orr. Eddie Orr."

*Eddie Orr, Eddie Orr* . . . Rita's overcooked brain turned the stranger's name into a mean-spirited playground rhyme. . . . *Had two hands, but not no more.*

"Another dude ran off into the woods," Hector went on. "We found him in a gas station bathroom ten miles away. He'd taken a bottle of bleach from under the sink and dumped it in his eyes. The bleach cooked the color right out of them. Things were white as gumballs."

He faced her now. "Who do you think dealt with those

shitstorms? Who talked to those wives, those fathers' kids, compensated them? Was it you?"

Rita didn't reply, but she did see their situation a bit differently now.

"And then *your* offering nearly cuts my balls off with a pair of garden clippers."

"Don't call him that. He has a name."

Hector collected himself, the polished professional. "The contract calls for one, Rita. It's not a negotiable item. It's *the* sole item. And if the chosen offering resists . . ."

"Why hasn't any one of us ever challenged the"—she searched for the right word—"the *rules?*"

Hector's lips twisted. "Don't you go thinking, Rita. Not now."

"It can't be that the others were cowards. My mother was a lot of things, but not that."

Hector's laugh was deathly soft. "Oh, you think your foremothers haven't tried?"

Pulling his glasses from his pocket, he slid them back over his eyes. "I've heard stories, Rita. I'll spare you the details, but . . . if you withhold the plaything, you become the plaything."

Reaching out, his fingertips brushed Rita's stomach. "*All of you* become playthings."

He withdrew his touch before she could knock his hand away. "Don't rock the boat. Be amenable, *sensible*, like your mother."

Rita caught Hector cutting his eyes at Milo. She caught the grimace too.

"Does the sight of my son repulse you?"

Hector gestured with one finger at the daisy-chain of yellowish nodules that had pushed from Milo's throat: a necklace of rotten baby teeth garlanding her boy's neck.

"It's, uh"—he swallowed—"pretty hard to look at, not gonna lie."

"Get the fuck out of here, Hector."

# 18

"**WHY, OH, WHY** *do we men keep handing over our birthright to devious hellspawn who say we did them dirty a thousand years ago?*"

Handyman Hank's face shone out of Trent's phone, angled on the lid of his toolkit. His voice boomed across the dirt with the timbre of a revival preacher.

"*If modern men want to live as castratos, their manhoods carted around in some woke carpet-muncher's ethically sourced hemp hand-bag, well, you won't see me lifting a finger to stop it. But I'll be goddamned if I'm joining* that *party!*"

Trent was perched up on his roof with his tools spread over the precarious slant. The night was cool and starless. Trent worked under the beam of his helmet lamp, wedging his crowbar under the shingles and cracking them loose like so many rotted teeth.

Trent peeled back a section of shingling to reveal the water-logged moisture barrier. After slashing at it with his linoleum knife, he abandoned the blade in favor of stripping chunks away with his bare hands.

*"I'm a man. Okay? A man who KNOWS things THEY don't want you to find out about, T-Man! The globalists, the New World Order, the hog-bellied gremlins and red-devil cheerleaders!"*

Trent ripped down to the ice barrier and the roof's wooden ribs. He saw one of them flinch in the lamp beam, squirming deeper into the blackness under the shingles.

*Oooh, you pink shits.*

Lying flat on his stomach, Trent plunged his arm into the breach in his roof. He rooted around blindly, arm sunk to the shoulder inside the congested gap. He couldn't see what he was hunting for, but knew they were there—his hand plunged into a pocket of pulsating warmth. He pushed in deeper, grunting in satisfaction, until his arm was encased in squirming softness to his elbow. It felt like a bagful of deformed, plump, skinned fruit.

He'd found one of their nests.

*"These rascals crawl out of the sewer stinking of sulfur with their gangrenous skin and snake-oil smiles, hobbling about yelling, 'We're gonna eat your daughters' ripe pussies at the roller rink and stab them at the sock hop!' It's true, T-Man! You can look it up!"*

The pinklings' bodies squeaked like organ-meat in his hands, a revolting mishmash of sacs and bladders that reached a thrilling tension before they burst, their insides squishing between his fingers like creamery butter. He sucked in his stomach and turned onto his side, shoving his arm in another few inches, pulping the sluggish bodies with machinelike efficiency.

*"Also,"* Hank added as a sage coda, *"sometimes a dolphin or two needs to get scooped up in a tuna net."*

"Fuck the dolphins," Trent muttered, squashing as many of the bastards as he could.

"*Preach, brotherman,*" Hank agreed. "*A righteous man needs his dolphin blubber.*"

Trent yanked his arm out. His sleeve was sodden and dripping with moist chunklets. The reek of the pinklings wept from the hole in the roof, gamy as snake piss.

"You feel *that*, you little bastards?" He stomped on the shingles. "I am Godzilla and you"—stomp—"are"—*stomp*—"Toky—"

The roof suddenly gave way like ancient fatback, sending his leg through a rotted cavity. He came down hard, nearly skewering himself on the crowbar.

Trent tore his leg out of the hole, childishly worried that something inside the house might try to grab him. He stared through it, down into Milo's room.

Trent scampered down the ladder and back into the unlit house, his helmet lamp throwing a coin of light across the walls. As he passed through the kitchen, his heel skidded and he caught himself on the mahogany island to keep from falling flat on his tailbone. There was a puddle on the floor—craning his neck, Trent peered up at the huge wet patch spreading across the ceiling. It sagged downward in a pulpy, discolored inverted meniscus. . . . The patch looked *pregnant*.

He got a broom from the recessed cabinet—nice touch, that—and poked the stained patch with the handle. Water rilled down the handle, stinking of human filth.

Filled with wordless fury, Trent carried the broom up to Milo's room. The bedcovers were soaked in the shucked-oyster remains of the pinklings. Trent gathered the sheets and knotted them on the end of the broom like a hobo's bindle. Hank always said a good handyman was a good sequencer. So first he'd wash the sheets, then tackle that hole in the roof. Make things right as rain, lickety-split.

He'd made it back down to the kitchen when his breath caught in a hiccup.

Figures waited on him in the murk. His helmet lamp beam brightened the features of—

"Rita—?"

It took a beat to register the uncanniness. But of course that couldn't be his wife. Or his son.

The flat-screen TV snapped on. Hank's face shone across the open living area like a lost deep-sea creature.

*"Look at 'em, will ya? Helluva job. Rarely have I seen better, and brother, let me tell you, I've seen a lot."*

They stood motionless as wax dummies in the darkened kitchen. Slats of scrap wood and flashing, ceramic and linoleum and rebar and pipe, duct tape and copper wire and hair . . .

*"It's okay to miss your family, T-Man. Okay to build a reminder too."*

Glancing at the TV, Trent saw the title of Hank's video:

"Easy-to-Assemble Replacement Family"

The tallest one's face belonged to Trent: high forehead, strong chin, thick around the waist. It resembled Hank a little too, didn't it, scraps of an old tartan work shirt clinging to its wicker chest. Blown fuses were stuffed into the wirework of its face. The female so much like Rita, brow set determinedly below the paintbrush bangs. Last was Milo, slumped against Rita's leg like a wire monkey with PVC poking out through its wallpaper skin.

"I didn't build these."

Trent's voice bounced around the deserted house.

Hank chuckled. *"Who knows what a man gets up to in the lost hours?"*

Trent touched his wife's constructed face. A wire eyelash slid under his fingernail, sharp as a thorn, eliciting a hiss of pain.

From somewhere upstairs came a rending *shrrraaaaak.*

Trent dashed up the staircase—each footfall earned a shrill *screeee!* on the stairs; they squeaked, they *all* fucking squeaked now. At the top, he flicked the switch to illuminate the blown-globe chandelier. The light was thin and brown.

He ran to the far end of the hall and threw the lights on in Milo's room. No worse than before. Trent moved back down the horseshoe hallway, checking things as he went. Bathroom, spare rooms, all fine.

The master bedroom looked okay, too. Flicking off his headlamp, he stared at his reflection in Rita's vanity mirror. His jowls were furred with the beginnings of a beard. A bone-white strip ran down the center of his chin—the same strip as on Hank's beard.

Pivoting, Trent went over to the closet, flinging the door open.

The crack was back.

Back, and bigger. The original home repair was now a jagged V in the wall. The frayed edge of mesh tape ran down one side like the teeth on a zipper; even as he stared, bits of the wall continued to crumble away, widening the crack, the *pitter-patter* of rubble raining down.

Trent's lower lip pulled into a doglike snarl. "Mother*fucker.*"

A sledgehammer—one of five Trent now proudly owned—rested in the bathtub, awaiting some project or another. He stalked back to the closet with it.

He smashed the sledge into the wall. The plaster seemed to dance and billow before his eyes, its surface taking on the shapes of faces: first Hector's sneering mug (*It's all about the dirt*), then that shithead from Home Depot (*I got no time for you Saturday guys*), that uppity dwarf Sarkasian from the car lot (*You wouldn't waste anyone's time, I'm sure?*)—Trent dug the sledge's head out, the wall shrieking as it tore apart, drywall dust puffing into his face—Rita's face appeared next, his wife smiling her secret-keeper's smile, her tongue a wet black succulent or the ace of spades; finally, gruesomely, Trent saw his son: Milo as a penniless bagman, his skin riddled with boils and his eyes yellow and sick-looking like an old basset hound's (*It tastes like peppermint, Daddy! A peppermint STAR!*)—and Trent swung that fucking sledge, swung it right between Milo's eyes with a slaughterhouse stroke, and next the wall was just a wall again, the crack a sucking vertical slash filled with darkness—

The sledgehammer hit a stud, sending an agonizing reverb down his arms. He staggered away, heaving. The crack now ran from ceiling to floor. Wind blew up the gap from someplace, causing the ragged edge of the gypsum to tremble in a manner Trent found labial: the lips of some enormous pale vagina occupying the wall of his closet.

He dropped the sledge. Stepped to the wall. Set his palms on either side of the crack.

Stuck his head through.

He stared downward. The structural ribbing of the house descended to a point of darkness past which he couldn't see—

*"Where have all the cobblers gone, T-Man? The blacksmiths and fix-it men?"*

The voice webbed up from someplace deep, down below the foundation and underfloor, past the frost-heave barrier.

*"You do not live in a society of repairers. When things break, you throw them away. Men do not know how to fix what is rightfully theirs."*

The voice didn't belong to Handyman Hank. It was not down-home-aw-shucks. It wasn't even remotely human. Yet it *was* Hank. Its resonance existed beyond sane calculation.

Staring down into the dark, Trent tried to picture the owner of that voice . . . and all his mind registered was a fossilized malignancy that by any logic should have been dead long ago but was in fact very much alive, oh yes, something that had existed here far longer than anything Dunsany Estates had constructed or Trent's small mind could comprehend, oh yes, *tee–hee*, down here amongst the moldering bones and worms. . . .

*"If a man doesn't care for the things he calls his own, well, something's liable to come along and take them from him."*

Somewhere beneath Trent, that darkness moved.

Taking one hand off the wall, he reached for the crown of his skull in search of the button on his headlamp. . . .

The beam shone off bulging battens of insulation. The darkness stretched farther than the lamp's capacity to illuminate it: an impossible distance, as if his home was balanced on top of a mine shaft.

When the fingers appeared down there, the light registered them immediately. But it took Trent's brain a split second to catch up.

The sight rammed home just how alone he was. A realization that a child would have known instinctively: when you're all by yourself, miles from any other human, anything could happen. . . .

And sometimes, just sometimes, it did.

Those fingers . . . they emerged from the space between the main floor and the basement ceiling: less than eight inches wide, too tight for any human to fit. Long and gray and curling at their tips like a genie's shoes.

Nothing came close to the terror that crushed into Trent then, not even how he'd felt under Ashley Greco's desk as Carson Aikles rampaged through the law firm with his hammer. There was an earthly logic to a man with a hammer. But there was nothing logical to what he was witnessing now.

The gray fingers hooked over a support joist. With a dry scrape, their owner pulled itself from that strangled cranny between the floors.

*Oh God. This thing's been here all along, hasn't it?*

It was made of dust. That was the best guess Trent's feverish mind could come up with. A face—a *kind of* face—cobbled out of packed grit and frayed twine and roofing screws and lumber scraps and those horrific pinklings, some wriggling but mostly not, and two carnival-glass closet knobs staring coldly as eyes.

Achingly, it began to climb up the suffocating passage between the outer and inner walls of Trent's house.

Trent's limbs locked. Messages were being sent from his neocortex—he could somehow feel them burping down his spine like sluggish air bubbles moving through hot tar—but they weren't getting to his arms and legs, not nearly fast enough.

A mouth split the compressed flatness of the dust-thing's face. The lipless mouth of a barracuda crowded with hooked nails, busted glass, a flapping electrical-cord tongue.

His inertia broke with the crisp snap of a glass pipette: *tik!* He lurched away from the wall on wobbly legs, his heels scuffling in the thick carpet and nearly dumping him on his ass. He could hear the thing whispering up the gap in the wall with the hiss of dead skin. It wasn't in any rush: Trent pictured ivy twining round a tree trunk, strangling it. For some stupid reason, he wanted— *needed?*—to see it again, just to know it was real, or real-ish, not some figment his overheated brain had cooked up.

He backed out to the bedroom door, eyes pinned to the trench in the closet wall . . .

. . . he forced himself to wait, his breath locked up under his ribs . . .

The fingers spidered through the crack and over the baseboard, long and chalky.

Trent slammed the bedroom door and ran like hell.

He heard the dust-thing heave itself through the crack: something as huge and porcine as a walrus that landed with a frightening thump. The floor trembled as it propelled itself across Trent's picture-perfect bedroom with a rubber-band-y squeak, *ree-ree*, perhaps moving with the peristaltic flex of a maggot. There was another, even more horrifying sound: a bone-like clatter inside the walls that told Trent the rest of its body was still *in there*, still disgorging itself from the crack.

Trent dashed down the upstairs hallway. The dust-thing battered the bedroom door. Next came the shriek of splintered wood. The cable and electrical cords tore out of the right-hand wall like veins through pale skin, whipping at his ankles.

Trent hit the stairs, taking them two at a time. The master bedroom door smashed open on its hinges and the thing steamed out like some lunatic freight train—Trent swore he could see the upper ridgeline of its body above the railing, tough and thick as rhinoceros hide—

Clutching the banister knob, Trent whip-shot his body past the now-silent TV, making a beeline for the front door. He had to get out of this house, first objective, no second one required.

Gripping the knob, he yanked the door open—

A fist rocketed out of the night and tagged him square in the face.

# 19

**BLOOD BURST BETWEEN** Trent's lips as he staggered back, ankles tangling as he landed hard on his ass.

A man stepped inside his house, stumbling on the now two-inch drop between the doorsill and the floor.

"Heya, chief."

Asscrack Al shut the door behind him. Trent cranked his head over his shoulder, his vision spitting cold fireworks. He couldn't see anything coming after him down the stairs.

Then Al was on him, dragging Trent up. He hit him again, a stinging blow to the nose. The crack of cartilage shot through Trent's skull. He sagged into Al's meaty chest.

"We hab to"—his words muffled by Al's overalls—"gedd oud of here, *now.*"

"Yeah, I don't think so."

Al guided Trent over to the sofa and sat him down roughly. His left leg sported a sleek walking cast. A forgotten memory surged back to Trent. *He'd* done that, hadn't he? In a storage locker. He'd near about broken this man's leg. And done something to his face too, which would explain the stitches near his ear.

Al said: "If you even think about touching my leg, I'll rip your fucking lips off."

Trent cocked his ear: over the tack-hammering of his heart, the house had gone still. Only cracks and creaks that you might dismiss as nothing. That the house *wanted* you to dismiss.

Al went to the sink and ran water over a rag. Trent's fevered mind twigged on the fact that his false family—the motionless replacements—no longer stood in the kitchen.

Al wrung the rag out and tossed it to Trent. "Here. For your beak. I didn't break it, but it ain't pretty."

Trent noted the pair of binoculars strung around Al's neck.

"I saw you coming out of Home Depot earlier this week." Al pulled a stool up next to the sofa and sat, bad leg stretched out straight. "Couldn't stay away, uh? Followed you back here. I thought about walking right in and breaking both your legs—tit *and* tit for tat." He gave Trent's knee a chummy slap. "But I said to myself, *Ned, you hold your water. Just watch.*"

He tapped the binoculars. "So, that's what your ole bud Ned did. The last three days. I watched. And you know what I saw, fella? Just you nancying around out here. No—"

The ceiling groaned.

Al's—wait, *Ned*; the guy had identified himself as Ned, hadn't he?—Ned's eyes darted up to the second floor before settling back on Trent.

"No wife, no kid," Ned continued warily. "Except I know you have a boy. Seemed like a good kid—better than a nutjob like you deserves. So I ask myself: *Ned, where's the kid?*"

Ned tapped the side of his head, then pointed at Trent.

"Hello! Crazyman's wife?" Ned called into the upper reaches of the house. "Crazyman's *kid*? You in here somewhere? It's okay, I'm not going to hurt you."

"You said your name's Ned, right?" Trent said pleadingly. "Ned, just listen to me for a sec, okay?"

Ned flicked him a distracted glance. "What?"

"We need to get out of here. I'll talk to you outside, in my truck or wherever you want—"

"Not until I see your boy. Proof of life. You and me, we've got trust issues."

"He's not here, okay? He's with his mother."

Ned computed this. "Well, that may be. But I'm gonna check all the same." He slung his binoculars off, laid them on the coffee table, and heaved himself up. "Sit tight." He tapped the hard bulge in his pocket. "Yes, I am packing. Try to run, I'll shoot your ass like a dog."

Ned made it to the stairs before Trent spoke. "Don't go. There's something up there."

"Yeah, pal," Ned said mordantly, "that's exactly what I'm afraid of."

"Please, I'm begging you. You need to get out of here."

"You're a total loonycakes, aren't you?" Ned's eyes held real pity. "What a sad life."

Ned clomped up the stairs. *Scree, scree, scree.* The chandelier globes fritzed and popped; in their uncertain light Trent watched Ned move along the upper hallway, his chest and shoulders bobbing above the railing. . . . Trent waited for something to zipper down the upstairs hallway, something so big it shook the house on its foundation—for Ned's meaty arms to fly up as his body got sucked out of sight—then for Ned's screams to start: those screams would be baffled at first, then drilling, and finally childlike.

Ned bellowed: "Whoever built you this place really chintzed you out! These doors are flimsy as soda crackers!"

A tremor passed through the flat-screen TV as something moved behind the kitchen wall, sinking down to the foundation.

Trent's truck keys were still in his pocket. The front door was ten steps away. Ned wasn't going to catch him, and he doubted he'd shoot him if he even had a gun. But Trent couldn't bear the thought of leaving Ned here with the thing in the walls. Couldn't sign the man's death warrant with such a cold hand.

"Ned . . . ?" No sight of him up there now. "My son's at the hospital, okay? If you don't believe me, I'll take you to see him."

After an endless gulf, Ned reappeared in the hall. He plodded back down the shrieking stairs.

"Gotta tell you—you ought to sell this place for scrap," he said. "It's falling apart."

The blood surged to Trent's head as he stood. "Yeah, it's a fixer-upper. Let's just—"

"If we go anywhere, it's the police station to file a report for assault."

Trent took two steps toward the door. "Fine with me. Let's do that. You can drive us—just go out with me, *now*, and—"

The cry came from somewhere beneath the main floor.

Ned's head snapped across the wide area to the basement doorway before whipping back to Trent.

The sound came again. Thin, despairing, *boyish*.

Trent darted for the door, but Ned was faster than he looked: he erased the distance between them in one heart-stopping lunge.

"It's not my kid!" Trent shrieked. "He's not down there, it's not *HIM*!"

Ned sent a fist crashing into Trent's stomach, pushing his wind out in a warm gust. He hit Trent in the temple. A fiery explosion filled his skull and he went down on the floor with his wires all cut, drooling blood.

Grabbing a fistful of his shirt, Ned dragged Trent across the kitchen to the basement door. He flung it open and flicked the lights on and muscled Trent down the staircase, hauling him like a sack of dirt.

"Stop it!" Trent managed, more terrified than hurt as his spine raked the stairs. "You're gonna—get us—*killed*!"

Ned deposited him on the basement floor. As soon as he let go, Trent popped up and took a wild swing, clipping Ned's chin. Ned wobbled not much at all and smashed Trent another good one, ringing his skull off the metal support pole and planting him back on the ground.

"You got him in a cage down here or something, you deranged bastard?"

How did Ned picture this going? Did he already see the newspaper headline: *Maverick Overalls-Wearer Rescues Child from White-Collar Torture Dungeon*?

Ned grabbed a screwdriver from the toolbox and hunkered down with Trent, his braced leg stretched out like a Cossack dancer in midkick.

"If you so much as move"—grabbing Trent's hair, tilting his head up—"I will put your eyes out with this thing. No fucking around anymore, you hear me?"

He left Trent slumped on the floor and took a few steps, craning his neck over the stacked boxes.

"Kid? Hey! Where you at? It's okay, the cavalry's here!"

"Don't," Trent croaked. "Just please, we need to go—"

*"Help me."*

Ned's chin sagged. His mouth fell slowly open.

A boy's voice. The one they'd both heard, clear and unmuffled. Not quite Milo's voice, but close enough that Ned wouldn't be able to tell the difference.

A boy's voice coming out of the basement drain.

Except it only seemed that way. That voice was coming out of the house, all parts of it: from the microscopic pores in the cement pad, from the knotholes of the wood beams and the dum-dum heads of the screws, from the cold guts of the furnace and the glazed panes of casement glass.

The voice wasn't even coming *from* the house, not really. Trent knew that now, finally.

The voice *was* the house, and in turn, the house was the voice.

Keeping his eyes on Trent, Ned toed the slotted cap off the drain hole with a deft flick of his boot. *Please don't do that,* Trent thought.

Kneeling awkwardly—his air cast squeaking—Ned squinted down the naked drain hole.

"Hey, kid. Say something. Speak to me."

*". . . down . . . heeere . . ."*

Ned's eyes flickered dangerously in Trent's direction. "You fucking sicko."

"It's not my son." If events had had a doomed taste before, they were presently moving toward a point of unchecked lunacy. "You have to know that."

"How the hell did you even do it?" Ned's gaze was nine parts loathing and one part grudging respect. "How did you bury your kid *under your fucking basement*?"

"I *didn't*," Trent nearly sobbed.

Ned looked around in search of a trapdoor. A way to explain that voice down there. But there *was* no explanation, not a sane one, anyway. His gaze fled back to the hole.

Ned stuck his hand down the drain.

It wouldn't fit inside. Not all of it, anyway. Ned's hand was big, his fingers thick as sausage links. Trent could only watch as Ned worked his fingers around the edge of the hole in search of a latch or hook or God knew what.

"Don't," Trent said, forcing the word past his lips. "Get your hand out of there."

Ned's look said: *Oh, you'd like that, wouldn't you, you crazy fuck.* He did pull his hand out, though—only to bend lower, putting his ear to the hole.

"Speak to me, kid," he called throatily.

The side of Ned's head hovered over the hole. Trent caught a sly note of suction and pictured a rubber ball clogged in the mouth of a vacuum cleaner wand.

Ned frowned. Bracing his arms on the floor, he propelled his skull up from the drain hole. The suction broke with a percussive *pop*. He dug a finger into his ear.

"Jesus . . . that's not right."

Ned's voice wasn't quite stable, his face pale and rigid as a granite headstone.

Trent pulled his legs under him and approached Ned, risking coming within striking distance. "There's nothing right about it,

Ned. So let's just go *now*. The hospital or the police or Venus, wherever the hell you want, I don't care—just not here."

"Oh, man . . . this is just too fuckin' weird," Ned breathed.

Given another few seconds, Ned might have readjusted his plan and cleared the hell out of that basement with Trent—

*"Heeeelp!"*

Piercingly close this time. Ned cranked his head over his shoulder, and when his eyes came back to Trent, the rage in them was a living thing. His arm pistoned out, catching Trent with the heel of his palm, stiff-arming him—

Trent came to gagging on his swollen tongue. When he tried to move, he was dismayed to discover that Ned had zip-tied his right hand to a basement support post.

Ned himself was at the wall, knocking on it with his knuckles.

"Hello?" he said. "Where you at, kiddo? Speak, for God's sake!"

"He's not here, Ned," Trent said, rallying his wits. "Jesus, can't you see? It's . . . Christ, it's the house, okay? I know how that must sound, but it's trying to trick you."

"Shut up," Ned said dully, fixed on his task.

He pressed his body to the wall, flattening himself to it. He inched along it, shuffling until he was in a soft patch of light a few feet from the water heater. Trent dragged himself up so he could see better, joggling his wrist to help the zip-tie up the metal pole.

"Ned, you have no idea what we're—"

When the voice came this time, there was something else knitted to it.

*"Ned Alders."*

It came from the drain again. That telltale echo of a voice bouncing off concrete, like a boy calling from under a bridge—except it wasn't Milo's voice anymore. Still boyish, but the mimicry felt purposefully malignant now.

Ned turned from the wall. Trent saw the expression on Ned's face, and understanding gripped him with a helplessness that made his bones go soft.

*"Come here, Ned. I want to show you something neat."*

"Ned, don't." Trent could barely move his lips. "Please."

But he could see—no, he'd *known*, the very instant Ned turned and Trent caught sight of his blank eyes—that Ned was in the grips of something he couldn't possibly comprehend. Trent, who'd spent too much time under this roof, could still scarcely understand it himself.

Ned sank to his knees in front of the open drain. His eyes were foggy. A timid smile rested on his face.

Trent felt a powerful animus wafting from the drain—God, he could practically *see* it: these cotton-candy strands, thin as spider's silk, bobbing and weaving as they tickled Ned's skin. . . .

*"I'm really close. I'm almost out, Ned. Just need a little help."*

"Okay, little buddy," Ned said dreamily. "I can do that."

Trent knew then that whatever force had gripped him from time to time here in the house—*the beet*, jefe, *the beet*—he'd never been exposed to even a fraction of its incalculable power. But Ned was getting something close to its full blast now, which could be no different from stepping inside the core of a nuclear reactor.

*"Come on, Ned,"* the voice commanded. *"SAVE ME."*

Ned stuffed his fingers down the drain.

The following sequence of events would be hard for Trent to piece together with any specificity later. A distancing mechanism must have kicked on in his brain. But during the minute or two (and that was all it took, though it would feel a minor eternity) when Ned fed himself to the drain, Trent saw everything with meticulous intimacy.

Ned's hand was far too big to fit, so he pinched his fingers and thumb together and kind of *screwed* them against the cement rim of the drain. He issued a goatlike snort as he hunched forward, making use of his 250-plus–pound frame to drive and twist his hand deeper in. . . .

"*Good, Ned. That's a good boy.*"

A fan of blood zizzed up, spritzing Ned's neck and upflung chin. If he noticed at all, it was with a grunt of satisfaction. The blood acted as lubrication; with his lips skinned back from his teeth, Ned torqued his hand downward in a series of stiff, unrelenting thrusts—a sort of meniscus curve developed, a point of tension where Ned's flesh and his unstinting determination met that unforgiving concrete hole—

Ned's hand disappeared a good three inches into the drain, straight down.

"*Excellent, Ned.*"

Ned's fingers and all the little jigsaw bones of his hand: the sound of them breaking was the high singing *snap-snap* of a child's cap pistol, the kind they didn't sell anymore. His hand went down the drain with a stiff crumpling as if he'd fed it into a compactor. His sleeve rucked up. Trent saw the bare skin go a gleamy white, veins bulging under that unthinkable stress.

"Aaaaah," Ned breathed, a sound of pure and almost orgasmic satisfaction.

"*STOP IT!*" Trent screamed, straining against the zip-strip around his wrist.

Ned's free hand skidded on the floor as he fought for balance; he gripped the handle on the candy-apple-red tool caddy positioned near the drain. *Good, Ned,* was Trent's wild thought. *Pull yourself out, pull yourself away—*

But Trent had it all wrong: yanking the caddy closer, its casters screeching across the floor, Ned used it as a fulcrum to drive his arm into the drain with even more force. His eyes rolled hysterically in their sockets, but his voice was calm.

"Almost there, little buddy. . . . I can feel your fingers reaching for mine. . . ."

"*You're getting closer, you dumb bastard.*"

The voice came from the vents and pipes, came from everywhere. Ned's grin stretched wider, a gruesome rubbery slash that threatened to tear his head apart.

Trent watched, awestruck, as Ned shoved more of himself into the drain. His arm went down in a smooth and sinuous motion like the swallow of an anaconda. The cement hole was the diameter of a tea saucer, and Ned's arm was at least twice that. It was like trying to stuff a boiled carrot down a McDonald's straw. But Ned managed it.

Ned let out a ghastly giggle. His free hand spasmed, popping out the caddy drawer; sockets spanged off the concrete with the sound of steel raindrops. The tape measure—that's all it was, Trent realized; not a pistol, only a harmless tape measure—fell out of his pocket as he planted his other hand on the floor, the tendons cabled and his eyes pushing from their sockets as he continued to feed his limb into the greedy concrete opening.

The fabric of Ned's shirt exploded off his arm with a shotgunning bark. His limb was swollen like a bodybuilder who'd swallowed the air hose, like Popeye, this grisly hypertrophic gourd. Blood needled out of splits in the skin like water from a thumb-capped garden hose.

Ned belched out a scream—*"Blllaaaaargh!"*—his arm wadding up in grotesque Michelin Man balloons. It was like watching someone roll the sleeve of a puffy winter coat up their arm.

Ned's head whipped wildly now, bloody froth dripping from his jowls . . . but ecstasy was painted clearly across his features too—this was a man witnessing a glorious sunset, bottlenose dolphins leaping on a glassine sea, a perverse euphoria that made the sight even more unbearable. . . . Trent watched the smaller bone of Ned's forearm, the radius, bow inside his skin, bending against the rim of the drain like overstressed bamboo until it gave with a high raw snap.

Trent strained against the zip-strip until it carved into his wrist like cheese wire, but Ned was too far away. Trent couldn't reach him.

The splits in Ned's forearm elongated past his elbow and the pressure caused the tendons to tear away from the bone: Trent couldn't believe skin could *do* that, watching as the heavy rags of Ned's biceps and triceps lengthened out over the floor like the tentacles of some ungodly octopus.

*"You're doing swell, buddy!"*

Trent knew that voice now. It belonged to Little Boy Blue.

Ned's arm wadded up where it met his shoulder, the cruel alchemies of pressure and resistance making his skin inflate as his humerus went down, down. . . . Blood jetted through the chest of his overalls, right through the weave. Ned's eyeballs rolled back but he kept shoving his limb down the drain even in this dream-state, a mindless compulsion like a dog straining at a leash. Trent heard the steady piss of blood and the edge of Ned's bone scraping inside the hole.

*"You're boring, Ned,"* Blue said dismissively. *"You're no fun at all."*

With that, Little Boy Blue was gone. That commanding presence deserted Ned's psyche, its exit making an audible *pop* in the basement.

The color drained back into Ned's eyes. With an unspeakable, inhuman strength, he ripped his arm out of the drain. The skeletal remains came jangling out, the bones connected like the baubles on a charm bracelet, the flesh stripped to bare cartilage except near the shoulder, where the skin hung in glistening tatters.

He stood abruptly, turning a bewildered circle with the remains of his arm flapping, the flesh hanging like waterlogged curtains. . . .

"Whu?" he said uncomprehendingly. "Whuzzat?"

Ned noticed his arm then. He began to scream so loud the vents shook.

*"SHUT UP."*

Little Boy Blue's absence had been short-lived. Both Trent and Ned cowered like little boys.

In the silence, Trent could hear . . . coring noises. The sound of bark beetles, perhaps, if one amplified their labor a hundred-fold.

*"I'll show you something, Ned, if you're a good boy."*

Oh God, oh Christ—that fog was back in Ned's eyes.

*"Will you be a good little boy?"*

Ned nodded, his chin bobbing down to touch his chest.

*"Good. Now, go look."*

Ned staggered to the wall with blood darkening his trousers. His unhurt arm came up, the flat of his palm moving along the drywall. He set his thumb on a spot, roughly head-high.

"Something back there," he said driftily. ". . . I feel the vibration. Feels nice."

Trent watched a small hole kindle in the drywall, a few inches to the right of Ned's thumb. A scintilla of drywall dust attended the circle, which was not too big and perfectly dark.

*"Take a peek, Ned."*

To his credit, Ned didn't look into the hole. Instead, he sensed the danger and threw his head away, his chin tilting back.

But too late—way too late.

A pink rope shot through the hole, steaming out like a freakish bullet train. But it was less a rope than a spike of obdurate gristle.

Trent caught the wet *squitch* as it sank into Ned's eye.

*"Goh!"* went Ned.

Ned's thumb slipped off the wall and a second rope needled through the hole his thumb had been covering, drilling into Ned's other eye.

Ned propelled himself away from the wall, planting his good arm and pushing with every fiber of strength. His body fell backward like a chest of drawers pushed out a window, but the pink strands simply stretched like some impossible taffy, letting Ned fall nearly to the floor before they retracted, reeling him back to the wall mercilessly—they must have spiked inside Ned's head, or ballooned up somehow, anchoring themselves. The ropes winched Ned back up until his face collided heavily with the drywall.

Ned's skinless arm flapped at his side as the pink strands went rigid, jettisoning him from the wall and simultaneously torquing, gyring Ned around with a chillingly balletic movement: his Caterpillars rotated, his air-casted leg flung out in a military goosestep before coming down, heels clicking crisply: *Herr Commandant!* Trent saw that his nose had been broken, his lips mashed brutally against his teeth. The ropes continued to funnel into his head, filing into his face through the wet doorways of his eyes. His skull bulged monstrously. The quivering pink ropes retracted tightly over his forehead—they looked like snail's eyes, eyes on stalks—pinning Ned to the wall.

Ned grunted in childlike bewilderment. *"Numma?"*

Trent scrabbled in his pocket—how had he forgotten it? He didn't carry his Beard Club razor anymore, but he did have his Leatherman multitool.

As Hank said, any handyman worth his salt ought to carry a Leatherman at all times.

*"What do you see, Neddy?"* Little Boy Blue tittered. *"Tell me what you SEE."*

More holes bloomed around Ned's body. It was like that midway game with the BB gun: Shoot the Star. Shoot out the star, win the stuffed animal. Boreholes dotted the drywall like cigar burns, dozens becoming hundreds becoming thousands:

they outlined Ned's arms and delineated his legs and belled over his head, and through these holes surged thinning bands of pink. They fired from the holes like grappling hooks—that same kind of floaty, limpid trajectory—crisscrossing his body like scar tissue. They shackled his arms and legs, mummifying his chest in struggling, soft bindings.

"Ned!" Trent cried wretchedly. "Get out of that, *please!*"

After a minor eternity, the Leatherman was in Trent's hands. He fumbled his thumbnail into the groove for the sawblade attachment, finally teasing it out.

The bands unfurled across Ned's face, clapping over his mouth and nose, and only then did Trent see something like fear express itself: a hard hitch of the chest like a man preparing to dive into deep waters.

The drywall detached in a single chunk, a unit exactly the size and shape of Ned's body.

The zip-strip snapped as he sawed through it, dumping Trent on the floor. By then, it was too late to matter.

The pinkness carried Ned's body back into the dark space behind the wall. It must be a lot bigger back there than Trent understood: the space accepted Ned's frame without any issue. The pinkness had to have some mothering root, because it effortlessly bore Ned's weight.

Slowly, at no more than an inch per second, Ned's body moved sideways, not down, drawn into the emptiness behind the drywall. Trent could hear Ned scraping along behind the water softener, the furnace, toward some terminus he couldn't guess at. He left behind a cutout in the drywall so perfect that his wife—if he had one—would surely be able to recognize him by it.

*"I can show you too, T-Man,"* Little Boy Blue tittered from the bloody drain. *"Would you like to see what Ned saw?"*

Trent stared at that yawning drain hole until his ears detected the silky whisper of the pinklings squirming up it. Without another thought—he had entered a realm past conscious thought—he staggered to the stairs and ran.

# 20

RITA AWOKE SCRUNCHED UP in the chair at Milo's bedside. She let her limbs unkink and checked her watch. Fifteen past midnight, the hospital ward running on phantom power. Milo's breath came evenly in the dark.

As her eyes adjusted, she noticed something in the second bed.

No, not noticed. *Felt.*

It sat on the other side of a privacy curtain dividing the room. The whole time they'd been here, nobody had occupied the bed beyond the curtain.

But something was there now.

It lay on the mattress on the far side of that filmy screen. An asymmetrical hump, like a heap of scrap metal in the crude outline of a body.

The stink of corruption grew thick in the room: a pile of old, green-fuzzed batteries and something much older, like a corpse bobbing up from a primordial swamp.

With a rusted squeal, the shape sat up.

*"It's time to go away now, kids."*

The silhouette of its arms elongated down the bed. Its fingers touched the floor. Its head cranked to her: the creak of its neck sounded like the snap of sunbaked rubber bands.

*"Time to get in the box."*

Milo jerked up in bed. It was the first time he'd moved in days. His arms reached out, his body straining mindlessly against the needles and tubes sunk in his arms.

*"Forever, little buddies . . . The long sleep . . ."*

Rita shot out of her chair and wrapped her arms around Milo as he lunged toward the shape, making kittenish mewls of want—

The door flew open, ushering in the harsh light of the hallway.

The room's lights snapped on. Trent stood at the switch, his face livid.

"Rita, we are never going back to that place."

Milo sagged back into the pillows. The bed on the other side of the curtain was empty again.

Rita's heart rate scaled down as Trent closed the door. His nostrils were crusted with blood, his shadow casting a frayed outline on the floor. He hovered over Milo, kissed his cheek, then pulled a chair up next to Rita.

"A man . . ." His face wrenched up. ". . . I watched a man die tonight."

Tentatively he outlined some weeks-old encounter at Home Depot. Some guy, and something to do with Milo's hair. That same guy had shown up at the house earlier tonight.

"It was the *house*, Rita." Trent stabbed his fingers through his hair. "*Jesus*, Rita, that house. It's killed him. It did something"—he pounded his thighs with his fists—"to *me*, to us, to Christ-knows-who-else—"

"Trent, look at me."

He did, with a sorrowful puppy-dog's gaze. She didn't *have* to tell him, did she? Her mother had never told her father a damn thing.

"You're telling me there's something in our house. Is that right, Trent?"

He nodded, his head bobbling like a windup toy.

"Well, I'm telling you you're right. Something is there."

The expression on her husband's face . . . it wasn't rage (but that would surely come), nor was it understanding (he couldn't make that leap with so little to go on), but Rita did see the *hope* of understanding like beads of sweat begging to break through his skin.

"How do you know, Rita?" He stared at her. "Have you been keeping secrets?"

Trent, or the caverned shell she now beheld . . . she'd done that. Ruined him. It had begun the moment their eyes locked at that law-society mixer sixteen years and forty-seven days ago.

The night she'd felt that dreadful spark in her chest: *There's the man I'll take.*

Everything that had happened to him since, every stumble and collapse that had steadily separated Trent from the person he was so sure he'd become—the man he *could have* been if not for her . . . her family's burden dictated that it had to be so. The men must be reduced and condemned. They must be left with no choice but to inherit the house in the dust.

The men Rita and her foremothers selected came blindfolded

to the slaughterhouse; each arrived holding the hand of a woman he believed loved him.

Trent now took her hands in his, squeezing so tight the bones ground.

"We're *never* going back, Rita. That house is poison. Tell me you'll never go back."

"I promise Milo and I will never go back," she said. "But you will."

When the realization dawned, his face dwindled somehow. "What did I do wrong? I'm sorry. We'll get away, okay? Go someplace new, and I . . . I can change."

"Oh, baby. Can't you see how badly you already have? You'll go back to that house," she said quietly, looking right at him.

"Like fuck I will."

"I know you believe that, but you can feel it, can't you?"

She'd often wondered how her own father must have experienced it. Rita imagined brown strings, half-rotted but unbreakable, sunk into Trent's head. The strings were attached to a wooden winch, the kind that castle guards used to raise drawbridges in medieval movies. That old crank kept turning, implacably turning, pulling its men back home.

She shook his hands off. She had to get away from Trent's childlike need . . . She could tell him to leave. He'd have no choice. Those strings would tighten mercilessly and he'd suddenly find himself outside the hospital, then soon enough in his truck driving home. She'd never see him again. She was sure of that now.

But Rita wouldn't do that to him, if only because of the night of that blizzard.

Milo had been only a few days old when they'd brought him

back to their apartment. It's a crazy kind of fear, the fear you had for a child. Rita felt it as soon as they got home from the hospital, away from the sensible maternity ward nurses who had all the answers. The second night home, a blizzard had rolled over the city. Twenty inches of snow drifting waist-high. Whiteout conditions. And they ran out of diapers. Rita had bought the wrong size and by then the few they'd been sent home with from the hospital were gone. Seeing as they couldn't wrap their newborn's bottom in old newspapers, Trent went out into the storm.

He was gone for forever, or so it seemed. New mothers felt time differently. She watched out the window of their twenty-third-story loft, down through the flurrying snow to the street that wasn't a street at all, just a flat white expanse too deep for even the plows to tackle. The only things distinguishing the street from the night were streetlamps whose light shone weakly, frayed by the gusting squalls. . . . She watched, cradling Milo, until Trent suddenly appeared: a defiant lump pushing headlong into the wind, his frame visible only when it passed under the ragged glow of those streetlamps, his legs punching into the snow, churning, pulling out and punching down again, determinedly marching home with a box of Pampers under his arm.

She'd loved Trent then, more than she'd love any other man before or after. It came to her that love was won with big romantic gestures—that, or perhaps it was simply chemical. But you kept love alive by getting those fucking Pampers in a blizzard.

"You know that motel off the freeway?" she said. "The one before the turnoff?"

"Yeah, the uh . . . is it the Tradewinds?"

"That's the one." She turned, pointing to the door. "Go now, okay? I'll meet you there."

Trent opened his mouth—

"Speak another word and the offer's off the table."

Trent's mouth shut with a soft click.

Before going, he took a minute with Milo, stroking his hair. Trent's hands had become those of a workingman, hard and callused. Just like her father's by the end. Her father, who before that cursed house hadn't known a T-square from a T-bone.

*I still love my husband.*

This fact startled Rita down to her marrow. She'd hoped their time at the house—the way that place would warp Trent into a bastardization of the person she'd met—might help her hate him, making it easier to let him go. But that hadn't quite happened.

A cold voice ran up on the heels of this realization. The remorseless voice of Rita's ancestors.

*Fuck him. You can always find another swingin' dick.*

# 21

THE TRADEWINDS WAS ONE of those horseshoe-shaped motels that sprouted beside highways like toadstools. Seventies-era double-deckers with names like the Capri, the Double Diamonds, the Lu-Lu.

Trent pulled in. The glow from the vending machines streaked yellowly down the Denali's paint job. He signed for his room using a pen attached to a chain, took his plastic key-fob, and walked up a concrete staircase to room 217.

The room's TV was an old box-style Zenith. He sat on the bed and stared at his reflection in the convex surface, then glanced absently down at his wrist. Something was gummed to his shirtsleeve. A tacky blot stuck there like a booger. But it wasn't a booger, was it? No . . .

That was Ned.

Numbly, Trent flicked the hitchhiking shred of that poor man (Ned's brain? his lungs?) off his sleeve.

. . . He ought to go home. Shit, what was he doing at the

motel when there were so many things that needed to be fixed and simply not enough hours in the day—

Trent bit his tongue hard enough to make tears spring into his eyes. His disordered thoughts cycled back to him.

He heard a vehicle roll into the lot and knew without having to look that it was Rita. When he opened to her knock, she stood on the landing shouldering a duffel bag and carrying a six-pack. Half of the rings were empty and she clutched the third can, killing it as she lingered in the doorway.

"Getting shitfaced while our son is in the hospital, huh?"

"He'll be fine." She stifled a burp. "I'll make sure of that."

Rita handed him a can of Pabst. Pulled off another for herself, popping the tab one-handed.

"You pissed at me, Trent?"

Weird voltages snaked down his legs. "Should I be?"

She nodded slow and deliberate. "Want to hit me? It might be the best way to start the proceedings. Take the edge off for both of us." She angled her head to offer her chin. "Go ahead. First one's on the house."

"Why would I hit you, Rita?" he said, baffled. "You didn't do anything. It's that *house*. We're both—"

"Shut up, Trent. I *want you* to hit me."

Hank's voice boomed in his ears like a foghorn: *Go on, T-Man, give her a biff. She's got a screw rattling loose, maybe a good sock-ola will get her gears meshing. . . .* But Hank had become ignorable. Whatever was going on, there was only room for two. Only Trent and Rita.

"I won't, Reets. It's a stupid thing to ask."

She shouldered past him into the room, which she began

to pace as if evaluating it for a suitability Trent couldn't guess at. She gave him a gentle order: "Sit," pointing to the bed.

Trent did as he was told. The can of beer rolled off his fingers, off the mattress, making a soft thunk on the floor. Rita remained standing, running one finger across the TV and picking up dust. She pulled an orange plastic chair over from the door—its legs raked the threadbare carpet, *skkkrrrrtch*, the peel of an endless scab—and sat facing him.

"Are you ready, Trent? Ready to want to murder your wife?"

"Jesus, Rita. Why does it feel like *you* hate me?"

"I don't hate you. I just never allowed myself to really love you."

"This is a hell of a time for a state-of-the-union about our relationship." He wanted to shake the daylights out of her.

"I don't talk about my family," she said. "You do know my brother Billy's in a care center, which is the PC thing to call a nuthatch. But I never told you what put him there."

Trent sat back on his hands. This wasn't about their marriage. Or not only that.

"Billy had his own Little Boy Blue. It had a different name but it was the same . . . it's always the same *thing*. Billy's friend called itself Li'l Patches. A character on a kids' TV show of the same name. At first it was on for a half hour every weekday morning, but eventually *Li'l Patches* was on all day. *Li'l Patches* never ended."

Trent heard the toilet flush in the neighboring unit, the water sluicing through the pipes.

"I don't remember any show called *Li'l Patches*," he heard himself say.

"It never aired on any TV set you owned. It only played at that house. Our house. Which was my family's house. It's always been my family's house."

"Stop it, Reets," he said, deathly soft.

He was suddenly more afraid now, here in this motel room, than he'd been back at the house earlier.

*Rita's so calm.* And that was it, wasn't it? *When I told her what happened in the house tonight—with Ned, the thing in the wall with the flapping electrical cord tongue, our son's voice coming out of the basement drain—she wasn't shaken even a little bit. She didn't call me a lunatic. None of it shocked her.*

Right then, Trent did indeed hate his wife with a heat to evaporate oceans.

"It's *our* house." Abruptly, he was on the verge of shouting. "Yours and mine and our son's. We're the only ones who've ever lived there. It's brand-*fucking*-new."

"It's always brand-new," Rita said tiredly. "I was eight years old when I moved into it the first time."

"Rita, we'll get you professional help." Oh God, she was sick, *sick*, her mind full of rot. "If I'd had any idea of the delusions you've been suffering from—"

For Trent, it was suddenly safer to forget everything he'd seen at the house—could he unsee that?—safer to deny the evidence of his eyes in favor of this much cleaner belief: that Rita had gone creepingly insane over these past months . . . better that, infinitely better, than being forced to confront the monstrous thing his wife may have done to him—to their son—the outline of which was now beginning to coalesce . . . a subterfuge so grand and so calculated (Oh Jesus, did you actually do it, Rita?), revealing a lack of care so vast, that it would stand as the most inhuman act imaginable.

"Trent, please."

"—shut up, will you? Just shut up and listen." All Trent had to do, right this minute, was make his wife admit for her own sake and the sake of her family that she was batshit nuts. "You're ill. I have no idea how you managed to cover it up this long, but, baby, it can't go on. For your sake. For our *son*."

Rita's palms settled possessively on Trent's kneecaps. It was all he could do not to flinch.

"You *know* that house is wrong. Some part of you knew all along, but that instinct was baffled. The house does that. Now, listen to me, okay? Billy had Li'l Patches . . . Milo has Little Boy Blue . . . and my father had Handyman Hank."

Trent's hands went to his knees, clamping hard over Rita's. He had to resist the urge to wrench her fingers back until they snapped like breadsticks.

"Why are you lying, wife of mine?"

"Am I, hubby? Am I lying?"

"I . . . I don't recall ever asking about your father. It was clearly a topic you wanted to avoid. So, if we're going to play out this theme of our new house somehow being the same one you grew up in, then tell me—where's your dad now?"

"He stayed behind." Her eyes bored into Trent's own. "In the house, with Hank. He's still there."

"*Wrong!*"

The bedsprings squealed as Trent jolted up. He felt his mouth pull into a leering, freakish rictus as he towered over his wife, his hand cocked back ready to piston forward into her face, which wore an expression of grave acceptance—*That's it, T-Man, give her a bop for sass-mouthing you!*—but instead he clenched his fist at the side of her head.

*"Wrong!"* he screamed again, his other hand doing the same, his arms flexed and trembling with her head pinned between them. *"WRONG, Rita!"* Blood filled his face—he could feel it, the swelling of some grotesque balloon—as a rope of saliva spooled over his lip to splash his wife's thigh. "Your dad's in a graveyard, isn't he? He's dead, stone fucking *DEAD!*"

"I bet Dad wishes he was dead."

Trent swung away from her, fists still bunched and veins cabling every inch of his flesh.

"Why are you *doing this*? I can't even . . ."—it dawned—"You want a divorce, is that it? Fuck me, Reets, I'll give you one! You don't have to drive me insane to get your wish!"

He collapsed onto the bed, finding himself near tears. He knew so many marriages ended like this—inanely, with shrieked accusations and hostility—but he'd hoped if that day ever came for them, it would be more mature, not some pitiful unraveling in a no-tell off the highway.

Rita sat beside him. Grabbing the duffel bag, she unzipped it across her knees. Took out a bottle of Jameson's and another six-pack, ice-cold.

"Drink with me, Trent. Like we used to." She cracked a beer and handed it to him, picking up her conversation where she'd dropped it. "Like I said, I moved into that house as a girl. Not the exact same house, but—"

"Rita, please, I'm begging you. Please stop."

She opened a can of her own and took a deep pull, sucking beer against her teeth. "Me, my mother, Billy, my dad. Five months later, three of us left. Me screaming, my mother stone-faced, my brother mad as a hatter."

Trent sipped his own beer. It tasted like wool. "If there's something in that house, why bring Milo and me there?"

"I had to," she said simply.

"Don't give me that. You've never done one thing in your life you didn't want to."

Her look was so cold that Trent was left wondering if he'd ever known his wife at all.

"We are tools, Trent. Both of us. I made you into one, but I was born one."

Rita killed her beer in a long chug, blinked her reddened eyes, and pointed at the TV.

"I think I can get it to come through there."

Rita grabbed the bottle of whiskey by its neck and walked to the TV. Despite how much she'd drunk, her words and limbs remained steady.

"There *is* something in that house, Trent. It's been there a long, long time. You know that's true."

*I do, don't I?* That impossible fact kept coring into his heart, making a home for itself.

She unscrewed the cap, tipped a solid three ounces of whiskey down her throat—Trent saw her throat flex as she glugged—let out a gasp, and began to tap the TV screen with the mouth of the bottle.

"Try turning it on," said Trent, weirdly disgusted with her.

Backtracking to the duffel bag, Rita removed a crinkly silvery bundle. She carted it over to the Zenith, where she unwrapped something from its tinfoil shroud.

The carcass—could've been a squirrel—resembled a lumpy

pancake of fur and red. The sight of it filled him with a cold species of horror regarding his wife: who she could be, the terrors she'd bottled up inside herself like poisoned waters. Once she'd positioned the remains between the antenna ports, she tapped the screen again.

"What's the harm," she said, crouching to talk directly to the TV. "It's not going to change anything, is it?"

She rose and took a step back as blue spiders of static began to crackle across the screen. The Zenith seemed to take a breath, the screen sucking into the guts of the unit, tunneling deeper than the back of the set itself . . . the tube snapped back, rippling, a pool of dark water. Trent realized without knowing quite how that he could actually reach through the glass now, sinking his hand inside the television. But he also knew that he'd pull back a mangled stump if he took that risk: it'd be no different from jamming his hand into a blender.

The screen tinted polar white. From the speakers came the sound of footsteps. . . .

Handyman Hank stepped into that unvariegated vista, right into the TV frame, dragging an ancient wooden box. He wore his usual workman's garb, but Trent could see bits of shattered bone and hardened rags that might've been dried skin knotted to his sleeves like the fringe on a buckskin jacket.

Hank sat on his box and smiled. His teeth were filed down to points.

*"Hail, hail, the gang's all here."*

Trent darted toward the TV cord with the intention of jerking it out of the socket—

Hank lunged at him from inside the set. The plastic housing

bulged as if under the stress of some unfathomable appendage, tiny cracks stressing into the screen. Trent froze.

"Sit down," Rita told him. "It wouldn't help anyway."

*"Listen to the wifey-poo,"* Hank said, tipping Rita a bawdy wink.

Trent sat. He had no choice. He'd lost all sensation in his legs.

"What *are* you?" he said in awe.

*"Who, me? Oh, I'm just some old thing."*

Until now Trent had resisted belief, or else it was like Rita said: the thing in the TV had prevented him from really seeing, ever since he'd set foot inside the house.

Keeping his eyes on the screen, he asked: "Rita . . . you really did know about this, didn't you? All along."

"Yes," she said. "I've always known."

Trent addressed the TV. "What are you doing in my house?"

*"Well, here's the thing."* Hank crossed his legs and stretched his arms. *"I've always been there, T-Man."*

"Why my house?"

"Your *house."* Hank clapped his hands. *"It's funny to hear those words coming out of your mouth. Let's call it an arrangement between your wife's foremothers and me."*

Without taking his eyes off the screen, he chugged the whole can of beer in his hand.

*"I'll tell you a story, my little ones. Many, many years ago—I'm talking not long after your kind were living in caves—I came upon a fire burning in the woods. Distant from the fire sat a hut."* Hank nodded at Rita. *"In that hut was your great-great-great-to-the-nth-great-grandma. She stopped me. Can you believe that? I said:*

*'Li'l ole me? Why, all I want is to sit by the fire and have a little fun.'"*

Never had the word *fun* sounded so sinister to Trent.

*"And you know what that silly old bitch told me? No."*

The roadkill atop the Zenith had begun to send up pinholes of smoke.

*"I could see she was a pariah, cast off from the very people she was risking her soul for. 'Why protect those by the fire,' I asked, 'who have exiled your entire bloodline?'"*

Hank—whatever Hank really was under the Handyman guise—laughed, a seemingly genuine sound. *"When she persisted, I showed her what I was. A hint, anyway, which until then had always been enough to drive your kind stark raving mad. But there she stood, still sane, telling me no."*

"You were scared of her," Rita said softly.

Hank's gaze drifted to her. Those eyes clashed and cycled, full of rusted things.

*"She made me feel, little one. Still, I had my games to play. I agreed not to approach the fire, if she gave me what was most precious to her. Can you guess what she said?"*

"No," said Rita.

Hank nodded. *"So I said, 'Give me the tiny one I can smell kindling in your belly.' Again, she refused."* Another bout of laughter, Hank's head swinging in mirth. *"Finally, I said: 'Give me what has least value to you.' And who do you think she offered?"*

Hank stared at Trent until his lips moved numbly: "Her husband."

*"Top marks, T-Man! And that fine fellow went into the box, and, ooooohhh, the times we had."*

Trent could see the simplicity of the arrangement. It was

out of a fairy tale, a concept even a child could understand. The women of Rita's family had to feed this thing.

"I'm not . . ." he said, enunciating each word, "going . . . *back*."

Handyman Hank peered out of the TV. The bones on his shirt jingle-jangled. The roadkill had gone wrinkly, collapsing in on itself. The smell was ungodly.

Trent faced Rita. "We can just leave, can't we? We'll go get Milo, right now. We'll get him discharged and just *run away*. It can't hurt us if we stop playing the game . . . right?"

"You have to go back," said Rita.

"No. I *don't*. I've always said there's nothing I wouldn't do for you or Milo, but that was before I knew the price of some things. If you don't think I won't get up right now, walk out that door, get into that stupid truck, and drive away, you're wrong. Whatever all this is, whatever debt's owed to *that*"—he pointed to the TV without looking—"it isn't mine to carry."

Trent's anger crystallized. "Why put me forward to pay it, you *cunt*? We had a *child* together. A good life . . . didn't we? Why would you *do* this to me? Why didn't you just *tell* me?"

"Because if you believed me, you'd never have come."

The Handyman—whatever it really was—had been listening in silence. Finally it spoke.

"*You're holding out on your hubby, darlin'. Are you going to tell him, or should I?*"

Off Rita's stony silence, the Handyman went on.

"*What your lady love's too shy to say is that if I don't get my piece of meat, I'll take it.*"

It didn't take much for its meaning to dawn on Trent. "Jesus, is it talking about *Milo*? Will it take our boy? Rita, what's happening to Milo—this *thing* is doing it?"

She just stared at him.

"And if I don't go back—?"

*"No matter what, T-Man, the box gets filled."*

No. There had to be another way. A new bargain, an escape.

"It's made the connection to Milo," Rita said. "Doesn't matter how far we go—eventually it will take him."

The TV set was melting now: the housing had gone as soft as fairground taffy and was sloughing to the carpet in marshmallowy runners.

*"Well, I see by the clock on the wall that our time is up. See you back at the hacienda, T-Man."* Hank gave a cheery wave. *"Looking forward to it—a lot!"*

The TV screen flickered as it slid from its liquefying frame like an eyeball from its socket, hitting the carpet dead.

Trent and Rita sat on the bed, knees lightly touching. Nausea trip-trapped up Trent's spine. He wanted to crawl under the bed and throw up like a poisoned dog. The fear in his gut merged with a sense of betrayal as vast as the Pacific. Treachery was as common as table salt in relationships. Husbands stepped out on wives, wives cheated on husbands. Men and women being fundamentally different organisms in so many ways, well, was it any wonder they came undone in the most unconscionable fashion? He could've understood Rita catting around on him—he wouldn't *like* it, but he'd get the banality of it, being a realist at heart.

But what Rita had done—what the women in her bloodline had evidently been doing for generations . . . there was a terrible perfection to their betrayal, wasn't there? They were offering up their men as—

"You've sacrificed me, Rita."

Setting his finger under her chin, he applied pressure until her head swiveled and they sat eye-to-eye. "That's what you've done. Made an offering of me, to that thing."

No response.

*"Say it."*

"Yes. That's the bargain."

"The bargain," he repeated dully.

Sixteen years. Two apartments, a dozen vacations, one crappy minivan, hundreds of dinner dates, thousands of hours together and as many whispered intimacies. . . . How many times had Trent told her he loved her? Ten thousand times.

How many times had she said it back?

Fewer. He realized that now. Significantly fewer.

"What are my options here, Rita?"

"You can run and it will take our son. Or you can go back and—"

"Do my fucking husbandly duty?"

"—and face it, I suppose. Maybe you can stop it."

Trent closed his eyes, exhausted. "You're just trying to get me to go back."

"You're right."

"There's nothing else you can think of? You've had your whole life to riddle a way out of this."

"You're a decent man, Trent. I'm so sorry."

A decent man. At what cost?

"How could you do this to me?" The sentence came out as a sob. "Why does your family keep doing this? What's the price of breaking the bargain?"

"It goes free, I think."

"*So?* Let it go, then. Let it find some other fire."

*You can fix this, Trent.*

The thought leapt unbidden into his head, causing his spine to straighten.

*You can neutralize it. Kill it, even! Go nuke that house. Wipe it off the face of the earth!*

His mind swarmed with half-formed, Rube Goldberg–esque possibilities, the product of countless home-improvement hacks: a bomb made out of fertilizer and wet gunny sacks; a homemade flamethrower fashioned out of propane tanks; some kind of medieval trebuchet that lobbed rotting carcasses—Clydesdales, moose—at the house from a distance until it was a crumbled shell of decay and disease . . .

*That's right, Trent! Give that Handyman feller what for!*

Then he felt those stealthy fingers plucking the wires in his mind. Trent gritted his teeth.

"Quit it, Hank. Don't bother. I'm coming."

*. . . Attaboy, T-Man.*

He stood on legs that were barely up to the task of bearing his weight. Grudgingly they carried him across the room. Rita sat in silence, watching from the bed. He made it to the door but couldn't get a good grip on the knob. He rested his head against the door.

"I'm so scared, Rita."

She came up behind him. Close, but not touching.

Reaching around his hip, she opened the door for him. "It's okay to hate me. I hate myself a lot of days."

"Thanks, I'll probably take you up on that. . . . Hey, Rita?"

"Yeah?"

"Don't ever go back there, okay? No matter what."

Down in the lot, Trent climbed into his truck. God, what a farcical vehicle. If he ever saw the dawn, he'd drive it right back to Rick Sarkasian and trade it in for pennies on the dollar.

# 22

THE DENALI'S TIRES POPPED gravel as Trent crept it down the unassumed road a few hours before sunrise. His house bloomed out of the night. Trent clawed his chest, massaging the skin; his heart resumed its beat but not steadily, fluttering behind his ribcage like a fat moth.

Bottles clinked in a milk crate in the passenger-side footwell. He'd stopped at an Esso station and hunted six glass bottles of Fanta out of the back of the cooler chest. Dumping out the soda, he'd refilled the bottles with high-test from pump number three, cramming a shred of chamois cloth into each one's mouth.

He parked at the end of the driveway. Fumbled the keys from the ignition, hunted them off the floor mat, and stuffed them in his pocket.

*Steady, Trent. It's gonna get a lot hairier than this.*

Trent lugged the milk crate out and set it down in the dirt facing the house. He lit the wick on one of his improvised Molotovs with a barbecue lighter.

The flame made a riffling note as he lobbed the bottle at the front window. It smashed through the glass to shatter on the terrazzo tiles that Rita had selected from the catalog. Dunsany claimed they were Italian, but who'd believe them at this point?

The fire caught with a leathery *whoof*, the friendly chuff of a Saint Bernard. He waited for the flames to climb the sides of the windows—oil-based paint on those walls, *highly* flammable—wondering why nobody else had tried this. Just burn this fucker entirely to the ground.

Flames licked inside the unlit house. Trent's heart took a triumphant leap—

The flames dimmed, then gradually died out.

"That's fine," Trent said to the house. "I've got a whole crate. And I can lay hands on plenty more."

He was lighting another cocktail when the garage door rattled up. His neck pocked with gooseflesh as the door rose three feet and stopped with a clunk. In the gleam of the Denali's headlights, amid the unused lawnmower and stacked winter tires, Trent saw a pair of legs.

Two thick legs in bloody overalls. One foot sunk inside a Caterpillar steel-toed boot. The other one swaddled in an air cast.

The security lights snapped on, pinning Trent.

*There's two ways to tackle any project, T-Man. The manly way and the bitch-ass way. What's it gonna be?*

Shielding his eyes against the glare with one hand, Trent watched the garage door begin to rise again . . . more overalls, then a bleached-starfish hand. Just one hand; a cold drizzling came from the other side. Trent knew that Ned—and that's what Trent was looking at, Ned or whatever was left of him—couldn't *still* be bleeding. He'd be all bled out by now, either from the torn-out stump where his arm used to meet his shoulder socket or from the other sockets, his eye sockets, which would be no more than pulpy cored-out pits.

Yet there Ned was in all his deathless glory, his blood dribbling onto the garage floor. And if Ned was still bleeding, he ought to be lively in other ways too. Trent guessed Hank had a lot of dirty tricks up his sleeve, but the first would be to let that garage door go all the way up and offer Trent a glimpse of what the house had done to Ned. Even though Ned was down to one arm and had no eyes, Trent was sure the man could still boogey a bit. Ned's lack of eyeballs would be a small hindrance because this version of Ned would operate on sonar, seeing through Hank's eyes, the eyes of the house, and using that unclean apparatus, Ned would chase Trent across the wastes, where the other houses should be, running him down like a dog, ole Ned snagging Trent's ankle and shinnying him like a badger up a greased pole as a new and infinitely more terrifying set of eyes swelled from the blasted pits where the old ones once sat—

Trent was on the front stoop before he quite knew what he was doing.

He stepped into the house with the crate of bottles rattling. They made each movement sound like a frenzy. He went still. From the upper floor came a bone-like skitter. Trent wasn't really worried about whatever that might be, or about Ned out in the garage. If he ever saw Ned again (*Please, Christ, don't let me see Ned ever again*), he wouldn't hurt Trent now. Ned was just Hank's way of getting him inside.

"You fooled me, Hank." Trent's voice bounced around his empty house. "But here's the thing: *I know* you're in my head now."

The kitchen drain gargled. It sounded an awful lot like laughter.

*If you say so, T-Man.*

"I do say so, you sadistic unfunny old bully," he answered with as much determination as he could summon.

The lights inside the house weren't working. He set down the crate and switched on his pocket Maglite. He didn't remember what it cost anymore. Money didn't matter. The tools had to fit the job. This one still had some use. The first thing he registered was the upstairs toilet smashed on the floor like a comet in the middle of the hardwood. A beautiful piece of ceramic, lovingly handcrafted. It had crashed through the mush-edged hole in the ceiling. Water streamed from a burst pipe, across the kitchen floor.

The second thing was a timid clopping sound behind the kitchen island. Trent's muscles knotted, sensing danger. But what tottered into view was only sad.

Morty the turtle, or whatever the house had now made it into. It staggered toward Trent on soggy cardboard legs. Its head was a burst lightbulb, fangs of blackness hanging from the broken glass. That head craned up to Trent with a glassy scrape.

Kneeling, Trent stroked its brittle shell. "I'll fix you, okay? I promise it'll be quick."

Straightening up again, Trent brought his boot down on Morty. The shell snapped, legs splaying out as he ground his heel side to side.

"Stay dead, Morty."

Trent tracked the trickling water over to the basement door. He forced himself to open it. When he tried the lights, they didn't come on down there.

"Is this the way it's going to be, Hank?" he called out. The absolute, consuming fear had him light-headed.

Trent followed the trickle of water down the stairs, taking each step gingerly. The beam of the Maglite illuminated the walls and floor in turn. There was no sign of Ned. Nothing to say he'd ever been down here, even the floor spotless, no blood. . . . The beam crawled toward the water softener, stopping dead. Was *that* blood? Yes, a light freckling of drops next to the hole in the drywall punched out in the shape of Ned—the image came of Ned's body quivering in the grip of those pink strands, so much like naked tendons, as it was drawn inside the wall.

The A/C cut out with a deathly rattle. In the raw silence Trent could hear something. It came from that hole in the drywall—no, from someplace behind it: a grinding machinelike note like the punch of pistons, but not metal ones, no, this was something more obliging. . . . Trent pictured Ned's body become an engine, some ghastly contraption heaving and cycling behind the wall, but that outline was so unspeakable his mind could only hold on to it for an instant.

The basement lights came on, the hot glare making Trent cringe.

Trent's family was waiting for him.

The blown-socket eyes of Trent's fabricated family regarded him with a feral species of intellect. He waited for the Milo-one's molded plastic jaw to unhinge and for it to whisper: *Welcome home, Daddy,* in the voice of a spider.

Flicking off the Maglite, he charted the water from upstairs streaming across the floor and down the hole he'd drilled weeks ago. It had felt good at the time. He didn't remember why, only that the hole was meant to be there. But it was just another one of Hank's games.

A ten-pound sledgehammer leaned against the furnace.

"Let's get to the heart of the matter, shall we, Hank?"

Trent picked up the sledge and sent it smashing down on the hole. A shockwave jarred up his arms. A bit of concrete stung his forehead. Blood beaded from tiny cuts, sliding down into his eyes, reminding him of those early videos, the ones where Hank actually seemed to care.

*You get hurt, you're worse than useless, T-Man. Protect yourself. No one else will.*

Trent tore a strip off his shirtsleeve and tied it around his forehead to catch the fresh blood. The safety goggles were there on the floor, mocking him. He couldn't do anything right. He pulled them on, hoping to see something new. It was the same basement. The same nightmare. The mask just scuffed the edges, making his desperation feel more real.

After a few swings, he got into a rhythm. Chips of cement flew. Some pinged off the goggles. The hole soon got big enough for him to step down into it. The cement became crumbly, more like sandstone. *Whoever built you this place really chintzed you out!* Dead-Ned shouted from the back of his mind. He stooped to hurl chunks away, sledging a wider and wider opening into the earth. . . .

The lights flickered out.

Darkness drenched Trent like a bucket of ice water. Terror spiked in his veins as he dropped the sledge and patted himself down. The Maglite. Where was it? Had he put it down?

The barbecue lighter, then. The one he'd lit the Molotov with, he'd jammed it in his back pocket, but maybe with all the swinging—

The basement stairs groaned.

The noise was distinct from the dripping water and the upcycling purr of the air-conditioner unit.

The next groan was louder. *Closer*. Not every step would make that noise though, would it? Some groaned, others creaked, but not all of the steps made sounds. . . .

The lighter! It was where he'd put it, jutting from his back pocket. He grabbed it, fumbled in the dark to find the safety catch and get the damn thing lit—

It fell from his nerveless fingers, clattering into the hole.

The groan gave way to the dry rasp of a bloodless hand sliding down the railing.

With his heart thundering, Trent pawed around in the hole he'd sledged. The stupid thing had to be here, unless it had somehow slipped down the original drill hole?

He caught a clumsy scrabbling over by the water softener. Trent's blood seized as the sounds became grittier—the rasp of dead fingernails on the cement floor as something pulled itself out of the wall and began to hobble toward him at a cumbersome drag, a huge blind thing hunting after Trent like some massive earthworm. . . . A congested exhale bristled out of the dark too, wet and bubbly, a man struggling to breathe through a crushed windpipe.

*Heck, you'll get guests dropping in uninvited at the queerest times out here. Fellas like your old pal Ned.*

Trent hardly needed Hank's prodding—his brain had already decided it *was* Ned, but not anything like Ned had been while alive. This figure was filled with the animus of the house, his blood foaming in the ragged hole of his trachea, this tubular calamari ring going down and down into the cavity of his chest but there was nothing in there now, just a cavernous emptiness full of a mad howling like the wind in a cave, and Ned was *pissed* at being left alone but now he had a new playmate to fix things with, and he was so happy he'd give Trent's hair a good tousling, oh yes, Ned would dig his dead meathooks into Trent's scalp and peel it right off, but by then Trent probably wouldn't care because the moment Ned's dead fingers touched him in the dark, he'd go utterly fucking loony—

Trent's fingertips brushed the lighter against the crumbled concrete. Grabbing it, he held it out and pulled the starter once, twice, three times—

The flame popped to life. Trent stared into the basement, wide-eyed.

There was nothing there. Only his horrible facsimile family. They wouldn't leave him. They were in it for the long haul.

The lights snapped back on.

Once Trent's heart rate decelerated, he got back to work. After ten minutes, his sledgehammer brought back a dry crumple. He scraped the hammer's head across what he'd uncovered.

A strip of fiberglass and bitumen. A shingle. More than a few. He scraped more dust away, felt the shingles scuff his fingertips. They were still holding their shape.

Trent mopped his brow with the hem of his shirt. He hammered away more rock to reveal a manhole-sized section of actual gable roof.

*My, my, T-Man, isn't that something?*

Hank was down there. Hank, or whatever it really was. The owner of Hank's voice with its own horrific face.

What choice did he have? Rita had explained the stakes, winnowed down his options until this was all that made sense. All that he could give. All that was left of him. He had been reduced to being an offering, or whatever the fuck she wanted to call it. A stopgap for the end of their family. Family sounded like something solid, but it could fall apart just like anything else. Families disintegrated every day. It didn't take much force to tear people apart. Sometimes all it took was a child or two. Milo could continue onward. Trent, though, would need to fill this hole or finish off whatever was down there. If he was going to embrace what lay beneath this house, stare it in the face, he'd at least do it with an exit strategy.

It took two trips to get the supplies he'd need. His first trip, Trent brought down the Molotovs, a Makita jigsaw, and his leather toolbelt. Retrieving his Maglite from the floor, he jammed it into a loop on the belt. On his second trip, he lugged down a Stallion 25,000-pound speed winch from the garage, the tendrils of Ned's hands always floating on the back of his neck. Every few feet he would turn around, waiting for that brutal embrace, a throttling that would allow him to finally give up. But Hank wouldn't allow that. Trent was still the one this place wanted most.

The house left him to his labor. No more sounds creeping down the stairs, no screams from below. Just his own breathing, in and out. The family effigies regarded Trent as he lashed the winch to a support pole using steel coils. He worked silently, professionally, testing his work as he went. Once he was sure nothing would snap under his weight, he hopped down into the hole with the jigsaw. The roof under his feet trembled and moaned.

The tungsten blade made quick work of the shingles. Trent ripped away moldy insulation to reach a slope. Ceiling plaster?

He punched a hole through the material with a screwdriver, big enough to fit the jigsaw blade. He used the Makita to cut a circle the diameter of a garbage can lid. The cuts met, then the plaster disc fell into darkness.

Trent shone the Maglite through the hole. He stared, awestruck. The plaster had broken into pieces on the carpet of a room down there.

The bedroom of a house under his own house.

"Okay, Hank. You've got my attention."

Clipping the winch carabiner to his belt, Trent belayed fifteen feet of cable. Anchoring his boots on the edge of the circle he'd cut, gripping the cable in his gloved hands, Trent took a deep breath and lowered himself through.

# 23

**MILO STAYED AT THE HOSPITAL,** somewhere with other voices, other bodies who could protect him with their sheer existence. Hank and that fetid earth needed to isolate their chosen champions.

The motel was depressing as hell. The gurgle of the sink, clogged with hair. Rita lay on the bed, wide-awake. A few nail heads pushed against the popcorn ceiling, as if the humidity in the air urged them to spring free.

Was this one of the pact's projects as well? Or was she just seeing these omens everywhere, now that the cost had been made flesh again?

She couldn't keep track of the boundary anymore; it wavered with each day that passed. The area was overflowing with human lives, people untouched by the curse she knew lay beneath their feet. They left their lights on all night, unburdened by the choices of their own flesh and blood.

The motel room reeked of ancient Pabst, but it was better

than the hospital. There were fewer screams in the middle of the night, no low moans as the morphine drip ran low in the room across the hall, the shuffle of nurses a constant hum. The motel existed in the no-man's-land off the highway among its compatriots, peering down on the new suburb that had sprung up below, the swath of parking lots that the big box stores had pounded into the earth around her. It was an outpost for a future that hadn't quite arrived yet, just on the edge of being anything at all.

Rita could call her mother, but the garbled answer she would get would be the same: *You have to choose, like my mother before me.* A long line of bent backs and warped minds, all aimed at the same hole in the ground that could never be sated. Hector had basically said the same thing to Rita at the hospital. Make a decision or lose everything. The game went on without you. Or took what you loved most. She cupped a hand against her growing belly.

Her mother and Hector shared weasel words, all their little machinations to keep the ground whole. The boundary was no longer isolated in the middle of a field, though—they had to understand that. People were getting too close, the wider world sniffing at the edges of what they could sense in the dirt—there was something hungry here, something that took from you if you lingered. It was Rita's duty these days to keep it sated, same as it ever was.

In the darkness, she slipped out of the motel room, trying to shake off the beers. She needed to feel herself move, to keep her mind occupied until what had to happen at the house was over.

*Does it* have *to be that way?* piped a frail voice inside Rita's head.

She remembered Trent's answer when she'd told him the

price of breaking the curse. Hank goes free. *So?* Her husband's naked disbelief opened a door that Rita was shocked she'd never even *seen*, let alone tested. On the other side of that door lurked one unalterable fact.

For centuries, Rita's bloodline had been forced to assume a burden of care for a community that didn't care about them at all. Care over people who probably didn't even *know* the sacrifice they'd made . . . but if they did, Rita suspected they'd simply expect it to continue without end:

*You've been doing it this long. Why stop now?*

*Better you than us.*

Each step down the motel's stained concrete steps was a reminder of Trent, trying to free himself from his new accomplice, the grinning manifestation of all the things he so desperately wanted to be, all the things Rita had never asked of him. She didn't care if he could build a woodshed or change a tire or rewire the living room chandelier. The old earth knew what ate at him, found the wounds the world made, and pulled them open until her husband was just raw, exposed nerves.

Duty drained you, pulled everything out of you and left it to dry in the sun. Her out-of-office email reply no longer offered a return date. There were other partners at the firm desperately trying to reach her on her personal account, begging for some explanation. The executive committee still needed her to vote on new hires. There was an HR review panel and three interviews sitting on her calendar. She kept deferring, delegating, and deleting. The entire life Rita had built to escape her family, all of it ashes in her mouth, tongue buried in the burnt dirt of home, whatever home meant now, a long fall and a short drop back into the life she'd never left.

She uninstalled the apps from her phone, messages flitting away into the ether with each forced deletion.

Milo would sleep for hours at the hospital. He had no screens of his own there—only a single TV watching over him. He would still need to be in the house, though, in that little box, to complete the pact—and Rita would never let that happen.

She left her phone in her pocket, ignoring the texts she could feel accumulating. A phantom vibration against her skin every few minutes. Was this how it felt to have Hank whispering in your ear, telling you to tear into the floor, to meet your true self in the dirt?

*"You should have taken better care of me."*

The voice crackled out of her phone speaker despite the inert screen. She wasn't like Trent or even Milo—it didn't want her. It wouldn't speak to her like this, she knew that much. Then again, what Rita knew was only pieces, fragments of a whole, the skeletal remainder of what came before.

*"I died in there, you know."*

The voice trembled as she climbed into the minivan. She didn't want to be inside a structure anymore, nothing rooted to the earth. She shut her phone down entirely and tossed it onto the passenger seat.

It was easier to drive, to travel through the landscape, faster than anything could move beneath the ground. She turned the key, headlights illuminating the great nothing, the world emptied of people, Rita alone behind the wheel, its only minder, the last girl in the garden.

The nothing turned into houses, slowly, gently, then all at once. The new suburbs spread out before her, an alien landscape. Humans could crush anything given enough time. They had manipulated the landscape around her, filled it with wisps of trees and sturdy bushes struggling to conceal electrical boxes. The dirt was theirs to move and control. Until it wasn't.

The dashboard crackled to life, the small, flattened center screen flickering. No image, just a voice, the same one from her phone, no longer garbled.

*"I'm still down there."*

Rita took a deep breath, spun the volume dial down to zero.

*"Still there, Rita. Always there."*

A four-way stop. No other cars waited for her. She blew through it.

"Shut up, Billy. I know exactly where you are."

A laugh, one that kicked out of the back speakers and loomed over her behind the wheel.

*"You know that isn't me."*

Billy with his cracked lips, his misaligned teeth, refusing to look her in the eye when she sat in his private room on the ward, running his hands over a crack in the wall that the staff claimed no one else could see. Now here with her, opening up to speak after so many years of silence. But there was nothing to touch, no crack to ponder, just his words bleating into her ears.

*"You know whatever they've got residing in that room is just what Mom could salvage."*

Another intersection. Rita's foot on the gas and then a small girl with her white dog, barely even glancing up from the pavement.

*"A fucking yard sale, that's all you see whenever it is that you actually see me."*

She slammed on the brakes, listening to them shriek for her. The girl and the dog barely reacted, only a nod from each before they continued down a brightly lit street, the houses all permutations of their neighbors.

Rita breathed deep. She could control this. There were still things she could save. The voice receded with the girl until she could barely believe it had spoken at all. Rita was alone with herself, the purr of the engine beneath her. She turned up the volume, Hall and Oates on the radio, smooth enough to let her escape Billy's ragged breathing. Rita ran a hand over her belly and then inched herself across the intersection.

She toured through the new suburbs, the developments that were actually completed. She counted streetlights, putting off the inevitable. She didn't see any other people out here.

Trent's voice in her ear. *So? So what, Rita?*

Time was running out, but what happened if she couldn't choose? She could keep spinning her wheels until the gas ran out, stumble into one of these houses begging for forgiveness, but each closed door told her they wouldn't care. They'd leave her out there on the lawn until the cops arrived. She was an outlier, meant to keep the rest of the herd safe. She was already marked.

*That thing goes free. So? Why is it fair that it be your responsibility? So-fucking-what?*

Maybe it was too hot. The sidewalks were untouched, free from chalk. Rita kept getting trapped in cul-de-sacs with every other turn. These lands were outside the boundary, but they would be the first to fall if she didn't let the house have Trent. The homeowners' association would not save them, no matter how level the lawns remained or how many garbage cans were put away before the kids got home from school. There was a price, always. It's what Hector had told her, what her mother would say if she even tried to phone. Who knew, Rita herself might end up part of the bargain if she went back to the house to see what was left of Trent.

Her own father had gone willingly in the end, but that was far too late for Billy. Would she continue the trend? Would she sacrifice a little bit of Milo just to see a little bit of Trent again? Continuity mattered.

There was no scale built to weigh these decisions. They rested on her heart like ancient, unmovable stones, squeezing it flat until everything inside her was rendered bloodless.

"A community that chooses itself," Rita muttered, sneering into the glass as she backed out of yet another dead end. "They don't know what hard choices are."

"*Is that right?*" her phone announced from the passenger seat. A face made of tin and wire flickered on the screen, the voice like Billy's pushed up and out of a clogged drain. "*You think you know? Really?*"

Rita didn't respond. She'd never known exactly what happened to her father, only that her mother had sealed the basement once the deed was done. Billy was catatonic on that final car ride out of hell. Away from a world where the walls were always temporary, where the door could disappear off your bedroom in the middle of the night. Windows shattered in the dark and were neatly swept up by unseen hands before morning arrived. No friends could ever visit, when the bathroom was often just a hole in the ceramic tile you had to squat over, dropping your waste down, down, down into what, she never really knew. She didn't ask. Her mother said it was just part of her father's process.

"*I know you want to blame all these people,*" the phone gurgled. She turned up the radio, the yacht rock serenading her even as the voice gained strength. *"It's just what happens over time. We expand. What do you say to that, Rita the Riveter? Remember the old man called you that? But that's what we all do. All these people. We're an invasive species. No real predators."*

Maybe that was how to approach thinking about it. A predator under the soil, finally ready to cull. And no one out here knew anything about it. Maybe that was what came next.

Maybe just leave the cage door open. It couldn't be that easy. But who was going to stop her? Hector?

Dunsany Estates had built a home for her out here, from spec. They had suggested a rich and fulfilling life to be obtained once it was all over, this final act to seal the deal. Her daughter would need to do the same in another thirty years, give or take a few. The daughter so few knew about, but few was all it took. Without one, Rita would be bound to find another to take her place, someone she could bind with blood. Someone for Milo and then for her. It could wait that long. Whatever dwelled in the earth there needed to feed, but it didn't have to gorge itself. It took only what was offered. Like a tree during a drought, it could survive off what it found in the soil for a while until the blood rushed through it again like warm, sweet water.

*"You go down there, you don't come back up. Not the same, at least,"* the phone sniggered. She tossed it into the backseat, where the murky tin face laughed. *"Come back smaller, maybe. With something missing. A lot of something. The kind of stuff people notice."*

Rita peeled around another corner, headlights catching a man out jogging, sweat drenching his shoulders like depleted wings. He ran in front of her, refusing to move to the side. She considered weaving around him—but instead pulled up beside him and lowered the passenger window. Maybe that would shut the voice up. Maybe someone else could tell her what was real.

"Hey, excuse me," Rita said. "Do you hear that? That sound? Sort of like a voice?"

He ignored her, continued plodding forward. No headphones.

"Hey, man, I'm talking to you."

He sighed. "What do you want, lady? I don't hear anything except you. I don't know anything about cars."

"I just wanted to—"

He stopped abruptly. She overshot him, had to reverse. He jogged in place. The phone stayed quiet in the dark. No spectral voices. She was on her own.

"I told you I don't know anything about cars."

"No, there's . . ." Rita began, without knowing how to finish her sentence. How could she explain the taunts emerging from every speaker around her? How could she prove they weren't just in her head?

The man continued to jog in place. "Look, lady, I can't help you here. And you're absolutely destroying my time on this run, all right?"

Rita shook her head, tried to remain calm. "Of course, sure, sorry to bother you, I just—"

"You keep following me, I'm calling the police."

An escalation. Rita frowned. "Um, are you fucking serious?"

"You basically ran me down in the street. And I will remember the license plate. I got a photographic memory."

"Ran you down? I pulled over!"

"And almost crushed my foot!"

Rita counted down from five. The man rolled his eyes and

continued his jog, putting one foot in front of the other. She could annihilate him right now like a bug if she wanted. The police? Like someone was going to save him. Good luck calling them after you're dead.

But of course, there was a greater authority out here observing her. How many cameras were watching Rita on this street, documenting her license plate, putting her into a database somewhere? They would all know her eventually. That was something people like Hector didn't understand. The world was becoming knowable. It was shrinking. The unknown was being exposed. You couldn't run. That didn't make it any less horrible—it just blended in with the surroundings. Each screen and camera was another portal for that awful grinning face, whether made of felt or human flesh, telling them to free it.

Once the boundary came down, it was open season. Trent had to stay down there.

"*You'd like to forget this?*" The voice was back in the stereo, crackling through the radio. Not her brother anymore. Billy in the background, weeping. This voice was older, more controlled, less concerned with guilting her. Confident and self-assured. "*You'd like to wake up?*"

Rita had never explicitly been told what had happened. She didn't need to be told. It still existed inside her. It flared off and on with the seasons, an old wound that throbbed when the pressure changed. She was allowed to reshuffle her memories. It was only during the visits to Billy that the old truths would bubble up like embolisms, slip back into the stream of her memory, rough stones that would jolt her out of bed, little wicker or wire families huddled in their boxes, accompanying the chosen ones down into the depths of the earth. And then they would fade again, become more indistinct, disappear into tamer anxieties. Teachers with wooden faces, exams held underneath a hedge, the boy she kissed asking her if she was ready to dig. She could handle those dreams, even the odor of wet dirt pressed into her face. It smelled like home.

*"Oh, I can help you with that,"* the deeper voice said. Patches, maybe. The other thing Billy knew down there in the basement. Li'l Patches. *"All you need to do is leave. Just stay away. Very simple."*

The wide streets gave her no support, no moral guidance. No one here had done anything wrong, not to her at least. Not that she could see, but sins were never worn openly, not in places like this. They were hidden in emails, buried in backyards, mounted over the fireplace in front of everyone and seen by no one. She didn't owe anyone out here a goddamn thing, and yet . . .

. . . she felt that tug inside her. To go into the house was to betray many centuries. But no one was truly going to stop her. There were no guardians. No other keepers. Her family had been chosen, and so the pattern continued. The same ritual repeated until it became the only truth you knew. Until you didn't think another world was possible.

Until now.

"I'm not leaving. You hear me? *I'm not leaving!*"

She tried to smash her fist into the screen. It barely cracked.

*"I know,"* Billy broke into the call, sniffling. *"No one ever gets to leave."*

Little Boy Blue stood in the garden outside a spacious bungalow, staring at her from across the lawn, his little fuzzy body molded in ceramic. Someone's latest licensed merchandise. Milo's keeper, the one friend he turned to every night after they all went to sleep. It was out here too. Keeping tabs on her.

"You little shit," Rita spat. The minivan roared as she bounced over the curb, spinning across the front lawn, tires thrashing the freshly laid sod. She turned in a wide arc, slamming the front bumper into Little Boy Blue, shattering its body and tossing its fat head with a crash through the front window of the bungalow. Lights flickered alive inside. She revved the engine again and spun back out into the road, her teeth grinding against each other.

It would be watching her until the bargain was fulfilled. There was no escape. It knew her. It had the patience to wait for her to decide.

Li'l Patches laughed on her dashboard. She wheeled out of the subdivision. High beams snapped on to urge her forward, turning the whole world into a road carved right into the country. Dead animals appeared on its shoulders, left and right, a grim path. The house didn't feed off them. It needed a human. For what, she didn't know—Hector had never really told her that part. He just said it couldn't be her. *You can't be the one.*

"I will get you out of there," Rita muttered.

Patches laughed before the radio faded back in, the opening chords of "Margaritaville."

*You don't need to lie to me.* This time Billy was inside her head. Alone.

When a skunk ran out into the road, Rita didn't swerve. She kept driving.

# 24

**THE STALLION ISSUED** a smooth *whir* as Trent descended into the hole in his basement floor, down through the roof of the house he'd uncovered. Three Molotovs clinked in the canvas sack slung over his shoulder as he entered this hidden, motionless world. The descent felt somehow like time travel: a disorienting sensation as the decades seemed to peel away, so vivid that Trent had the fleeting impression that he was getting younger with every foot he dropped, so that by the time his feet touched down he'd be a child again, his clothes hanging on him and his hands so small that his wedding band would slip right off.

His boots hit the carpet. He glanced up through the hole. The lights still shone in his basement. This was real, no illusion. He wasn't any younger—he was still middle-aged, still soft, still terrified.

He'd dropped into the bedroom of a house buried directly under his own.

He trained his Maglite on walls covered in faded *Star Wars* wallpaper: a knobbed root system pushed through the wall where Chewbacca's face should be, spidering over the Wade Boggs poster and the Sega Genesis console on the desk. Dirt bulged against the bedroom window, the glass splintered by the grind of the earth.

Trent flipped open a notebook on the desk. *BILLY'S IDEAS.* He thumbed through pages of designs and diagrams. The notations gave way to ragged scrawls of boxes, dozens clustered per page, drawn so forcefully that the pencil had ripped through the paper in places.

*LI'L PATCHES AND BILLY LIVE HAPPILY EVER AFTER*

He shone the Maglite up through the hole, needing to stabilize himself. The shadows of the effigies now loomed up there in his basement. Had they crowded closer to the hole? He thumbed the remote control on the Stallion winch. Obligingly, it played out more cable.

Trent opened the bedroom door and stepped into the hall. The air in this second house was stale—like the first whiff after cracking a sarcophagus, which Trent figured this house really was.

*Hell of a way to meet, father-in-law,* Trent thought morbidly, hoping like hell that face-to-face never actually came to pass.

Trent's boots left imprints in the cream pile carpeting. Portraits hung from the second-floor walls. The faces had worn away to blank circles, but Trent knew who they must be.

A device made out of a Buster Brown shoebox, Lincoln Logs, and the guts of a crystal radio rested along the wall. Its handwritten label read: A BILLYCO PRODUCT.

He went down the stairs, the railing wrapped in Christmas garland studded with icicle bulbs. The bay window had blown inwards under the weight of the earth. The layout was the same as his own home, but this house—the Underhouse—felt smaller. Maybe only a half-foot all around, but the knowledge pinged on some deep register of his psyche.

The family room bookshelf held a series of Time-Life volumes, the ones salesmen used to hawk door-to-door. Trent brushed the dust and cowled spider's webs off their spines.

*The Handyman Method.*

Trent pulled out volume 1. Hank grinned from its cover. Trent flipped the book open. The first entry was: "Fix That Crack, Hank!"

Trent paged through the whole series. By the time he got to volume 4, the projects had become increasingly obscure and un-tackle-able.

- "How to See Through Your Neighbor's Skin"
- "How to Tell if Your Wife Is Fucking the Mailman"
- "How to Make Your Children Love You Again"
- "What to Do When Your Daughter Just . . . Won't . . . LISTEN!"

When Trent was finished, the books lay in a drift at his feet.

He hit the winch control button. It took a while to play out enough cable to let him move into the kitchen. A photo was tacked to the olive-green fridge with a California Raisins magnet.

DAY I—MOVE-IN DAY!

One of the two men in the photo sported a Magnum, P.I., mustache and mirrored sunglasses. The resemblance was so uncanny that Trent understood he must be looking at Hector Hannah's father. Hector Senior stood in front of a house in a familiar dust bowl. The girl next to him was Rita, Trent knew at once. The others had to be her brother, Billy, and Rita's mother, with an expression too terse to call a smile.

The final person in the snapshot, Rita's father—now, *he* was just *beaming*.

Blue light filled the dark expanse as the TV flickered to life behind him.

Trent turned to face the living room. The unit was a Panasonic cabinet model. The horizontal and vertical resolved into the face of Handyman Hank, grinning at Trent from under decades' worth of caked dust.

*"Do you believe you had a choice, Trent?"* it asked, its teeth huge and its burly beard sprouting from its face with an audible hiss. *"What your kind calls self-determinism?"*

Trent's skin didn't even crawl. That part of his brain's circuitry must have burnt out: a bad sign, but one easily disregarded now.

*"From where I'm sitting, you were always going to end up right here, right now, with me. You and your wife were fated to fall in love. Which means you and I were on a journey to be with each other, too."*

Trent realized some part of him would continue to love Rita, despite what she'd done. This fact was inexplicable to him, but then love itself was inexplicable, wasn't it, seeing as that love for his wife was inextricably wedded to a species of hatred.

"But hey," he said with a grim little smile, "nobody promised married life would be a bowl of cherries."

The basement door squealed as it opened wide. Darkness lay clotted down the staircase. Trent's pulse went haywire, but mostly all he felt by then was exhaustion.

He pulled a Molotov from the sack and lit the wick. Maglite in one hand, bottle in the other, he went down.

Trent had reached a plateau where the terror was manageable. A palace of clean thinking, his mind traveling on straight lines. It was here he could reckon, finally, with who he was. A fuck-up? Yes, in the commonplace ways. He could've been a better husband, father, human. A better man, whatever that entailed. Here he was, trying to fix things. A man like any other, forever prone to the Big Gesture: carving their faces on mountainsides and spoiling their neglected children at Christmas and hurling themselves into the jaws of certain annihilation, slaves to their Y chromosomes.

So down he went. Trent Saban, knight-errant with his bottle of flaming Fanta.

His boots gritted on the basement floor. He felt a presence—the sour tang of breath at his neck. He spun, the flame fraying, muscles tensing to hurl the bottle—

Something protruded from the basement wall. A kind of bubble, but it wasn't. A sphere of wood, six feet by six. It looked exactly like the foundation-less nest Milo had found in the woods that day. But this one was *in* the wall: it was migrating through the concrete, pushing its way out of the house like . . . like ambergris, was the only image that came to Trent, the waxlike substance sperm whales excrete from their digestive tracts.

He eased around the rusted water tank for a closer look. The Maglite took in the nest's bulging contours. He wrapped his fingers around one of the staves and applied pressure, hopping back as the wood splintered and something tumbled out onto the floor.

An effigy, same as the ones that had taken up residence in

his own basement above. This one's face was sloughing away, its candle-lightbulb eyes staring blankly. Trent knew he was looking at a version of Rita, a girl who must never have been happy: Trent could see that sadness in the cruel bend of her gooseneck-lamp spine.

The Maglite picked up something else, behind the water softener. Trent eased over the effigy until he stood by the hole in the basement floor, as big as the one he'd dug in his own.

He shone the light down it, the beam reflecting off cement chunks littering seventies-vintage shag carpeting.

There was another room down there. Another bedroom.

"Hello?"

His voice sank down, passing through what felt like a warren of substructures, vaults, and dark spaces in the earth. Trent pictured a Russian nesting doll, but instead of houses hidden within one another, they were stacked on top of each other. Dozens of homes, each slightly smaller than the last. A vertical neighborhood drilling down and down into the earth . . .

Trent balanced the Molotov on top of the water softener. The bottle had gotten uncomfortably hot. When he turned, he noticed the Rita effigy had crawled up behind him. Its steel-tube finger brushed his heel.

He slid around the hole and away from the Rita-thing, hissing in disgust at its dry touch on his skin. He tried to get a better look at the bedroom down through that hole. The Maglite caught the angle of an open door down there, but the light couldn't reach past it, into the hall—

Trent's ears caught sound where his light couldn't reach. The palsied scrape of something crawling down that hall. Dragging the unguessable wreckage of their body over the hardwood with the scrape of fingernails or maybe naked bone—

*"Where's the respect for the Old Ways gone, T-Man?"*

Trent reeled away from the hole. He collided with the Rita effigy, its wire-and-stick fingers clutching possessively. He kicked them away with a screech and tiptoed around the water softener, heels stuttering at the edge of the hole. He spied what he assumed to be a chest freezer across the basement, a common enough sight. . . .

Except chest freezers didn't squirm. They weren't fleshy pink.

As he watched, the covering carpet of pinklings shucked away. Trent could now see what they'd been obscuring.

A box.

The smooth surface was perforated by holes bored into the luxurious wood. It was made of two pieces, left and right, hinged where the halves met and held shut by dowels.

Trent hunkered down, setting his ear to one of those holes—

A breath. Tortured, frail, but there. Something was inside.

He crept to the rear of the box. Two openings had been carved at its base. Trent shone his light inside: something was clogging the holes, an inch or so in. Wrinkled and cracked, like rawhide left in the sun until it wore away to transparency. Trent's breath whistled into one of those holes—he saw the rawhide twitch . . .

. . . were those *feet?*

Trent crawled around the front of the box. Two smaller holes, side by side, were tunneled into the wood. He listened at one of them . . . a whisper of air drifted out.

Understanding clicked in Trent, pushing the darkness back just a bit.

"Ohhh . . . that's *you* in there, isn't it, Hank? And you've been trying to make me let you out, is that it—I've got to submit myself, is that how this curse works? And you think I'll—"

*"It's an old contract."*

The voice didn't come from inside the box. It lay in an unexplored part of the sunken basement, a place Trent couldn't see—didn't want to see.

Trent watched the wooden dowels push out of the box one by one, clattering on the floor.

*"They used to be more common, when people respected the old makers."*

Panicking now, Trent hit the winch button. But nothing happened. Was he too far from the remote? No, that wasn't it. It was the cable, lying slack at his feet. He watched in hopeless despair as the rest of the cable snaked down the basement steps in a loose coil. The end was clipped, the tungsten braids blown apart like the hull of a firecracker.

Trent pictured the effigies in his basement, the Milo-one holding a pair of bolt cutters: $25.99 at the friendly Depot.

The last dowel popped free. The box hinged open in two halves like a clamshell on its side.

When he saw what was inside—what he could only hope was the final, unimaginable horror—Trent's mind snapped cleanly in half.

Of all possible ways to go completely mad, it was merciful in its swiftness.

But that was the last mercy Trent Saban would be afforded in this house under his own.

The box's occupant crawled past him, making a noise somewhere between a gag and a giggle as it hauled itself over to an easy chair in the corner, set before a TV/VCR combo. The thing clambered into the chair like a bug and sat there, shuddering obscenely.

The TV sprang to life. The VCR whined as a tape began to play.

*The Handyman Method.* Tape one of an endless set.

Theme music rang out. On the TV, Hank appeared. His body glowed like a deep-sea life-form. He laughed . . . those dimples, so merry!

The last clean sight Trent had was of Handyman Hank . . . of what Hank *really* was, its truest outline. And he bore witness to the biggest trick of all.

It bulked in that unexplored part of the basement. Its posture broadcast a complete indifference, perhaps even an eternal boredom. Trent beheld its wrinkled flesh that fell in dewlaps like pleated burlap, those cold yellow eyes and teeth gray and durable as iron . . .

. . . those sagging, dusty breasts.

"*Easy math, T-Man.*" Unmistakably feminine, that voice. "*One goes out, one goes in.*"

Trent got down like a dog within the open clamshell of the box, kneecaps and palms flat on the floor. The box slid closed around him sideways, like the mouth of a puppet. The wood had been lovingly carved to fit his body and no other. It felt like being encased in solid Lexan.

As all went silent and dark, Trent's mind settled on a scene from a night not long ago. The three of them sitting on the sofa hip-to-hip-to-hip, Milo bookended between his mom and dad, each reading a book. No one talking, only the occasional flip of a page.

Broken things can be fixed. Objects and people, marriages, entire lives. Sometimes an ill wind blows through a man, releasing a temporary ugliness. But the storm clears. That part of him goes away and never resurfaces.

The box closed with a soft click.

# 25

**THE HOUSE BENT** toward the earth. The moon traced its declining arch. Last time, they'd had only a few months living here in the almost wilderness until her mother couldn't take it anymore, until Billy was so quickly warped into someone else.

Now Rita beheld a shrinking tomb. The world moved so much faster now, the cycles speeding up. Once the ground was satisfied, the house was no longer needed.

The driveway did not meet the lip of the garage. All the little details that had so enraged Trent on a daily basis were apparent to Rita now, the tiny imperfections displayed as glaring flaws. The skeletons of the other homes watched her scramble out of the minivan, her phone swinging a weak beam of light. Billy's voice no longer taunted her; he had been pushed aside by Li'l Patches, a low murmuring in her ear. She wanted to throw the phone away, but she ultimately had to know what it wanted. The pact shouldn't be hers to bear alone, not with Milo in the hospital and another life clawing itself into existence inside her.

The phone gnawed at her wrist, Billy's accomplice shaking its matted head at her on the other side, breathing onto the glass.

*"You could've let him stay."*

Rita had returned to her childhood home only once, as a college sophomore. Billy was up in Briar Ridge by then, but his shock wouldn't have equaled Rita's. Billy had known. When she'd arrived, only the peak of the roof remained visible amid the dust. Rita had knelt by the little shingle pyramid, the place you'd stick a weathervane, pressing her ear to it. Through the layers of wood and insulation she heard a scream from way down inside. She'd told herself at the time that it was the wind.

*"You shoulda left him here."*

The house changed every time based on their needs. The land still smelled the same from when she was little. The dirt too was the same, filled with sulfur, iron, touching the edges of her tongue as she entered the house, the door struggling to escape from the frame. Inside, the angles were warped, the ceiling sagged. She continued using her phone as a flashlight, afraid of what the wiring might have become in her absence. The murmuring pile of metal and dirt pulsed on her phone, a grinning face that if you stared long enough revealed a hint of Billy around the eyes.

*"He belonged down here."*

The house was warm, a giant incubator. Rita made her way through the main floor, tracing her husband's final path through the house. She paused at the constellation of small cracks in the west-facing wall, the ones Trent had repaired now reemerging as hungry slits. She watched her hand run over the cracks, fingers pressing into the holes, entranced by the systematic destruction around her. The house had turned all of Trent's hard work into outright parody, stripped it back to reveal the crumbling infrastructure beneath.

*"What kind of man do you usher into this?"*

This was the question she'd once asked her mother, spat back at her now from Patches' crumpled grin on the screen. There were options, depending on how much you knew or were willing to know. Some distant relatives before her took up with criminals, one even a pederast. Awful specimens who deserved their fate. One smothered her tribute with a pillow, leaving him in a comatose state in the hopes it would hurt less. There was no evidence that helped, but still. All of the women had been steered by an ungovernable instinct beyond attraction, shared interests, common goals. Their men had stumbled to them with arms outflung, like boys clutching for their mothers after a bad dream.

"We didn't even get to change the backsplash," Rita joked, but the words came out too heavy. The face in her phone sniggered, continued its muttering. It didn't want her here, but it certainly couldn't stop her. It could only suggest and cajole. She was still necessary. It had no force to apply yet.

Rita headed toward the basement, the source of all that heat thrumming in her home.

*"You can't bring him back."*

Of course, there were whispers about a place like this. It just had to stay out of official records, which became harder as the years passed. There was so much data, so many ways you and your actions could be tracked. But there was also space to flood the world with false stories, to spin so many variations on a theme that the actual thing itself disappeared from view. This was how it had found her son, how it had found her husband, insinuating

NICK CUTTER AND ANDREW F. SULLIVAN

itself into their worlds, speaking to them through the screens, finding new methods to infect their minds with its single need: a life source. A want that went all the way down into the core of the earth itself.

Rita staggered down the tilted basement stairs. Warm air climbed into her lungs as she crept closer to the bottom, her phone light wavering over a hole in the floor, hacked and smashed into the concrete. Tools scattered around like diminished offerings.

Closing her eyes, Rita could see Milo in that hospital bed, his breathing barely present, Hector leaning into her with a snide look. Milo's inventions were still hidden around the house: barely coherent constructs Little Boy Blue had directed him to build, binding the boy even closer with the house. Lego intertwined with copper wire that must have come out of the walls. Melted action figures holding burnt-out fuses above their heads like trophies. Little Boy Blue. Li'l Patches. Handyman Hank. They all offered up that unwavering support, that devotion a boy craved.

She took a few steps forward to the edge of the hole her husband had hammered in the floor. Heat rose from it in waves, as if the earth itself was exhaling.

*"You can't bring it back up."*

She deliberated her next actions for only a moment before tossing her phone through the hole. Li'l Patches' face morphed back into Billy's tortured features before it bounced off the carpet down there.

*That's Billy's room,* Rita dizzily thought. *My kid brother's room, where we used to sit on the bed drawing ponies together.*

A winch was bolted to the basement support pole. The cable snaked down through the hole. *Smart move, hubby of mine.*

When she gave it a tug, she felt no resistance from below. When she pressed the green button, the winch activated, playing out more cable. Okay, good. She could pull herself back up using the winch—although that must've been Trent's plan, too, and the house had a way of screwing with those.

A pair of work gloves lay on the floor, coughed out of one of the tool caddy's drawers. Men's large, but they'd have to do.

Gripping the cable high and stringing it between her legs, gripping the trailing length behind her butt, Rita eased herself over the lip of the hole, belaying herself down. The cable sang through her fingers. Even with the gloves, the friction stung her palms.

*"I'll take the head off that bitch!"* the Billy voice shrieked, the high notes all wrong, Patches losing the finesse it had displayed earlier when it still felt in control. *"The whole fucking head!"*

Her sneakers settled onto the bedroom carpet. She shook the gloves off, blew on her reddened skin, forced herself to pick up the phone. She could hear scratching sounds coming from somewhere below, claws raking back and forth against the wood in the sunken walls.

Maybe she should turn back and leave Trent down here, flee back to fresh air, a son who might still have a normal life, a daughter Rita could shelter from her terrible burden until she was a teenager. . . . Her husband could stay, the most recent tribute stacked upon so many others before him, in bungalows, cabins, shacks, huts, all blind as earthworms, all writhing until they served their purpose in this place, sinking into a maw that only asked for more.

*"He really should have stayed down here,"* Patches said, swapping faces again. No more Billy on the screen.

Rita held the phone away from her like a torch, keeping its heat from her skin. She remembered this room. The walls trembled under the weight of the house above them, but this was Billy's room. The faded *Star Wars* wallpaper, the shredded white pile carpet. She could hear the earth sucking at the house, pulling it taut, making it shudder above them. Maybe they simply couldn't go back. Maybe this was what happened when you tried to undo a ritual. It took everything, swallowed your temple whole.

Second thoughts filled her head, brought on by a lifetime of preparation for this moment. Nobody would fault Rita if Trent disappeared. She had overwhelmed him, subsumed his life into her own. His law career was gone, especially after the head-scratching hoax he'd perpetrated in the aftermath of Carson Aikles's office rampage. A desire for some old glory, the kind that was in short supply these days. He wanted to be a hero, even if it meant sitting with that lie in his throat. No one would wonder why she left. Too many holes in the walls.

Billy's little television sparked to life in the corner. Little Boy Blue looked out to wave at Rita, the shattered face of the lawn gnome she'd left on the cul-de-sac only an hour before. There were things you pushed down so deep they ceased to exist, until your world fractured, and it all came spurting up like so much crude black oil. Little Boy Blue laughed and sniggered.

Outside, the hallway slanted away under her feet, almost shunting her down the stairs at its end. The same symbols carved into the walls down here, the recurring circles, the same loops, the same message. A pattern she knew. Books strewn all over the floor. *The Adventures of Li'l Patches. The Handyman Method: Fixing It Up the First Time.* Notes scrawled in the margins. Drawings spattered over the pages, blocking out the text. Some of them looked like Billy's own hand, as if she could still remember the cadence of his writing. The phone chittered at her wrist, Patches doing its best to transmute into Little Boy Blue again, rippling around the edges. All things return to their place, she knew. All things revolve around a center. You are never in your own orbit. Your circle always belongs to something larger than yourself.

Dirt pushed through the walls around her, dust in the phone light filling every sense, though Rita could smell the rot beneath it, the decaying loam that allowed the surface to continue blooming. She shuffled past portraits hanging from the walls, family faces melted and discarded. The Christmas bulbs along the railing flickered on and off, rustling in their garlands.

*"You could have left me here,"* Billy Patches pleaded, a seam splitting along its chin on the phone screen. Another battered TV in the far corner of the living room crackled to life, showing a cartoon Milo plummeting down a hole. The screen was cracked and bleeding. *"You could have left us both."*

Through the trashed living room, amid the sputtering lamps plugged into nothing, Rita saw the basement door yawning open before her, beckoning. Another descent. Another confrontation. Billy Patches screeched another laugh. Rita set her phone on the floor, Billy and Patches both grinning up at her. She lifted her foot and smashed the screen, slamming her foot down again and again until there were only glass shards and black fragments. The flooring gobbled them up. The TV in the living room began to scream, shrieking like Billy back in that little room, and then it whimpered, cursed, sparkling and sizzling into nothing.

Billy was gone. Rita would need to make this part of the journey alone without her jeering guide. The lamps sputtered when she drew close. Old videotapes unspooled on the carpeted floor. Bracing her hand against the wall, she made her way down into the basement, her feet weighing every step. There was light down here too, a fuzzy light that she could feel sputtering with hunger, calling for her from an older television, the one her father used to watch while talking to himself alone down here, plotting for a future without them.

Each step pulled her closer like a chain winching itself tight. Rita had no choice in the matter. She crept past the rusted water heater, entering a space now filled with figures she almost recognized. Herself and her mother, repeated again and again in wire and bulbs, reaching out toward her. Duplicates, company for the world ahead. Every time she glanced away, they moved closer, tiny adjustments she could barely trace. Inch by inch. One of them looked just like Billy, metal teeth too big for the tin mouth where they'd been shoved in place. She yanked at a loose chain dangling from a bulb above her head, and the whole room snapped into yellowed focus.

In the far corner, her father's TV crackled not far from a rectangular wooden trunk, larger than whatever they'd found Milo inside that night in the basement above. The TV and VCR appeared to feed off the hot air down here. Nothing was plugged into the walls. A face watched her on the screen, a big man in his coveralls, grinning at her with an inhumanly wide smile, surrounded by trunks like the very one that sat before her. This was not Billy or Patches or Milo's little friend. This man was very pleased with himself, looking like he'd just finished licking his plate.

"*I won't be opposed if you join him,*" the handyman said.

Rita ignored the thing on the screen. It wasn't a person, just a mask for the hunger down here, the earth that asked them to give up a piece to save the whole. This was its home, not hers and never had been. She spied a slim controller on the ground. The winch control, must be. She slipped it in her pocket.

*"We'll have to make you your own box, though. Your own little friends to travel with you."*

Rita ignored the screen and gripped the slit in Trent's prison, just enough space for her fingers to slide in between the smooth, polished wood. The two sides cracked apart as she applied pressure, doing her best to block out the voice. This voice was stronger than Billy's had been, more real than the slivers spiking into her palms, more vivid than the pain. The words bit into her.

*"Now, I wouldn't be doing that,"* the man on the screen said, flickering and crackling. He stood in a basement just like this but with a bright fire burning behind him. The boxes around him then burst into flame, each one's contents shrieking in unison. The man was growing younger, teeth getting whiter, hair getting brighter. He flexed his arms to show off his inhuman strength. His overalls sagged around him like robes. *"He made his choice. And you helped him make it! You brought him here. You let him come down this deep."*

The trunk cracked open wide, its dowels splintered. The screen continued to rage at Rita, blustering against the scratched surface. *"You better fucking be climbing in there with him!"*

Trent was still in his clothes. The body had been taken as it was offered. She could see him breathing, the otherworldly box sucking at him from below. She reached down to pull him out in the sickly yellow light, felt a thick, warm appendage cower away from her touch. She pushed through the disgust filling her throat.

*"You can't undo the choice!"* the screen bellowed again. The VCR whirred with its rage, tape melting in its slot. Startled, Rita released her hold on Trent. He tumbled back down inside, hungry noises beneath him suckling and slurping. She turned to the wailing TV screen, a handsome, striking face pressed up to the camera, lips snarling, nostrils flared wide and red. She crashed a foot through the screen, felt its edges bite into her ankle, but denied herself a scream.

"That's enough," she said. "Come on, Trent. Come on."

Mumbling, burbling, what remained of her husband began to stir to life. She got him half out of the box again, arms swaying over its side. Splinters clung to his skin, slipping through him like old butter. He was already wasting away. His mouth dragged against her skin. She yanked on his loose body until it fell onto the floor. A pile of hay. She couldn't get him to move. Only bones inside the skin. Only bones and what was left of his heartbeat.

*"Now, I can't let you keep doing this,"* the voice announced, just like the one on the TV screen, but deeper now, a bass note that thrummed through the cavern of this old, buried house. *"Hector's orders. The old guard remembers. Not that he's the one telling me what to do these days. What goes in the ground, stays in the ground. You'd do best to remember that."*

The far edge of the basement floor crumbled as the voice shook the room, emerging from the stacked structures buried below. Dirt-packed features, arms full of wire and pipe. The figure was Handyman Hank crafted out of the innards of the house. Eyes from old faucets, but still capturing the essence of her family's ages-old antagonist, an innate competence that wasn't belied by the garden hose serving as its coiled neck muscles. She knew by how it moved that the thing could see every inch of her down here, had mapped the entire place inside its brain, whatever it was speaking to her through this shape, reaching out into the house itself to grow stronger. The sickly bulbs above sizzled.

Rusted nails and screws glittered like hairs emerging from its shifting skin. No eyes behind those faucet glasses, just dirt in the crumbling sockets. Soil ran down its cheeks in thin lines like tears, as if it had been hiding in the corner laughing silently until she destroyed the TV, mocking her attempt to thwart it. No need for a screen anymore. No projection, just the reality of the thing swaying here before her, its heat forcing her to cower. Maybe it wasn't a man at all—something sweeter and sicker underneath its voice.

*"I knew Billy well, very well, dear Rita. Even better than Li'l Patches. They used to play together all the time. Did you know about his pal out there in the woods? I taught them each so much, playing in those little trees. Built a whole world out there together. Our own animal kingdom, our own kind of physics, if you will. You can make anything out of dirt. You can get people to build entire lives out of dirt. Entire futures. That's what I gave him. And that's what he lost. I was prepared to bring him down here, but your mother beat me to it. He left part of himself down here. But now . . . that Little Boy Blue . . . ? He's almost enough. Don't you think? Better than half a boy. Better than a wisp of a man."*

The weeping dirt spasmed with thick pink tendons that appeared to breathe, pushing through the thing's thin clothes. She could see a smoke alarm ticking away inside its chest, the carbon monoxide detector spasming in its foot. It laughed and watched Rita stagger under Trent's insensate body, tucked its thick copper fingers into its waistband. *"We wait, though. For second chances, for another cycle of seasons to pass us by. Billy got away, but this one stays. You're gonna put him back in that box. What goes in the ground becomes the ground, Rita."*

Rita stared at this hungry shape before her, the most sophisticated of the duplicates. This unknowable dweller, emerging like an ambassador from the ground. It smacked its hands together, fingernails formed from the grout and yellow tile in her en suite bathroom upstairs.

*"Hector is a good man,"* it continued. Its tongue sparked when it spoke, little blue arcs on each syllable. *"He keeps the Old Ways. Just wants to make sure everyone plays by the rules. It makes things easier to have a deal arranged. To know when you will be fed."*

Rita spat on the ground, adjusting Trent's weight in her arms. She would drag him out of here if it killed her. Fashion a harness and winch him into the daylight world above. She owed him this. The house could have her if it wanted.

Her next words came out clean, words she had never expressed before in this life, words entirely alien to her self-conception, the woman she knew in the mirror.

"I don't care."

The thing that had once been just a human fragment on the screen cocked its head, a smile spreading under the dirt, teeth flaking paint chips. Thick pink grubs thrummed in and out of its cheeks, pulsing off-tempo, rhythmless. A tongue of wire slowly circling out in glee. *"Oh? A new choice. Do you understand what you say?"*

"No, I don't," she said, her voice flat. This wasn't a place to win an argument. She had no case to argue. She refused the terms and conditions of the arrangement, the one that had been passed down from one generation to the next. Instead of looking for a loophole or desperately searching for an escape clause, she would let the whole thing burn. Let it end here under the ground. Let it all crumble. She would walk away. "I don't care."

The thing laughed, no longer any voice she recognized. *"Okay."*

"Okay, what?" she snapped, but it only laughed in reply. It used whatever form it could find to make its point, even the glibbest answer in its repertoire. Something Billy taught it once. She dragged the scarecrow of Trent toward the basement stairs, past the other duplicates, her mother, herself, her mother, herself again. Old offerings. Company for the eternity spent down here until every drop was wrung clean. The TV set still sizzled, dripping some kind of ichor, a thick pink spasm in the dirt. Her own blood mixed with it.

*"More than okay, actually,"* the thing croaked at her. The pink pulsations slowed, satisfied. *"No need to stay here any longer. No pact."*

It was only on her way to the basement stairs that Rita saw the other body sitting in its chair. This one was not a duplicate. It was desiccated, bones beneath a paper layer of skin, but still a human form. A living corpse. She could push her fingers through it. A husk. The long hair was gray and scraggly around the temples . . . the same temples her father picked at when he was worried, fingers probing at that skin, the same freckle-spattered scalp. Each vibration caused it to shed a few more flakes of skin, settling back into dust. The body appeared to reach for her, but she would not take his hand. He could not help anyone down here. She would not play the same role, would not become the same tool. She took a new shape.

The wooden receptacle lay empty. Trent had replaced the previous donor for only a few hours, yet already her husband was almost gone, eyes barely flickering. A hint of pink feelers slipped away under Trent every time she touched him, the earth still trying to draw some more sustenance out of the drained body. But she had him, could feel his heart against her arm, still alive, still human. Not like whatever stood like a shambling man before her, smiling with its gritty mouth, not even attempting to stop her retreat to the fresh basement above.

*"You've made your choice,"* it said. *"We have no pact anymore. As you say. No more boundary. No rules. Nothing to bind anyone here. You or . . . this."*

The last of the effigies crumbled behind them, the versions of her family that her father had obsessively built. He would be pushed out eventually, found on the edges of the boundary once every single bit of sustenance was gone, accompanied by his mute entourage. There was nothing to mourn here. So much waste pushed out of this den into the supple earth.

"No more boundary," Rita said. Whatever it needed to hear. Whatever made it happy for now. She was leaving. Trent gurgled in her arms. "No more pact."

*"Ahhh, yes."* The deep, sultry voice of the earth ringing through it, thoughtful, considering. Pink flesh stippled against one of the walls, reaching for Trent, cowering from her touch. *"The fire, so bright. I may approach it now. I may play."*

It didn't follow her. It seemed content—the earth couldn't force her to do anything here. It needed to honor this dissolution.

*"A welcome choice."*

She continued through the living room, her shattered phone glittering on the floor before her. Rita could taste cold air ahead. Trent kept breathing. The surface world was getting closer.

Trent slurred against her, spit dripping from his mouth, but moving like a human again, holding his own weight. She tripped on the winch cable lying on the stairs. Locating the control in her pocket, she pushed the red button. She heard the winch whir to life up in the basement; the cable retracted over the stairs. It still worked, thank Christ.

Her heart pounded down here in the filth and dust. *Just don't look back. Don't look.* If you didn't look, you didn't have to believe. If you didn't look back, there was no body down there, no tomb, no empty altar. It was just a hole in the ground.

They reached Billy's bedroom. The cable rose up through the hole like the magical rope from a fakir's basket. Rita snugged the gloves she'd left behind over Trent's hands. His eyes were filled with a brokenness that scared Rita.

"Hold on to the cable, okay?"

She took his hands and put them where they needed to be. She expected the house to play some final filthy trick: the cable would snap, the ceiling would cave in, or her husband would abandon all care and sink to his knees, refusing her help. They'd made a deal, she and the old thing below, but such things rarely played fair.

Steadying Trent's neck with her hands, looking as if she was strangling him, Rita kissed him full on the lips. "Hold on. You can do that for me, can't you?"

Trent's fingers tightened on the cable.

"That's it. Just as hard as you can."

Her husband mumbled something. His words were too mushy to make out. She held her ear near his lips. "Say that again, darling."

"I wish I never met you."

Below, the hungry earth trembled, pleased with itself. Finally, irrevocably free.

# EPILOGUE

## FIVE DAYS LATER

**RITA PULLED THE SIENNA** up to the house. Milo sat in the passenger seat stiff as a mannequin. She patted his thigh.

The skin jumped along his throat. "Don't go in, Mom. *Please.*"

Rita's eyes skated to the rearview mirror. Trent was laid out across the back bench seat, all buckled down. He'd remained motionless—only the shallow stirring of breath in his chest—until they'd gotten close. Now he was shaking, his eyes wild with fright.

"Watch your father, okay? I won't be long."

She switched off the minivan and got out. Went up the weed-strung driveway, the interlocking bricks that Hector had crowed over now sinking into the dirt.

Milo had woken the day after she'd gone down after Trent. The next day, the lesions on his throat began to clear. The day after that it was as if they'd never been there. The doctors were baffled—but of course they would be.

As for her husband . . . his recovery was always going to be a lot trickier.

Twisting the knob, Rita let the front door swing open. She stepped down onto the foyer tiles. As soon as her foot touched them, she felt the emptiness. The presence that had always raised the hackles at the back of her neck had vacated the premises.

The house had sunk at least a foot in the past few days. Heading across the living room, she noticed it wasn't just sinking—it was deteriorating. Chunks of drywall crumbled from the heaved walls. The buckled floor had dinner-plate–sized holes in it, as though acid had been poured onto the wood.

The house, simply put, was dying. The structural equivalent of necrotic leprosy, bits rotting and falling off. Rita took in the decay with a dry eye. There were new challenges ahead. Distant landlords and burdensome security deposits, the chain on the flimsy rental door threatening to snap in the middle of the night, all the fresh, raw ways the world would threaten to break her again and again. Nothing worse than what lay beneath the earth, though, that thing which knew her name, knew her heart. She'd severed the old roots so something new could grow without fear. She would not hand off this poison to the next generation. Would spread it around instead. Let it all rot and fade away. Dunsany could deal with the remains. No bank. No insurance company at the door, at least not for Rita. Let it be a scrap pile sinking under its own weight into the earth.

She went upstairs, avoiding the steps that issued ominous cracklings. The hallway's mildewy carpet was covered in cables that had torn through the walls. She stepped over them as she would sleeping snakes—one gave a lively jerk, blue sparks spitting from its naked wiring.

She gathered nothing from the master bedroom. There were items in there that she'd have liked to hold on to—some drawings Milo had done, the bracelet Trent had given her on their first Valentine's Day—but some inner caution told her to leave it. Bargains were ticklish, especially those of the nature she'd made.

In Milo's room, she got down and peered beneath the bed. For a split second, she saw a man's face under there: a head growing out of the carpet like a bolus, covered in cobwebs and dust-bunnies, with a bone-white stripe running down the center of its beard.

She squeezed her eyes shut. Let out a breath. Looked again. Nothing there.

But it always *would* be there. She'd have to live with unpleasant surprises like this from time to time, reminders of the pact she'd made and what she'd made it with.

Reaching under the bed, her fingers closed on Milo's tablet. The conduit the thing had reached out to him through.

Standing, she brought the tablet down hard over her knee. The screen broke, glass crunching, as she folded it in half. Satisfied, she kicked the mangled thing back under the bed.

She went back downstairs, absently running her hand over her gently rounded stomach. She'd begun to show just a bit. Milo hadn't noticed yet. She'd explain everything in time. To her son and her daughter to come. Would she have a daughter, even? The pact called for one, of course. But that was all null and void now.

Before leaving for the final time, she cast one last glance over the living room and kitchen—

The basement door was open.

Darkness webbed from that slit, leaching up the stairs to spread across the kitchen area like an oil the sunlight couldn't reckon with. Somewhere past that stain, down those stairs she'd never descend again, she heard laughter.

Gibbering, insane, endless laughter chaining up from that place under the basement.

"I'm so sorry, Dad," she whispered.

Rita stepped outside and shut the door behind her. Got in the Sienna and drove to a crossroads that was truly that—the suggestion of an X marked in the dirt—and accelerated past it, the house dwindling behind them until it was gone.

She opened the windows to let in some fresh air. The *whoosh* of the wind concealed her husband's whimpering, which he did more or less constantly: the whimpering, the trembling, the drooling. But there were small signs of recovery. A pinprick of light that occasionally danced in his eyes. She didn't think she was imagining this.

Rita pulled into the nearest housing development, named Oak Bridges despite the lack of oaks or bridges. The tires quieted once they were running on asphalt.

The inrush of air was now broken by the unmistakable sounds of industry.

The Sienna cruised past an old colonial home. A man in a bespoke suit, his paisley tie loosely garroted around his neck, took wild swings at his front-yard maple with an axe while his wife looked on in paralyzed wonder.

"What in Heaven's name are you doing, Cedric?"

"It's gotta come down!" The man swung again and again as lacy foam collected at the edges of his mouth. "I'm telling you, it's gotta come down!"

Rita stopped at a four-way intersection. With the engine idling, she caught the whine of power drills, the shriek of table saws, the endless *dak! dak! dak!* of hammers pounding nails, so many nails.

Trent shrank on the bench seat at the noise, curling into himself like a potato bug.

Rita stepped on the gas.

The neighborhood's men were out in their yards or occupying their driveways. They all had tools hanging from belts strung around their waists, most of the items fresh out of their packaging. Their laptops and phones were out too, arranged just so in their respective work areas, and collectively from them came the voice Rita knew all too well.

*"Now, friends, it's like I always say: women dig men with calluses on their hands. Soft hands equal a soft mind, yes indeedy."*

That voice rose up to the tips of the old-growth maples rowing the streets. These houses had been here a long time, in one fashion or another. And these people too: their forefathers and foremothers, on back through the years.

Rita knew that after she and Milo and Trent continued on, once dusk gave way to night, the sounds of pounding and drilling and sawing would persist until the early dawn hours, after which the makers of that din would retire to bed, sleeping only long enough to gather the strength to start all over again.

Rita's eye caught on something lurking in the shadows of a corner lot's wraparound veranda. A burly shape squatted under the bell of a mulberry tree, sitting on an old box. The silvery glint of those pointed teeth was barely visible under the mulberry's manicured branches.

*So long, but let's not say good-bye, okay? Farewell for now, see you again soon.*

She stopped at a house near the southern scrim of the development, idling at the curb. A man was up a ladder, feverishly pounding nails into his aluminum siding. His wife was in the yard on the phone.

"I don't know what to do, Mom! He's been acting this way for two days!"

The man on the ladder spied the minivan at the curb. The sparkling discs of his aviators pinned Rita behind the wheel.

"*You!*"

"Mom, is that—?"

"It's nobody, Milo."

Clambering down the ladder, the man staggered down the driveway, clutching the hammer. His sunglasses dangled off one ear to reveal a pair of bloodshot eyes.

"You *bitch!*" he screamed. "You fucking traitorous welshing bitch—I'll *kill you!*"

From the backseat, Trent let out an uncontrollable giggle.

Rita put her foot on the gas. Milo craned his head back to see the man lurch into the middle of the street, his shrieks giving way to wails as he sank down onto the asphalt.

"Is he going to be okay, Mom?"

"No, Milo, he isn't. But it's just Hector. Hector's not all that important."

The Sienna's brake lights glowed at the corner of Cranbrook and Appleseed as Rita turned westward and left the development behind.

In the high heat of the afternoon, the *burr* of power tools was uncommonly loud.

# ACKNOWLEDGMENTS

## NICK CUTTER

If you're one of those perverse individuals (I say so being one myself) who skip to the back and read the acknowledgments before finishing the book, I give you the same warning medieval cartographers wrote on the uncharted portions of their maps:

*HERE THERE BE SPOILERS.*

Thank you to my friend and coauthor Andrew. He's a fearless writer, even when he's writing stuff that is acerbic or painful or just plain strange. I've never known him to write scared. His ideas possess an originality that mine (as a more meat 'n' potatoes horror writer) sometimes lack. Almost all the truly electric, blow-your-hair-back ideas in this book came from him; my job was to take the gold he'd dug for us and spin, spin, spin it like hell. . . . Beyond that, he put up with my fussiness and overanalysis with good Oshawa-bred grace, plus he wrote his ass off the whole way through.

## ACKNOWLEDGMENTS

All that being noted, it should come as no shock that the initial seedling for this story came from ole Andrew's noggin.

Let's journey back, shall we? Four-odd years ago, pre-pandemic, Andrew and I met at a bar. We'd had this notion to write a short story together and decided to kick some ideas around. Andrew had a great one about a malevolent entity who starts beguiling a dude via a YouTube home improvement channel. The poor guy's stuck out at this house in the middle of nowhere, trying to fix it up, and goes progressively more insane.

Andrew wanted the vibe to be something along the lines of "Unedited Footage of a Bear," which I loved, so I was very much down for the idea.

We figured 5,000 words ought to do it. A quick-and-dirty rocker of a story.

Fast-forward to that story's completion at closer to 8,000 words. We sent it to my film agent, thinking he might be able to convince some deep-pocketed producer to option it. But my agent came back with the feeling it wasn't quite fleshed out enough. Needed more beef.

So back to the forge Andrew and I went, emerging with first a 12,000-word story, then 15,000, then 18,000. The beast kept getting bigger!

The story had morphed aesthetically too. Less the frenetic tone of "Unedited Footage," more domestic, the satirical bones starting to protrude. The main character now had a wife and a son, and the wife knew some stuff—the wife had *history*, boy howdy—plus there was something hinky down in the basement.

But the idea of the malignant, supernatural handyman stayed the course; it allowed Andrew and me the freedom to comment on some of the stuff we saw happening in society, with our friends, under our own roofs, and (for me at least) inside our own heads.

My agent sent the novella to Ed Schlesinger, my longtime editor. Ed said: "Hey, I'd publish this . . . but it'll need to be longer!"

With Ed's guidance and encouragement, Andrew and I worked on a lot of drafts, in fits and starts, through pits of writerly despair, navigating the tricky cowriting process as the novel took shape in a protracted, oft bizarre and head-scratching manner. . . .

So, what started out as a 5,000-word story idea gradually became *this!*

Thank you to Andrew, and to Ed. There were some rough waters to chart, but at this point in my career, I understand that such waters need to be sailed to reach a safe harbor. I was grateful to be on board with you both. Thankfully we didn't have to resort to cannibalism . . . this time.

As for the inspiration for the book, I should dedicate a paragraph or two to that.

The "haunted house" narrative is one of the fundamental tropes of horror literature. And the storyline of a character in an existential crisis going nuts in some isolated hinterland . . . any hardened horror reader has been taken down that road before. There are quite a few books that can be fairly seen to influence *The Handyman Method*, at least from where I stand.

Of course, there's *The Shining*. Can a line be drawn between Handyman Hank and Delbert Grady? Surely, though to me Grady seems a bit fussier and stiff-upper-lip, whereas Hank is earthier (quite literally). I also love Robert Marasco's *Burnt*

*Offerings* (in that one, it's the wife who goes crazy), *The Amityville Horror*, *Hell House*, *The Haunting of Hill House*, *Slade House*, and Anne Rivers Siddons's *The House Next Door*. These are my influences. I can't and won't speak for my cowriter.

Readers may detect aspects of those works, or perhaps others, woven into the fabric of the book you're holding. My ambition with *Handyman* was to have fun playing in that hoary old sandbox of the Haunted House Novel and, I hope, add one or two twists to the proven formula.

As for Hank . . . he was a ball to write, in the way that deplorable fictional characters can be. I always imagined that if Hank had a closet, you'd find a hard hat in there, a white hood, a MAGA cap, and a blister pack of Infowars-branded male enhancement pills.

As for the demise of Ned, I was inspired by Deke's gory end in Stephen King's short story "The Raft," as well as a scene in the 1988 remake of *The Blob* involving a kitchen sink.

And clearly, I must have something against turtles! First in *The Troop*, now poor Morty. No actual turtles—or any other critters—have ever been hurt in the writing of any Cutter book.

Thank you to my erstwhile agent, Kirby Kim, and to everyone at Gallery, the best home ole Nick's ever had. Thank you, Joal Hetherington, for your wise and thorough copyedit. Thank you to my mother and father, my brother and sister-in-law. Thank you most of all to my wife, Colleen, our son, Nicholas, and our daughter, Charlotte. Hubby/Daddy can be a mess sometimes, a frayed bundle of insecurities, but he loves you so very much . . . just make sure you don't catch him watching YouTube videos in the witching hours, chuckling throatily and talking back to the screen.

## ANDREW F. SULLIVAN

The first time I read Nick Cutter, I was sitting on a crumpled box of nylon rope nestled thirty feet up on the shipping mezzanine in a liquor warehouse, waiting for another case of red wine to come hurtling down the rollers toward my head. The stories in my battered library book spoke to me in ways few writers had before. They were crafted with care, covered in grime, dripping bodily fluids, and filled with a beating heart that labored just beneath the weathered surface. Between stacking pallets six feet high with bottom-shelf whiskey, I devoured that book over a single shift. I then drove home in the middle of the night, weaving around the roadkill that hadn't quite been pulverized yet, hoping each almost-corpse wouldn't lock eyes with me. The whole time I knew I could now tell these kinds of stories, the ones that felt true to me, the ones Cutter had made feel so real. I just had to figure out how to do it on my own.

It would be a few years before we met, and even more before we worked together. I'm extremely grateful to Cutter for his support of my work and his resolute faith in what I do. Through our friendship and working relationship, he has taught me so much about what it takes to be a writer and a human being, and what it really means to choose to do the right thing, even when it isn't easy, even when it's the last thing you'd ever want to try. It's our characters who consistently fuck that part up. They just can't seem to get it right. I blame the algorithms.

Beyond Cutter's faith and dedication, big thanks to Ed Schlesinger, whose enthusiasm, attention to detail, and commitment to the project have been unwavering. Thanks to Steph

## ACKNOWLEDGMENTS

Sinclair for helping me get to this point, and for the Cooke-McDermid team carrying me forward. Thanks to the Gallery Books crew for bringing me along with Cutter, pretending I didn't just slide in with the morning mail delivery. And big thanks to my wife, Amy, the support of my family, and my number one good-time boy, Iggy, the dog who may or may not just be an animated loaf of bread.